ANCHORED

at

Mackinac

ANCHORED

at

Mackinac

CARRIE FANCETT PAGELS

HEARTS OVERCOMING PRESS

ISBN: 978-1-7366875-4-3

This is a fiction book. Places, names, incidents are either imaginary or they are used fictitiously. Any similarity to actual people, events, or organizations is coincidental.

Hearts Overcoming Press

Printed in the United States of America

DEDICATION

To:

Linda Borton Sorensen,
who inspires me with her friendship
and our mutual love of Mackinac Island.

&

In memory of

Jacqueline Hyacinth Croteau Williams,
who encouraged and believed in my writing.
I miss you so much, Jackie.

Praise for Carrie Fancett Pagels' Books

Behind Love's Wall
Carrie Fancett Pagels creates a wonderful story of intrigue and romance in *Behind Love's Wall*. Set on the amazing historical Mackinac Island, the author makes a creative balancing act of time periods and characters, bringing it all together in one story that I found hard to put down. I believe readers will enjoy the twists and turns, and I highly recommend *Behind Love's Wall*.

~**Tracie Peterson**, bestselling, award-winning author of over 125 novels including Ladies of Lake and Heirs of Montana series

Butterfly Cottage
This lovely novel centered on three generations of women as they face a summer of change, will resonate with readers long after the last page is turned.

~**Suzanne Woods Fisher**, bestselling author

My Heart Belongs on Mackinac Island
An enchanting love story, *My Heart Belongs on Mackinac Island* is sprinkled with warmth and humor, grace and faith. A highly enjoyable read!

~ **Tamera Alexander**, *USA Today* Bestselling Author

Character Chart

Gentle Readers: I offer this chart in the event you need to refer back from the story and check names and relationships.

Heroine: **Sadie Duvall** –twenty-two years old, Maude Wellings's best friend.

Frank Duvall – Sadie's father, an alcoholic who has gone missing after his wife's death.

Bea Duvall – Sadie's sister, teenager, works at the Winds of Mackinac Inn.

Garnet – Sadie's sister

Opal – Sadie's youngest sister

Hero: **Robert Swaine**, thirty, only surviving child of Carter & Jacqueline.

His parents, the Swaines: Carter Swaine & Jacqueline Cadotte Swaine (both deceased)

Terrance Swaine, deceased eldest son, father to Lily

Lily Swaine, daughter of Terrance (deceased) and granddaughter of Jacqueline (deceased), cousin of Robert. Singer at the Grand Hotel Born in 1860s during the war.

Eugenia Swaine Welling, their only daughter (deceased mother of Maude and Jack and wife of Peter Welling.)

Maude Welling, almost twenty-one, has become a maid at the Grand Hotel.

Jack Welling, twelve, the fastest runner in the state of Michigan in his age group.

Second eldest Swaine son, deceased during Civil War, served in the Union army. Never married, no children.

Aunt Virgine/Virgie, elderly islander sister to the late Jacqueline Cadotte. Aunt to Robert. Great-aunt to Maude and Jack Welling, and Lily Swaine.

Dr. François Cadotte, Island doctor, cousin to Maude and Jack Welling and Robert and Lily Swaine.

Izzy, Dr. François Cadotte's beloved Labrador Retriever, Islanders' favorite pet dog.

Second Heroine: **Ada Fox**/Adele Schwartz/**Adelaide Bishop** – wealthiest woman in the world—currently the Housekeeping Manager at the Grand Hotel. Her parentage is a secret—I'll let you figure that out in the story! Peter Welling was her first love when she lived at a Poor House and his family owned the farm next door.

Second Hero: **Peter Welling** widower (father of Maude and Jack, his wife was Eugenia Swaine Welling)—Proprietor of Winds of Mackinac Inn, widower whose first love was Adelaide Bishop/Ada Fox.

The Christy Family:
    Garrett Christy, esteemed Grand Hotel craftsman who is married to Rebecca Jane Christy. They own and Rebecca operates the Christy Tea Shoppe on the island which is also a bakery. Friends of the Duvalls and Wellings and others.
    Richard Christy, runs a lumbercamp in Newberry. His wife is a former librarian.
    Jo/Josephine Christy Jeffries, owns and operates a bakery in St. Ignace, Michigan. Her husband Tom is an educator.

Dr. Stephen DuBlanc – young psychiatrist on staff at the Grand Hotel, love interest of Lily Swaine.

Winds of Mackinac Inn Staff: Mr. Chesnut – gardener, Jane - maid, Mr. Roof – handyman

Greyson Luce – Maude Welling's former fiancé now married to Anna Forham Luce, wealthy daughter of a newspaper magnate.

Grand Hotel staff: Mr. Costello – Manager, Mrs. Stillman – Assistant Housekeeping Manager, Alice – Lily Swaine's maid, Zeb – shoeshine man, Dessa – maid and Zeb's wife.

Canary/Cadotte Cottage/Robert Swaine's staff: Matilda - maid, Mr. Hastings - butler.

Patrick Byrnes, renowned island builder.

Prologue

Mackinac Island, Michigan
June, 1894

All of Sadie's aspirations crumpled into a rubbish heap as Robert Swaine's fist connected with Lt. Bernard Elliott's square jaw, and her beau crumpled onto the grassy knoll

"Stop!" The very word she'd been repeating to the handsome officer was now aimed at her best friend's young uncle.

Robert rubbed his fist, his face red, as he scowled first at Bernard and then at her. "Elliott deserves a sound thrashing."

Tears coursed down her face. Years had been invested in this moment—when an officer from the fort would ask her to be his wife and take her away from Mackinac Island. Away from the decaying French–Canadian cabin her family called *home*. Away from Pa's drunken tirades, and the sight of Ma working herself to death trying to support them.

The man who should have become her fiancé this night groaned as he rose to his feet and brushed at his navy woven-wool pants. With undisguised disgust in his eyes, Bernard pinned her there, beneath the lilac trees, the faint scent of their new blossoms taunting her. "We're through, Sadie. Do you hear me?"

She sucked in a breath. A year of courtship ended by Robert, a man who'd been so dear to her—a man who should understand what she really needed. Which wasn't this outcome. Her best friend's uncle, Robert Swaine, had watched out for both Sadie and Maude for years. But they weren't children anymore. Sadie, a year older than Maude, was now twenty-one. And Robert had just now destroyed her only chances.

"Through? Good!" Robert narrowed his eyes, his fists yet clenched. "Be gone with you, then."

"No…" But Sadie's weak protest was greeted with Bernard's disdainful glance as he slapped his new forage cap back on his head and headed up the hill toward Fort Mackinac.

Robert took two steps closer and gently grasped her shoulders. "Did Elliott hurt you?"

"No." Not physically at least.

He frowned, as his eyes narrowed to half-closed. That was the same look he'd always given her when he'd not believed her. The same expression of consideration when she was fifteen, infatuated with him, and he'd had that awkward, embarrassing, little discussion with her about his engagement to Miriam.

"Here, let me dry your face." Robert pulled a linen handkerchief from his breast pocket and gently patted her cheeks, the fine cloth soft but not soothing.

She stood there like a ninny, letting him treat her like the child he thought she was. If only he'd realized that she'd been a grown woman for years now. If only he'd realized that before Miriam had trampled his heart like a runaway horse.

Sadie hadn't seen much of Maude's young Uncle Robert since he'd been jilted and had gone off and begun acquiring more ships on the Great Lakes. Since he'd become a captain and sailed one of his vessels. Why did he think he should intervene? Surely Bernard would have stopped, would have come to his senses, and then finally proposed to her.

If he'd not been away and so busy running his shipping interests, Robert would not have had to physically correct Lt. Elliott's misconception that Sadie Duvall was his for the taking. Thank God, Robert been watching the twosome from the dock, where he'd just moored his ship. A man leading a woman into a secluded part of the fort's gardens was up to no good. Why hadn't Sadie realized that?

"Let me walk you home." The anger, fear, and care he had for this young woman caused his voice to rumble.

"No. I'm all right." She brushed dirt from her dress.

The cad didn't even have the decency to bring a blanket with him.

"Do you realize what you've just done?" Her voice quivered in anger.

Saved her from being compromised? "From the tone of your voice, I suspect you don't understand, yourself."

"He was my last chance, Robert, and you've ruined it!"

Last chance? Elliott had been about to ruin her reputation. "I rescued you."

"Bernard wouldn't have hurt me." Sadie nibbled on her lower lip; her eyes averted to the ground.

Snorting, he jerked his thumb over his shoulder. "You told him to stop, and he didn't—I *heard* that."

"He was supposed to propose to me tonight."

Robert grasped her arm, the cotton fabric of the sleeve soft beneath his fingers. "Did Elliott tell you he'd marry you?" He turned her to face the direction they'd need to travel to get to her home.

A street sweeper passed by, eyeing them.

"Well, no, but from everything he said…" Her cheeks suffused with color. "And we've been courting for over a year."

"Courting?" When Robert had been on the island, he'd never seen her anywhere in public with the young man, a dashing golden-haired dandy several years Robert's junior.

"Yes." She looked up; eyes wide. "We picnicked every Sunday afternoon on my days off. We went fishing, too."

"Like we used to do?" Picnicked for years on the bluffs, by the Fairy Arch, by Sugar Loaf, and laughing and telling stories—he, his niece Maude, her sweetheart Greyson, and Sadie.

"He even came to church with me…"

"When?" He had no reason to be jealous, but the green-eyed monster squeezed his heart.

"Once."

"Did he ever take you to the roller rink or to dinner at Astor's?"

"No."

Robert had. Many times to both. "Ever out to eat at *any* of the restaurants in town?" He'd sported Maude and Sadie around to every single establishment on the island. That was before tongues began to wag about him and the too-young island beauty. Before he'd courted Miriam Beckett and become engaged.

"You're just jealous that I can be happy and get married." Her full lips formed a perfect pout. "You're angry with me because of what Miriam did."

His fiancée had eloped with one of the officers from the fort only a fortnight before they were to have wed. He swallowed back bile. "I'd never have treated Miriam like that jackal just attempted with you."

"Well, you're not him."

"And thank God for that." He wanted to tell her what he knew about the officer from the fort, but he dared not. She'd never believe him anyway. This wasn't the time.

"Just go away, Robert. Leave me alone!" Sadie stifled a sob as she pulled free from him and ran.

The flimsy pine door slammed behind Sadie as she entered her family's home—which was little more than a log shack. The stale scent of bacon grease and wood smoke assaulted her nostrils and she wrinkled her nose. She was supposed to escape this sour smell. She'd hoped to become an officer's wife—to live in a beautiful two-story home at Fort Mackinac, or at a fort far away from here. Where she'd serve guests with fine china dinnerware and crystal goblets. Where there would always be enough to eat. Where she'd awake to a warm cozy house even on a chilly winter's day. But that was not to be. And she'd run out of options.

"Sadie?" Ma's voice carried from the back where Sadie and her sisters slept, sharing an old rope bed that perpetually sagged.

"Yes, Ma?" She began to cry again, a hiccup starting. She dabbed at her eyes with Robert's handkerchief.

"Come here, love."

Luckily Pa was nowhere in sight. Likely Frank Duvall was down at the bar, drinking away his worries over being unable to hold a job.

In several strides, Sadie crossed the open family area, where the hearth was flanked by two wooden benches, covered in pillows. Between them sat an overstuffed velvet chair that Robert had brought in during the winter for Ma's comfort, after her long days at Witmer's Steam Laundry. Sadie rounded the corner to a short hall, which led to her sisters' and her room.

Ma cocked her head slightly, her lips pursed, and set down the undergarments she'd been folding when Sadie had joined her.

"Where are the girls?"

"Maude and Greyson have your sisters right now. They were taking a carriage ride and asked if all three—Bea, Garnet, and Opal—wished to come." Ma shrugged. "Saw no harm in it."

Sadie drew in a slow, fortifying breath. Maude, her friend, was all-but-engaged to the handsome son of Sadie's employer, Mrs. Luce. "No harm other than *you* were left to do their work."

"The quiet has been nice, though." Ma smiled gently, though sorrow, and some other emotion, disappointment, washed over her pretty face. She reached into her apron's deep pocket and pulled out a newspaper clipping.

"What's that?"

"*You* read it." Ma's lips disappeared into a thin line.

More tears slipped down Sadie's face. Ma cut out obituaries and other special notices from the leftover papers from the laundry. This didn't bode well. And after the altercation with Bernard and Robert, she wasn't sure she could hold back the sobs that threatened.

She unfolded the newsprint. A beautiful young woman with fashionable upswept dark hair, dark eyes, and a pale complexion smiled back at her from the paper. Sadie tried to place who she was. "I don't know her, Ma."

"Keep reading." Ma sank down onto the bed and began to roll socks together.

Miss Antonia Gaston of Lansing, Michigan, is engaged to Lt. Bernard Elliott of Mackinac Island. A September wedding is planned at the bride's parish church in Lansing. The paper slipped from Sadie's hands. She gasped. "Oh! Oh no."

No wonder.

No wonder all the excuses why Bernard couldn't squire her around on her one day off each week. No wonder when Mr. Foley, the island photographer, was making images in the street in front of Astor's, that Bernard hadn't wished to be seen. When she and Bernard had walked past, the handsome officer turned away from the camera, claiming it wouldn't sit well with his superiors if he were in a promotional picture for the restaurant.

Did Robert Swaine know of this engagement? She dabbed at her eyes.

Ma took her hand and gave it a gentle squeeze. "Is this what you were crying about, love? Did Bernard finally tell you about his engagement?"

Her lips parted but she couldn't respond. Robert saved her from humiliation, and her mother had shown her the truth of the matter. A chill went through her, and she rubbed her arms. Three years of redoing Maude Welling's hand-me-downs, fixing her hair on her day off, and attending any officers' mixer event that Sadie could—all to get off this God-forsaken island, and for what?

"I'm sorry, love. I know you thought that young man was special, but me and your Pa never trusted him."

Nor had Robert. Clearly. Or he'd have not rushed up there to intervene. But Robert Swaine had no right to give his opinion. No right to keep caring about her and her family. No right to make her want more in life.

But he had.

Detroit, Michigan
December, 1894

Mrs. Adele Schwartz. That didn't sound like a spy's name, although she certainly felt like a spy, working at this men's fraternity house—especially since her childhood sweetheart, Peter Welling, was sponsoring one of these boys at university. Schwartz had been, however, her third husband's surname, may he rest in peace.

"How are you doing today, Mrs. Schwartz?" Fraternity member, Greyson Luce, a senior at the college, grabbed an apple from the bowl of fruit she was carrying to the dining room. Leave it to that young whelp to grab and take without asking.

The young man was accepting dear Peter Welling's assistance because he was supposed to marry Maude, Peter's daughter. Since Adelaide arrived there, almost a year earlier, Greyson also squired a society girl around town, especially to some of the swankier events. And she'd overheard Greyson boast that he had a great many businesses on Mackinac Island that he'd be responsible for once he'd graduated. But those must be Peter's to manage, since the boy was there on scholarship and aid. He did a great job concealing that fact from others, but Adelaide made it her business to know what was going on around her.

She looked first to the apple, now half-eaten, and then to the young man's eyes. "I'm fine. How was your Christmas vacation on Mackinac Island?"

His cheerful countenance crumpled. "I'm afraid two of my dear friends' mothers died."

"Oh. I'm sorry." Her own husband's passing had made this Christmas a very quiet one.

"Mrs. Welling took ill and was gone so quickly. And so was Mrs. Duvall."

"Mrs. Welling?" Peter's wife had died? The breath caught in Adelaide's chest. She'd just seen the woman at the old Welling farm in Shepherd, in central Michigan, a couple of years earlier. She pressed her hand to her chest, where her fingers brushed against her broach's cold brass metal.

"Yes, did you know her?" The young man's incredulous expression caused Adelaide to force her face into a mask.

"Yes, I met her at my childhood home in Shepherd—where the Wellings have a farm. And I knew Mr. Welling when I was young." She omitted that her late childhood residence was a poor house and that Peter had been her true love. "They run an inn on Mackinac Island, where you live—isn't that right?"

He cast her a strange look. "Yes, they did. Mrs. Welling inherited it from her family."

"Mr. Welling grew up on a farm, next door to me. I'm so very sorry for his loss."

"As am I."

He'd referred to the women's deaths, as mothers of friends. So, he considered Maude a friend? Not his betrothed? It was her understanding that the two were to wed this coming summer. "Your friends must have been quite distressed."

"Yes. It was quite shocking. Both ladies had children still at home."

Peter had a young son about eleven or twelve. "I can't imagine." She'd not had children—and that was a deliberate choice. How could she ever explain her background, the horrors of her early life, to any offspring she might have?

Greyson leaned in. "Have you stayed in touch with Mr. Welling?"

"Oh, I'm afraid not." She made a face of regret—realizing Greyson likely didn't want her in communication with his sponsor. "His wife simply happened to be at the farm when I was there on a visit. The poor dear."

"I see." His gaze darted about the dark room with its heavy black Eastlake furniture. "Will you be sending a condolence card? I could include it with my correspondence."

His tight smile unnerved her a bit. Only a bit.

She touched his arm lightly. "Oh, no, Mr. Luce. I don't think that's really appropriate, do you? After all these years to send him a letter."

"No. I suppose not."

"Then we are in agreement. But thank you for sharing that with me. And I'm sorry for your friends' loss and yours."

"Thank you, Mrs. Schwartz."

Poor Peter. His poor family.

No, it would not be appropriate to send him a letter.

But she'd not let her old friend suffer alone. She'd lost three husbands and had started over so many times that she'd lost count.

Adelaide knew exactly where she'd spend her summer. *On Mackinac Island.*

Chapter One

June, 1895

Sadie shaded her eyes and scanned the deep sapphire waters of Lake Huron, to no avail—Captain Robert Swaine must have taken her words, uttered a year ago, to heart. When would she once again spy his ship coming into port? Her gut clenched. She could have taken a boat to the mainland—if she had the funds. Instead, the Straits of Mackinac hemmed her in, their zig-zagging currents too strong and her poverty too deep for her to escape. And now she was truly stuck, without the strength to procure her way out because she alone must care for her sisters.

Jack Welling, Robert's twelve-year-old nephew and her best friend Maude's brother, raced down the hillside toward her. He skillfully dodged the cows who were making their way up the hill to the fields near the former fort. The federal government would no longer be managing the National Park but would transfer ownership to the state. Mackinac National Park was now being converted to Mackinac Island State Park

So much had changed in the past twelve months. *Ma gone. Pa missing. Younger sister, Bea, now working. Sisters Opal and Garnet under my care.* Sadie exhaled a sigh.

Slowing his pace, Jack hooted, and then stopped. He bent over and clutched his knees, panting. "Hi ya, Sadie!"

"How're you doing, Jack?"

As he looked up, a knowing expression creased his eyebrows. "Prob'ly the same as you and Bea and Garnet and Opal."

Not so good then.

"Maybe so." At least the boy had a father and his older sister to care for him. *And someone to pay the bills.*

The boy straightened. "Sorry that carrottop fired you from Mrs. Luce's place."

Sadie flinched. "She didn't fire me—Greyson's wife said they didn't need my services any longer." But Jack was indeed correct that the rude woman's hair was as orange as a carrot. Obviously, that didn't detract from her beauty, because Greyson had jilted Maude for her. How astounded Sadie had been when Maude's fiancé marched into the Luce home, with a wife on his arm gowned in some fancy get-up. Even more astonishing was when the newcomer had sneered at Sadie and announced they didn't require her assistance now that they'd arrived.

Jack shrugged. "Let you go, though. Same thing."

No more wages, regardless. "And all this activity and building on the island, yet no one willing to hire me except for Mr. Foster." At the tavern. The place where her father used to be found quite regularly.

"Maude's still lookin' around for a job for you."

"And we're grateful for Bea working at your inn." God knew they needed her younger sister's wages to help with expenses.

"Yeah." He rolled his eyes.

"I hope she's behaving." They badly needed her position. Bea was well known on the island for her saucy ways and tart tongue.

"Sure! Hey, guess what? Mr. Hardy, the owner of the sawmill in Mackinaw City, stayed with us—givin' folks estimates for buildin' more cottages on the bluffs—and I asked him about your dad." He scrunched up his face. "He ain't seen him. Good thing, since somebody got killed down there recently, and it weren't him."

"Yes, that poor man who perished. Thank God for small mercies it wasn't Pa." She and her sisters had prayed for the man's family. What a tragedy.

"Huh? How can mercy be small?"

"Mercy from God is a big thing." She sure needed some. "So, you're right." She winked at him.

"I'm right a lot!" He grinned, but a shadow quickly passed over his face. "Would ya please write my uncle Robert and tell him to get back over here?"

"Me?" She raised her eyebrows. How many times had she begun a letter to Robert and then tossed it in the fire?

"Yeah. I know he'll listen to you." He crinkled his nose.

"What do you mean?" She patted at his arm but hit air as he swooshed away from her and raced the rest of the way down the hill.

She pressed a hand to her chest; sure she felt her heart beating through her worn cotton blouse. Why did Jack think Robert would listen to her? Was she truly responsible for him not returning? Maude said her uncle had things he simply had to work out and one of them was the loss of her mother—his beloved older sister.

"Sadie, girl!" Mr. O'Reilly called out as he passed by in his dray. "Ye're lookin' lovely, lass!" He pulled off his blue work cap, revealing a shock of thick, white hair and waved at her.

If his idea of lovely was being dressed in a dowdy tavern maid's uniform, then lovely she was. "Top of the day to ye, Mr. O'Reilly." She pulled her skirt to the side and dipped into a mock curtsey.

The man's laugh carried over the sound of his draft horse's heavy *clip clops* down the street.

A gust of lake breeze ruffled her skirt and apron. Sunlight flickered over the Straits of Mackinac as a ship headed toward the port. *Not Robert's ship.* Why did that realization bring so much sadness with it? Because once upon a time long ago, she had imagined her future, only and ever, intertwined with his. But oh my, what a young girl she'd been then. And she was a woman now and must make plans of her own. Somehow, some way, she'd eventually get a position that would allow her to care for her sisters until they were fully grown.

She'd have to leave Mackinac Island.

If she had her way, she'd become a fully trained nurse. She'd show those people who looked down their noses at her, because of her father, that she was a useful member of society.

She'd not rely on others to take care of her. Sadie would be a respectable member of the community—on her own.

Robert's steamboat sliced through Lake Huron; its cerulean waves punctuated by foamy crests. What an inauspicious return to such a beautiful place, with him attired in lumberjack's clothing aboard his own ship and not at the helm. His face heated. Why was he slinking into his own hometown like he was some kind of criminal? If finally listening to his doctor was a crime, then so be it. His many months of a healthy regimen had brought a level of vitality back that had vanished years ago.

Would Sadie Duvall, along with his niece, Maude, recognize him despite his many changes? He rubbed his clean-shaven jaw.

A young woman and her mother, Mrs. Lindsey and her daughter, if he remembered correctly, stood near the ship's rail. The daughter pointed to the water, "The water in the Straits of Mackinac is as blue as sapphires."

Sapphire—like Mother's ring. Now that Robert knew the truth about that fop, Greyson Luce, who'd jilted Maude, he'd be sure to winch the family ring out of his claws. The cad had never actually placed it on his niece's slender finger. And with Sadie's lieutenant married and a child on the way, Robert had his own plans for that sapphire family ring—for his niece's sweet friend who'd grown into a beautiful young woman. The railing, cool in his hands, felt slick from the spray. Was he putting himself on a slippery path? Putting up with her father, Frank Duvall, as a potential father-in-law had deterred most island men from even considering courting her. Frank epitomized the sobriquet "sot."

"Even from miles out, you can see the outline of the Grand Hotel—so expansive." Mrs. Lindsey pointed to the cliff.

"We're staying there the entire season." Young Miss Lindsey, a pretty blond who reminded him of Sadie, blinked up at him.

"I hope your stay on the island is very restful." Not that most of the guests were planning to rest. The vast majority were there to be entertained and to enjoy every bit of beauty the island had to offer.

"And I hope Mr. Bobay will be here as well." Mrs. Lindsey's words were full of unexpressed emotion that simmered beneath her clipped comment.

"Charles Bobay?" The railroad magnate had also turned thirty recently and like Robert was unmarried. "I believe all the shareholders should be here soon." Robert wouldn't mention that he, too, would be attending the meetings at the Grand. Talking about such things was not "done" by islanders. Mother had drilled humility, respect, and gratitude into him from the time he could utter the words, "Great Lakes' schooner," and would point out at the harbor.

"That's exciting news." Mrs. Lindsey smiled approvingly at her daughter, who blinked several times. The girl stared down at her crocheted gloves and began to tug at the fingers.

"We best be getting to our seats now." Mrs. Lindsey maneuvered over the ship's deck as though she'd had previous experience at sea. Her daughter, however, clutched the rail, her gait unsteady.

A blast sounded from the ship's horn as they entered the harbor. He should have been up there steering this ship. Instead, he'd arrived what he hoped was rather incognito and wouldn't be staying at the Winds of Mackinac, but hiding out at Aunt Virgie's, or the Grand, where he had business to conduct. It had been Peter's terse letter that drew Robert home for the first time since his sister's funeral. That and the remembrance of a certain beautiful young woman who believed that he'd spoiled her chances at matrimony.

Soon the ship docked. Robert tugged his cap low on his brow. He'd meet with family and friends on his own terms. Robert disembarked, weaving in and out of the crowd to avoid the passengers. He caught his reflection in a plate glass window by the dockmaster's office. Did he look young enough for Sadie Duvall to consider him? There were about eight years between their ages—not the twenty that she'd once assumed. How he'd laughed when twelve-year-old Sadie believe that he was over thirty because his dark hair was threaded with silver. He'd only just turned twenty. He'd allowed her to retain that mistaken notion for a long time afterward.

He made his way toward the boardwalk. He hoped to see a carriage waiting from the Danner Stables.

Little Billy Lloyd, a wharf assistant whom Robert had trained, came alongside him. "Hey, don't I know you, sir?"

"Maybe." Stifling a grin, Robert slipped a coin into the boy's pocket, just like he had every day when he was on the island's main wharf and ruffled his mop of curly hair.

"Mr. Swaine!" Billy's green eyes glowed. He shook Robert's hand so soundly that a few passersby turned to look.

"Shh!" He leaned in. "Quiet, Billy, I'm not announcing my presence." *Not yet.* He didn't need Peter hearing about his arrival until Robert was ready to see him.

The boy made a motion as though buttoning his lips together. "Shoulda known you by your eyes."

Billy had previously described Robert's eyes as *odd.* Like the Cadotte men before him. Green, blue, and light brown swirled in his eyes like stormy waters near the island. "The color is called hazel." As he'd told the child many a time before.

"That's a girl's name, though. It ain't right."

"I don't know what I'm going to do about you and your notions, young Mister Lloyd." Shaking his head, Robert glanced toward the street for a dray driven by his cousin Stanley.

Stan was supposed to take Robert up to Aunt Virgie's place. The elderly woman lived in one of the oldest structures on the island, and far from town. He had an open invitation to stay with his beloved aunt. Better than the secrecy her place provided was the fact that she knew all the goings on in town, on Mackinac. She'd get him caught up with happenings.

"Don't worry about me." The boy patted Robert's back. "But hey—Captain Swaine, where'd you leave the rest of you?"

He laughed and reached into his rucksack and pulled out some Beeman's gum. "I'm chewing this instead of eating your mother's good cooking." Mrs. Lloyd was the head cook at Astor's. His stomach growled at the thought of eating some of her fine cooking. Robert offered the boy a piece of gum and Billy took it.

"See ya, Mr. Swaine." That grin was going to one day break a few ladies' hearts.

"I mean it now—don't tell anyone you saw me, Billy." Robert dug into his pocket and pulled a five-dollar bill from his wallet. The boy's eyes widened as he passed it to him. That was two weeks' wages on the docks.

Billy heaved a sigh. "I can't take this, sir."

Robert wrapped his hands around Billy's knuckles. "Worth every penny to me for you to keep my secret."

"You sure?" He scowled.

"I'm positive, Billy."

"Thanks, Mr. Swaine." The kid sped off so fast that Robert was sure his nephew, Jack, was going to have a potential challenger in this year's island youth leg race.

Robert headed off toward the street. He ducked his head and avoided the many dockworkers who unloaded early season arrivals' belongings. Some of the men were bent with age while others weren't much older than Billy and Jack. The youngsters had mastered bike riding even with a full load in their wide baskets while the older men pulled wagons down the street.

When Robert lifted his gaze, he spied a young woman, attired in old-fashioned work clothes, head bowed and obscured beneath a wide bonnet. Her arms were wrapped so tightly around her middle that she appeared about to be ill. When she raised her head, Robert caught Sadie Duvall's beautiful profile. Her gaze was directed at Leon Keane, who stood at the entrance to the mercantile, a smug expression on the manager's narrow face.

Sadie's brow furrowed and she rolled her lips together. She appeared oblivious to Robert as she wiped tears from her cheeks.

I'll have a word with Keane sometime soon and see what nonsense he is up to—treating Sadie so rudely.

Robert strode closer to Sadie, and she glanced in his direction. She gave him a quick onceover, showing no recognition. Or did she? And want nothing to do with him? Did she still blame him for setting that officer in his place? Robert watched as she brushed at her ugly faded skirt, turned on her heel, and walked away. His gut clenched. She looked as pitiful as the girl in his niece's favorite childhood story—a stepdaughter, named Ella, who was covered with cinders from cleaning out the fireplace each day.

Someone tugged on his sleeve. "Hey, sorry to bother you." Billy ducked his chin. "Wondered if maybe you'd seen Frank Duvall in St. Ignace—Sadie's been asking everyone who's returned from the mainland if they've seen him."

Unspoken were the words *whom she could trust*—Sadie would have only inquired of people who wouldn't judge her or denigrate her father even further. "No, I haven't." And a stumbling, bumbling sot roaming about St. Ignace would have caught his attention.

"She's got it awful rough, Mr. Swaine."

He flinched. Mrs. Duvall had died near the time his sister had passed on—both of pneumonia. "How long has Frank been missing?"

"Quite a while—I think all winter, at least."

The man might be a ne'er-do-well, but he was Sadie's father, and now she had the entire responsibility for her sisters. *Poor Sadie. And what have I done to help?* He'd secreted himself away and focused his attention on healing his body from all the neglect it had suffered while he'd captained his boats and expanded his business holdings.

So Frank Duvall was gone. Missing. What should he do? This might present him with an opportunity to put himself in Sadie's good graces. But he couldn't have her knowing what help he could provide. What was that the pastor in St. Ignace had said? "He who knows the good he could do but withholds it…" Didn't he say that was a sin?

For the first time in months, he had a concrete plan for what to do with himself on the island. And he'd pursue his mission with passion. He spied Stan driving his dray in his direction.

Robert had to help Peter, he had to determine his niece's and nephew's needs, and Lord willing he'd determine what room Sadie had in her life for him. He'd help them all if he could.

He'd start by reconnoitering with his Aunt Virgie, his mother's surviving sister.

Robert waved for Stan to stop.

"So, you're home, Stranger?" His cousin's eyes danced in merriment as Robert scrambled up beside him.

"Yes. Yes, I am."

Home.

Of all the cockamamy things Adelaide had done in her life, hiring on as housekeeping manager had to have been the worst. But it had put her closer to Peter. And it had also put her closer to the young woman who'd just left her office. Maude Welling, a beautiful but obviously naïve girl, wouldn't last two weeks here at the Grand Hotel. Adelaide would bet all her electric and railway stocks combined on that outcome.

What was I thinking? I was thinking of all the wonderful days I had with Peter, that's what. I was thinking how he'd lost his wife and the boy he'd sponsored through school had betrayed his daughter. She patted her upswept hair, generously laced with silver. How different this hair was from the reddish hennaed hair she'd had at the Fraternity House at Detroit University. And having listened to that ninny Greyson Luce at her fraternity hall job, she'd been sure this move might be helpful—now that that young Greyson had thrown over Peter's daughter, Maude, for a newspaper mogul's daughter.

A knock sounded on her door.

"Enter," she called out.

"Mrs. Fox?" Zebadiah, their shoeshine man, removed his grey, soft, slouch hat as he took two tentative steps into her office.

How many names had Adelaide "tried on" since settling on this latest one? *Ada Fox.* Her maiden name, her adopted name from

Captain Fox, seemed most appropriate. Her adoptive mother preferred to call her Ada, complaining that Adelaide was "too French." Truly, though, her adoptive mother likely objected to the reminder that Adelaide's birth mother had chosen the name.

"Close the door." She rose and pushed her seat away from her desk.

Perspiration beaded on the man's dark forehead. She waved her hand. "Please relax, this is an entirely friendly visit." One in which she needed to kill two birds with one stone.

"Yes'm."

"I called you here because I need a favor. And I'll pay generously for your eyes and ears." And possibly for his silence—although he'd not yet breached that.

His dark eyes briefly locked on hers. "What do you need?"

"All I ask is that if you hear anything that concerns you, or see anything, from any of the guests that you'll come to me with that information." If she'd learned anything on this job, already, it was that she needed more help in keeping track of her own agenda. And also, to do her work properly. If this man was as observant as she believed him to be, though, he also knew her secret.

The man's stiff shoulders relaxed beneath his boxy brown jacket. "I already do that, ma'am, though."

"You've been very helpful. That's one reason I've asked you to come speak with me. What I need is a little more than that."

A crease formed between his dark brows. "What can I do ma'am?"

"Discretion is of the essence." So far, he'd displayed that trait.

"Yes'm."

"I want you to particularly look out for a new hire we have. Her name is Maude. She'll be a maid here. Make sure no one bothers her in any way. Do you understand?"

"Yes'm."

"And Zebadiah, I'll be calling on you for some other things." She returned to her desk and unlocked her center drawer. She retrieved the cash envelope and brought it back around to the employee.

His eyes widened as she handed it to him.

"This extra work is between you and me. If I hear of you telling anyone else about what I ask you to do, you'll be fired. Do you understand?" She hated how tough she sounded, but she'd not gotten this far without learning that you couldn't risk information leaks.

He made a cross over his heart. "I won't even share this information with my wife."

"It's better that way and I'll never ask you to do anything that is illegal or immoral. Be assured of that fact." Adelaide clasped her hands at her waist, one of her techniques to convey that she was finished with a conversation.

"Mrs. Fox, how did you know you could trust me?" This time, the worker's dark eyes locked on hers. "Did you remember me?"

She gave a curt laugh and dipped her chin. "If you could keep my secret all these weeks since I've been here, then I'm sure you can manage a little spying for me."

He laughed. "I'm a pretty keen observer. Was even then—all those years ago."

Adelaide wagged a finger at him. "You're the reason I stopped showing up to clean on the nights when the board met."

He raised his hands. "I'd have never told anyone about that. And I never planned to."

"I'm glad." Only a handful of trusted people knew her true identity. And she planned to keep it that way.

Chapter Two

The scent of stale beer permeated the air at Foster's tavern—much of it spilled onto and soaked into the wide-wood planked floor. Sadie exhaled a breath. When she inhaled again, the pilsner odor battled with the stench of working men's sweat and the sardines that many Norwegians savored like candy. Not that she blamed them—they were accustomed to such food. It was probably like a steak-eater from St. Louis wandering into a Mackinac eatery and inhaling the scent of whitefish. But whitefish odor didn't seem to cling to clothing like sardines' smells did.

She wiped her brow. After working all day, she certainly wasn't perfumed like a rose, either. She stretched her neck, wishing she could sit down.

Although their piano player was allowed a break each hour, and had stepped outside now to smoke his pipe, Sadie was allowed no such luxury. She tried to bite back her irritation at the inequity. Without the lively music in the background, the sounds of conversation, of mugs being set on tables, of men scraping their chairs back all coalesced into a kind of low buzzing noise.

Sadie approached a table of lumberjacks. "What would you three like to order?"

The first man, with a blaze of red hair that bristled around the knit Frenchman's hat that he hadn't bothered to remove, didn't even look up at her. He thrummed his thick fingers on the tabletop. "We're from a lumber camp on the mainland in the Upper Peninsula and we can't get any good hard liquor."

"Yeah, because of our boss." The dark-eyed man spoke the word *boss* like an epithet.

The third man, with greasy blond hair, dressed in a black and red checkered shirt like his tablemates, made a circular motion with his index finger. "Your best whiskey all the way around."

"All right." She took a steadying breath. She needed to know if her father was alive. Normally she'd not inquire of strangers, but no one had sighted him. Not one person recognized the name. "By any chance have you come across a lumberjack by the name of Duvall?"

The dark-eyed man, the youngest looking of the trio, frowned. "Why do you ask?"

The other two men looked up, their eyes widening as they took in her appearance. Sadie's cheeks heated. "My father is Frank Duvall and he's not returned from the lumber camps."

"Which camp was he in?" The red-haired man looked around for a moment, then spat a stream of tobacco into a nearby spittoon.

Sadie stifled the urge to gag. But she needed help. Why did she need to know about her father so badly? It wasn't like he was truly going to help her and her sisters financially. Nor would he do much in the way of parenting the younger ones. But he was her pa. She needed to know. She had to know.

The piano player started in on one of his favorite tunes and Sadie had to raise her voice to be heard, "I believe he started out around Mackinaw City and then moved on to a camp near St. Ignace or maybe even Newberry."

"We're with Graveau's outfit between them two cities. Ain't never heard the name." The blond man scratched his head. Hopefully he didn't have lice in that greasy mane of his.

"What's he look like? And does he like his drink? Because if he does, we'd have probably run into him at one of the saloons up there." Dark eyes sparkled with amusement as the other men laughed.

Dare she admit her father's proclivities? She exhaled a long breath. "Yes, he does enjoy the taverns. As far as appearance—he's what I'd call a wiry build. Has graying hair and blue-gray eyes. Is about average height." She raised her hand slightly above her head to indicate how tall Pa was.

"Not that many old-timers in our camp." The tobacco-chewer launched another stream across to the brass spittoon, almost missing it.

"What about you, miss? Who's looking after you?" Deep chestnut eyes fixed on her face. "Are you on your own?"

She averted her head. "Oh no. I have the rest of my family with me. But we'd really like to get Pa back home." She offered them a tight smile. "I best put your order in."

She hurried up to the bar, sure that the men's gazes were affixed on her retreating form. It wasn't really a lie, was it, to say that she was with her family? Her sisters were all she had left.

"Sadie, we got a big group comin' in from the docks in a bit." Mr. Foster raised his thick eyebrows high. "The foreman down at Mackinac Transport is retiring and they're bringing the rest of their party over here."

She nodded. If only he'd brought in another girl to help her tonight. But of course, he hadn't, the old tightwad.

Her next few hours were spent running trays of drinks back and forth and trying to avoid knocking any of them over. The lumberjack trio continued to cast sideways glances at her. With each round of whiskey that she delivered, they continued to ask about her—not her pa. She finally had to make up crazy answers.

"Miss Duvall, what do you enjoy doing around here?" The *spitter*, as she'd begun to call him, leered up at her.

"Why I enjoy dancing with the bears, out by Arch Rock, in the moonlight." She kept her face deliberately devoid of expression.

The other two men gawked. Dark Eyes hiccupped. "Thas danjrus." His words definitely were slurring more.

"Oh no." She smiled at them. "Brown bears are very adept at waltzing. I'm in more danger of having my toes stepped on if I were dancing with a human."

Spitter guffawed.

Sadie shook her head as she walked back to the counter. "I think we better cut them off."

Her boss wrinkled his nose. "Stop going by their table. We're closin' up soon."

The retirement crew had dwindled down to a handful. When Sadie served them what she knew was heavily watered-down rum, the retiree raised his hand. "That's enough for us I believe, miss."

The other men murmured their agreement.

Sadie pushed back a lock of hair on her damp forehead and examined the oak clock in the corner. She returned to the counter and leaned against it, well aware that she, like the rest of the place, wasn't smelling at all sweet now either. "Looks like we may be done with orders."

"Good." Mr. Foster, the tavern owner, pushed up his rumpled shirt sleeves and repositioned the black garters that held them there. He cast her a sly glance. "Hey, Sadie. Want a closing time brew?"

"No, thank you." She needed to get out of the tavern before the odious man had thrown back a few too many Stroh's Bohemian beers.

Blue ribbon winner at the Columbian Exposition in Chicago or not, too many Stroh's caused the man to leer at her like he'd done every night for the past week.

How different this horrid job was from her position caring for Mrs. Luce. She absolutely loved looking after the infirm woman. Unbidden tears welled in her eyes at the memory of Greyson's new wife's callous dismissal of her. Mr. Welling, Maude's father, had been the one who'd paid Sadie for her work with Greyson's mother. That was because Greyson was to become his son-in-law. But still, it seemed that Mr. Welling, not Greyson's nasty wife, should have been the one to have spoken to Sadie. Mr. Welling and Mr. Foster might be the same age, but these two men could have been from two different worlds, in the way they behaved toward her. Mr. Welling had always treated her with courtesy and respect, like he did his daughter.

"Suit yerself then." Foster scowled and filled his mug to the top with the pilsner.

She exhaled a sharp breath and tugged at her now-filthy apron. Like every night since starting, she'd have to wash and hang that and her work dress before she went to sleep. Right after she checked on her sisters and made sure they were safely tucked into bed.

Henry Harrison, the piano player, shut the keyboard cover with a bang. "That's all there is, fellas!"

The brawniest of the men pointedly turned in Sadie's direction, and she averted her gaze. She should have never talked with them about her father being missing. *Foolish, foolish girl.* Apparently, they'd misinterpreted her questions as interest. Or they just saw her as fair game without a father to protect her. But she still had God. Didn't she?

And thank the Lord, she'd no longer have to listen to Henry repeatedly playing "Daisy Bell," and singing other songs with lyrics so bawdy she had to tune them out. A dull throb droned in her aching head.

Sadie dipped her washrag in the soapy bucket of water as the trio of men slowly walked past her, the oak floor planks groaning beneath them. Without looking up, she wiped the shellacked table clean, then dried it with another towel. Too bad it didn't sop up the odor of the whiskey that had spilled there.

"Goodnight, Miss Duvall." The third man had paused at the door.

No, no, no. Now he knew her name. She really had been stupid. Sadie's knees began to shake. Staring down at the table, she called out, "Have a blessed evening, sir!"

He made no reply, but the other two men's laughter overrode the slam of the heavy front door shutting.

What if they waited in the old fort gardens, which she had to pass when she left? Sadie had a knife and a horn that Robert had given her several years earlier. Although he'd meant it as a souvenir of sorts, the thing made enough noise to at least startle someone. Now Robert was gone. He was the first man who'd stolen her heart, though he'd taken it unwittingly. He'd rescued her from the officer whom she'd dreamed would give her a better life but had lied. And how had she repaid Captain Swaine? By fussing at him and sending him away.

"Lock the door, Sadie."

She followed Mr. Foster's command and turned the brass bolt on the door. Outside, darkness had finally cloaked the island. She'd never worked an evening position before, other than the few times she'd had to stay over at the Luce residence. What a contrast this job was to the task of caring for poor, frail Mrs. Luce. But according to Anna Luce, Mr. Welling had refused to pay Sadie's wages anymore. That seemed only right since Greyson Luce was no longer engaged to his daughter. And neither Anna nor Greyson wanted Sadie there. Still, she wondered if Anna had lied. It wasn't like Mr. Welling to not be direct—and kind.

Sadie had only a day to make other work arrangements. At least there hadn't been a scene. Anna, the new Mrs. Greyson Luce, was too cold, too reserved, too utterly disdainful to stoop to arguing with a servant. Not that Sadie had protested. It was Greyson's mother who'd raised her thready voice to her new daughter-in-law. Sadie had spent a good ten minutes soothing the older woman and assured the invalid that she'd see her at church. And that she'd find a job quickly. No one, though, would offer Sadie a position. The bar owner was the only one who would hire her.

"Can I pour you one, Henry?" Mr. Foster hoisted a large mug as he called to the pianist.

"Not tonight. I'm gonna hit the hay."

Oh no, that meant she'd be alone with her employer. *Deal with the wolves within, or the wolves outside?* Sadie tugged at her suddenly too-tight collar. *Lord, help me now.* But she couldn't go running off.

She had to finish her job. She had to pay for her sisters and herself, so they could eat and have a roof over their heads. Footfalls headed toward her, and she unlocked the door for the musician.

"Goodnight, Miss Duvall." Mr. Harrison tipped his bowler hat at her as he headed out the door. "I'll keep my ears open for any news about your father."

"Thank you." She relocked the door and then flipped over the CLOSED sign, the bottom sticky with something. Sadie cringed. Was this to be the rest of her life? A barmaid in a rundown island tavern?

"Don't forget those tables in the corner."

Sadie retrieved her leather bag from behind the piano and set it on a bar stool. Tonight, she'd finally receive her wages to make all this misery worthwhile. She grabbed her cleaning items and moved on to the corner tables, her back aching. From the corner of her eye, Sadie caught a fleeting movement outside, in the shadows beyond the gaslight. Were the lumberjacks waiting for her? She shivered, and then quickly moved on to finish up her tables.

"Sadie, you almost done? Time to close up." The owner's words slurred slightly.

Time for her to get her first pay. She'd worked hard. By her accounting there'd be enough for rent, food, and a little treat for each girl. Her tips that week had kept them fed at a bare minimum. If she never ate another baked bean in her life, she'd be happy, and certainly no more bean sandwiches *ever*. Her heart began to hammer at the thought of the money about to be pressed into her palm. It would be worth it all… They'd be fine. For one more week, they'd be okay. But she'd not let him touch her. If he thought her pay entitled him to anything more than her waiting on customers, then Mr. Foster had another thing coming.

After putting her cleaning supplies away and hanging up her apron, Sadie approached the counter, and the till. She picked up the tooled leather purse that Grandpa had made for her years earlier and fingered the design of the pines pressed into the buttery soft deerskin. Mr. Foster was locking the cash register. She saw nothing in his beefy hands. She waited. At least he wasn't ogling her. In fact, he seemed to be avoiding eye contact.

"You can go on now." His gruff voice made her flinch.

Not without her hard-earned cash. "My pay, Mr. Foster?"

He blinked and his jaw shot up a notch, but he looked past her at a painting of the Tahquamenon Falls, centered on the far wall. "Well, now, missy, the way I see it—you've just worked off your pa's debt to me this week."

"What?" Bile rose in her throat. Her head throbbed; the droning noise in it ratcheted louder. She was being robbed. Suddenly light-headed, she placed her hand on the oak countertop.

Foster sniffed. "He stiffed me for a large tab he'd run up here before he left." He shrugged his shoulders but still wouldn't look at her.

"I didn't cause his bill—he did." Anger burned like fire in her chest, and she fisted her hands. "You owe me my week's wages."

"He's your pa—and now we're squared up. I'll start paying you next week." His tone wheedled.

Next week she and her sisters would be out in the street, starving.

"No!" Sweat trickled down her brow. She had to have that money now. Must pay their bills or they'd be given notice. Her sisters couldn't go without food. "You'll pay me, or I'll report it."

He laughed, a wicked low chuckle that began in the middle of his dirty, blue-striped shirt, his large belly jiggling the fabric. "And who'll you be telling?"

The sheriff who routinely put her father in the brink for the night? *No.* She fought back the tears overfilling her eyes, but she'd not let this bully see.

"Maybe there's another way for you to earn some money?" His tone sent shivers through her.

Mouth agape in shock, Sadie whirled on her heel and strode to the door. She'd not come back to work here. The holes in each stockinged foot pressed against the thin leather of her shoe soles. She couldn't trust this evil man, and she'd not return.

Sadie unlocked and pushed the door hard, letting it slam behind her. She didn't care if the glass in it shattered to pieces—Mr. Foster had deceived her.

Oh Lord, what am I to do? Oh God, I've struggled so hard, so long. Like a blur, the past year of working and caring for her sisters ran through her mind. Sadie wrapped her arms across her midsection, and rocked back and forth for a moment, trying to stem the tide of rising nausea inside her.

What about the lumberjacks? Were they hiding nearby? She dropped her arms from her waist, a cool chill of evening air washing over her. If only she had a cloak. If only she had something, someone to protect her. But even if her father was here, he'd be of no use.

Pa had never been the same since the winter he'd hauled wood over the ice covering the Straits of Mackinac for the Grand Hotel to be built. The men who'd transported the timber had to remain deadly quiet during their work, straining to listen for the sound of ice cracking—which could have meant instant death. Although the ice never had given way, thank God, something in Pa's very nature had snapped, changing his nature.

She was well and truly on her own. Not a buggy, not a single person on a bicycle rode past. Movement on the hard-packed road behind her hastened her forward.

"Wait!" From a few steps ahead, a familiar man's voice warned right before she ran smack into his solid chest.

"Oh!" She inhaled the light scent of cedar and spruce, the soft wool of his jacket familiar. She took a step away as the man grasped her upper arms. Faint light from the stars and the sliver from the moon reflecting on the water provided only the barest illumination, making the man's face impossible to discern.

"Sadie, what are you doing out so late?" *Robert Swaine?*

Recognition of the baritone voice opened the floodgate of her tears. *Such a good man.* He'd saved her from Lieutenant Bernard Elliott, who'd had no intention of marrying her but every intention of stealing her virtue and ruining her reputation. Robert was the man she'd foolishly spent years pining over but who'd been so far out of her reach. A bit older than her and a wealthy man; her time spent mooning over him as a young teen had been wasted. But he'd been the one she could always count on, before Miriam had crushed his heart.

"You're back." Her control vanished, and she sobbed into his shoulder.

Comforting arms slid around her, settling like angels' wings on her back, strong but gentle. "Now, now—it can't be as bad as all that."

Oh, but it was. *God knows it is.* She shook with sobs.

Several sets of footsteps came in their direction.

"Gentlemen?" Robert's stern voice held a warning.

But something wasn't quite familiar about *this* Robert. Muscles bunched beneath his wool jacket. This was a sturdy man with no hint of pipe smoke on him, no faint wheeze in his steady breathing. Was she mistaken?

Sadie sniffed. She couldn't get out any words. This had to be Robert. She needed him. She leaned in against the man. How many years had she and Maude run to her handsome young uncle, so he could fix their little injuries? He'd been a rock for Sadie—an example of a stable and godly young man who contrasted with her father's poor behavior. Of course, she'd never been held in his arms like this before, either.

"They're gone." His voice certainly sounded like Robert's, but this man was more compact and strongly built. Worry niggled against her comfort. He loosened his hold, but she remained leaning against him.

The wind rustled the lilac trees, wafting their sweet fragrance. Robert smelled nice—not like the men at the tavern and free of his pipe smoke. She, however, carried the odor of smoke and stale beer on her. Maude's uncle would have scolded her had he caught her in this condition—would have asked what she'd been doing.

She'd failed to bring a lantern with her because she'd been so excited about getting her pay. Fresh tears welled up, and she began to hiccup.

"What happened? Did old Foster try something with you, Sadie?"

She stiffened and pulled away. "No. But he didn't pay me."

A sob escaped her throat. Humiliation burned her. She couldn't tell Robert Swaine, a wealthy man, that she and her sisters were penniless. He'd think she was begging. Or worse.

"Well, Sadie girl, what does that matter? Why are you working for that worthless toad?"

She swallowed. "I...my father..."

"I just heard that he was gone." Robert squeezed her hand. "Do you have any idea where he might be?"

"He was supposed to go find work at a mill on the mainland or in a lumber camp in the Upper Peninsula."

"I saw him in St. Ignace quite some time ago. About a month after my sister, and your mother, succumbed." He drew in a deep breath.

"But not again?" She sniffed.

"No. I'm sorry. Now that I know, I'll start sending out word along the railroad."

"Oh." She'd forgotten he owned stock in Michigan railroads. She'd not been ashore on the mainland in years, and on a train only once in her life.

"And although that miscreant Foster didn't pay you, there are sufficient funds at the Island General Store to provide for you girls."

Girls? Her sister might be girls, but Sadie was a young woman. Obviously, he still thought of her as a child.

Spine stiffening, she recalled the pain she'd experienced when she'd pined away for him, her best friend's uncle, who could never be a match for her. "My father...did he send..."

There was a long pause. Waves repeatedly lapped against the shore nearby.

"You didn't know?" Something in Robert's voice held tension. Or was he fibbing? "I'm so sorry Mr. Keane didn't send word to you."

Not only had the pinch-faced shopkeeper never sent word, but when she'd asked for a line of credit, he'd refused her. "No," she drew the word out, then chewed her lower lip.

"I am sure that you girls have funds on account there." There he went again calling her a girl and he used the tone of voice that he saved for instances when he wasn't being quite honest—which was rare.

Pride warred with gratitude. She blinked back tears. Robert had to have set something up for her and her sisters, that was the only explanation she could imagine that made any sense. Robert was allowing her to keep her dignity by not disclosing that he was being charitable toward them.

I'm just a girl and a charity case to him. She stiffened.

One day, though, she'd make something of herself. She'd take care of her sisters, too. She'd find some way.

"I'll inquire at the store soon, thank you." Her voice sounded clipped to her own ears.

The kind man wiped her face with his handkerchief, gently dabbing her tears away. She didn't want to feel like a child. Robert's presence stirred a longing in her for more. More than being his niece's friend. But all those feelings she'd had for him were just childish dreams—weren't they?

"Let me escort you home, my dear."

"Thank you, Robert." She sniffed. "We're staying at Mrs. Eleni's boarding house."

Grunting what sounded like disapproval, but saying nothing, he looped her arm through his and walked her up the dark street toward the boarding house. As her arm brushed against his side, where she'd leaned in on so many occasions over the years, Sadie hesitated, then stopped. She'd never been in Robert's arms before, until this night, but many times she'd leaned on his shoulder, his arm wrapped around her on one side, and Maude on his other side.

Captain Robert Swaine told the most wonderful stories about ships and boats on the Great Lakes. And at Christmastime, Robert made the best Santa Claus. Had he been unwell? Because the Robert she knew required little padding for that role. He used to powder his hair and beard. When her face had pressed to his neck tonight, there was no beard.

"You're awfully quiet." Robert slowed his steps. "What is it?"

Ahead of them was the gaslight on the corner by her boarding house. A tiny niggling worry pursued her. What if this was someone impersonating Captain Swaine? But who could have known such details?

"Where have you been, Robert?" He'd been gone too long. Even Maude and her father had become worried about him.

He drew in a sharp breath. "Here and there."

He didn't say anything about being out on his ships. She'd heard he'd lost two. Should she press him for more? Sadie's palms began to perspire. The Captain Swaine she knew would have mentioned how he'd felt about such a plight.

They moved closer to the gaslight.

No beard, the man was clean shaven. And handsome—very handsome indeed. A man with a trim and muscular build who looked only a few years older than herself. Sadie tried to catch her breath.

"Something wrong?"

Robert Swaine had sported a bushy beard for as long as she'd known him. "So how long will you stay?" Sadie's mouth felt full of marbles. She was exhausted, distressed by her scoundrel of an employer and by those leering lumberjacks who'd hidden in wait for her. Was it possible that another man possessed a voice almost identical to Robert's?

He released her arm. "As long as it takes—perhaps even the summer."

The man her young heart had first pined for would never have said such a thing. His greatest desire was to be aboard ship, at the helm. "Captain Robert Swaine would sooner swallow his tongue than say those words."

Sadie backed away from the man, shaking her head. She ran toward the boarding house, as confusion warred within her.

Chapter Three

What was journalist Ben Steffan doing at the Grand Hotel, masquerading as a wealthy foreign industrialist? Adelaide crossed her arms over her chest and paced back and forth over the thick wool rug on her office floor. *Friedrich König indeed!* The reporter had certainly picked an impressive sounding faux name. She'd seen Ben Steffan in action, over her years in lower Michigan, enough to know that he was *hungry.* He was searching out a story that would launch him further in his career.

Was the journalist there to expose her secrets? She'd caught the handsome, young, social news reporter eyeing her suspiciously when she'd shown up at a number of Detroit events—always in different attire. It was as if he *knew.*

A lone tear trickled down her cheek and she wiped it away. *But he doesn't know everything. He knows nothing of all I've endured.* Uncontrollable shivers coursed down her arms. She reached for the cut glass decanter of water on her desk and poured herself a cupful, hands trembling so hard that water dribbled down them and she had to pull the cup away from the desktop.

A little girl. A ship. A young woman's patois half-comforting her and half-scolding her. Arriving in a seaport full of people speaking both French and English—and something in between. A house that smelled of fragrance so sickly sweet that Adelaide almost gagged—and had received a smack on her bottom. *"You behave, girl, you hear me? You lucky you got to come with me. We's lucky we ain't both dead."* But it hadn't seemed like luck—more like evil.

The door to the office swung open and Assistant Housekeeping manager, Mrs. Stillman, barged inside without even bothering to knock on the door. The woman scowled at Adelaide, making her almost-feral features even sharper. "Broken, I say!"

"Who has broken what?" Adelaide worked hard to make her countenance appear calm.

Definitely getting a lock installed on my inner office door.

"That new maid is gonna be the death of one of our workers or maybe even a guest." Mrs. Stillman scowled at Adelaide. "She was dusting a crystal bowl, decided to lift it to the light to admire it, tripped, and dropped it onto the floor."

Adelaide shrugged. "Accidents happen."

"Accidents happen? That's all you have to say?" Her subordinate glared at her—and not for the first time did Adelaide wonder how this woman had been hired for the Grand Hotel.

"I'm sure we've all broken things." Of course, not several expensive objects in one week, but luckily Mrs. Stillman didn't know about the other objects Maude Welling had laid waste to.

The assistant housekeeper wagged her finger at Adelaide. "You best take that money out of her wages if you're not going to fire her."

Adelaide stiffened. She didn't take kindly to be admonished by a woman whom she was increasingly becoming to dislike. "That will be all Mrs. Stillman. You may return to your work."

"Well, I never."

Adelaide shot the woman a warning glance before she departed. If this continued, she'd definitely have a conversation with Mr. Costello about Stillman's behavior and attitude. Adelaide sighed and rose from her desk as Stillman closed the outer door none-too-quietly as she departed. She shook her head as she felt for the pins on her bun to make sure they were still secure.

She strode down to the shoeshine station. "How are things going, Zebadiah?"

He looked up from buffing a pair of wingtips that had been left for polishing before dinner. "Fine, ma'am, just fine."

"Good." She clasped her hands at her waist. With no customers at Zeb's station and most guests out for afternoon jaunts, things were quiet.

"We got some shady lookin' gentlemen here this week." Zeb spoke his warning words quietly as he continued to work. "And Mrs. Stillman is constantly having fits over something that Miss Maude does. I helped the girl clean up a mess she made with her cleaning solutions this morning."

"Thank you." Adelaide briefly closed her eyes.

"The new singer—Miss Lily—she's got some secrets might be as big as yours." Zeb shook his head.

Time for the Pinkertons to be contacted. "I'll look into that. Thank you."

And time for Adelaide to finally step out and do what she'd really come to this island to do—to reconnect with her old friend, Peter Welling, in any way that would be helpful to him. She shivered. How could someone who'd traveled the world over be afraid of journeying less than a mile to the Winds of Mackinac Inn?

Someone banged on the Duvalls' door, rattling its rusting iron hinges until they might break, and then paused. It had to be their imperious landlady. Sadie locked eyes with Bea, who was dividing a long loaf of bread into five pieces. As the pounding resumed, Sadie flinched, but her younger sister simply scowled. Little Opal ducked under the table while Garnet stood shaking, clutching the back of a narrow unvarnished chair.

"Your money tomorrow or you're out." Mrs. Eleni finally stopped abusing their door. "Do you hear me, Miss Duvall?"

Cringing, Sadie hugged Opal to her chest.

Bea stomped across the narrow room and unlocked and flung open the door. "Sure, my sister heard you, and so did everyone else in this place, Mrs. Eleni. Now let us eat in peace."

The elderly woman tugged her dark scarf closer around her head, her beetle-like eyebrows drawn together in her wrinkled face. She muttered something in Greek, probably an epithet, by the way she ground out each word. Then she turned on her squat-heeled black pumps and returned back downstairs, mumbling in her native language the whole way.

Bea exhaled loudly and closed the door with a thump.

Garnet popped up from beneath the wobbly table, nearly knocking it over. "Bea, I'm hungry, what did you bring us?"

"There's ham and cheese to go on the bread." Bea unwrapped the waxed paper from the meat.

"Yum." Opal snatched a paper bag and opened it. "Cherries! I thought I smelled some."

Sadie waggled her finger at her youngest sister. "Go rinse them first."

"Ok."

A line formed between Bea's tawny eyebrows. "I can't keep doing this."

"I'll get another job soon." Sadie forced her lips into a half smile. "Cook sent this."

"Bless the woman." She'd always been kind to Sadie when she'd visited at the Wellings' inn.

Bea cocked her head at her. "But Sadie—Captain Swaine told me there was money for us at the mercantile. I saw him this morning. Papa must have left something there."

Sadie's lips parted but she bit back her response. Their father hadn't left two dimes for them to rub together. So, he certainly hadn't left funds at the store, despite Robert's implication.

"Why haven't you gone there?" Bea glared at her.

"I…didn't know." Not until last night when Robert mentioned it. "We've been there many a time, and the clerk hasn't said a word."

Bea shrugged. "And the captain said you know we could all stay upstairs above the store, too." Her angry tone left no doubt that Bea was done providing anything extra for her sisters.

"You saw Robert Swaine, then?

Bea's brow wrinkled as she divided the ham onto the pieces of cut bread. "Huh? What kind of dumb question is that? I just told you."

"No, I mean—didn't he seem different?" What she meant was—didn't he look even more handsome?

Bea blinked at her; her green eyes luminous. "Well, he's awful quiet. But he gave me candy like usual. And he's not staying at the inn, so something must be different like you say."

"I…see."

The girl's eyes softened. "I like him an awful lot. If only he wasn't so old."

"Bea!"

"Well, he's gotta be at least thirty. Maybe forty."

"Not forty—barely thirty—but too old for you." Sadie laughed. "Come on. Let's say the prayer and then eat." As they slipped into the chairs that island craftsman, Mr. Christy, had made for them, her shoulders relaxed. At least their fellow church members had tried to help them the best they could. They sat at the narrow table, another of the Christy family's gifts, and prayed over their meal. The craftsman had made the pine table for them, and his wife regularly gave them baskets of left over baked goods from their tea shop, but they had their own family to feed. And she wouldn't ask their pastor for any further help. Reverend McWithey had been very kind to them, too. She had to hang onto what little pride she had left.

When that was gone—what then? She had to find a way to gain the skills she needed to be able to support herself and her sisters.

"I'll pick up some things from the mercantile for us." Including a copy of the mainland newspapers. Somewhere out there, her future was waiting.

This past Sunday, Pastor McWithey had said sometimes people would step into the gap for you. She hated to call upon her friend, Maude, who was grieving the loss of her fiancé, but there was so much at stake here.

Tomorrow, she'd put aside her pride and call on her friend. Maybe she had some ideas about employment for Sadie. And if worse came to worse, Sadie could humble herself and beg for a job doing laundry for the Wellings or down where Ma had worked.

Hot tears threatened to spill. She'd promised herself that she'd never become like her mother had—aged before her time. And now Ma was gone.

But if it came to it, Sadie would do what she needed to do to help her sisters survive.

She wanted more for them, though.

And she would secure it.

Early morning rays of light pierced the filmy curtains in his absent cousins' room, as Robert woke from a fitful night's sleep at Aunt Virgie's massive cabin in the island's interior. He'd been unable to shake Sadie's words from his head. As she'd opined, the Captain Robert Swaine of years past wanted only to escape this island, onto the Great Lakes. And with his bequests from his parents, Robert had indeed pulled his anchor and set off onto the water.

He rose and stretched as a soft knock sounded on his door. He grabbed the worn flannel robe that Aunt Virgie had made him when he'd earned his captain's license and put it on.

"Robert? Are you awake?"

"I am." He opened the door.

She patted his cheeks. "Oh, don't you just look the picture of health now? I'm so glad."

"Me, too."

Aunt Virgie peered past him into the bedroom. "I sure miss my sons, but they've got their own families and pretty soon I may even have some great-grandchildren to boast about."

"And I imagine they'll all want to come and visit their Grandma Virgie."

She cast him a sideways glance. "In the summer. But neither of my daughters-in-law would venture up here for one of our winters."

The scent of bacon wafted up from downstairs. "That smells good."

"Oh! I better get back down there." She turned and moved with an agility he'd seen in his crew members but not in his elderly aunt.

He followed her downstairs.

"Just in time." She pulled the pan from the stove.

They enjoyed their breakfast together and Aunt Virgie caught him up on island news.

"What have you got planned for today, Robbie?"

"I can't wait to take my horse out for a ride."

"I know the stables in Harrisonville have taken good care of him."

"They have, but I want to get that Thoroughbred reacquainted with his master."

"Good idea. I imagine you've missed him."

"More than I realized." He'd missed so many things, so many people, including this dear lady, more than he'd realized.

"Do you know what I've missed besides seeing you and your dear sister, God rest her soul?"

His uncle had passed away quite some time ago. Virgie didn't like anyone bringing him up, though, so he'd not mention him.

Aunt Virgie covered his hand with hers. "I miss my time visiting with the tribe and the tribal elders."

Oh no. She's starting this up again. "Given that it's been so many generations since we've left, are you sure you're not more interested in learning more scary stories to share with your great-nephew, Jack?"

She shrugged, and grinned. "There's that. But as I near the end of my life—"

"Aunt Virgie don't say that."

She raised her hand. "It's true. I'm old. But I'm finding myself drawn back into the stories of my Ojibway ancestors—of your ancestors, too."

Mother had barely been involved with the tribe. Oh yes, she was very glad for the prominence her Native family had brought her in the local community. Yes, she was happy to make donations and help. But no, she'd not wanted to be involved in actual tribal functions. She'd left all that to her sister. And Aunt Virgie had made sure her children and all her nieces and nephews understood Chippewa lore. "Why don't you take Jack with you sometime?"

"Ha! As if Peter would let his son be associated with the tribe."

"Have you ever asked him?"

"Well, no."

"Ask."

"I think I will."

"Somebody needs to take that boy in hand before he's lost to us, Robbie."

Sadie had received some miracles in the past by stepping through these doors and into the Wellings' world, and today she really needed at least one.

As Sadie stepped inside, Jack Welling, in striped short pants and a navy shirt, crinkled up his nose. "Maudie ain't here."

She bent to the side and craned her neck to look around the boy and into the Winds of Mackinac Inn's large foyer. "Maude's not here?"

"Didn't I just say that?" Jack grabbed an apple from a nearby crystal bowl on a cherrywood table.

"Do you know when she'll be back?"

"Nope." Jack crunched down hard on his apple and chewed.

"Please let her know that I was looking for her." Sadie's voice sounded pathetic, even to her own ears.

Jack nodded and if she was right, there was a bit of sympathy in his expression.

Bea descended the stairs, arms full of sheets. "What're you doing here? Come to spy? Or gloat that you're not having to work right now?"

Sadie gaped at her younger sister. When she realized that her jaw remained open, she shut it tight. How could Bea think such things about her?

Mr. Welling's office door opened. *Oh no.* She didn't wish to speak with him. *How embarrassing.*

"Sadie, girl, it's good to see you." Mr. Welling gestured her toward his office. "Come in my dear, I wish to tell you something."

Bea glared at her. Hopefully he wasn't about to tell her that her younger sister had also gotten herself fired.

Sadie lifted her skirts and followed Maude's father into his office. Although the odor of pipe smoke still prevailed over a citrus scent, apparently Bea was telling the truth. She'd claimed recently that she'd conquered the dust motes in the office with a lemon oil-soaked rag.

"My dear, I'm dreadfully sorry about that Anna Luce thinking she had the right to dismiss you without my approval."

But if he wasn't planning to continue paying for Mrs. Luce's care, then wouldn't he have been the one to have done the firing? Sadie chewed her lower lip. She wasn't sure what to say.

"I heard you had a run in with Foster." He shook his head. "If he has robbed you of your wages, as I overheard Bea saying, then you could press charges."

"I don't think that would be necessary." She certainly did not want that horrible man sharing in court that her father had never paid his liquor tab.

Mr. Welling stepped toward the window, his back to her. "I wish I could do more for you, Sadie, but right now I find myself in a bit of a dilemma. I could end up in the situation you find yourself in."

What on earth did he mean by those words? "Surely not. You have a beautiful inn and you've worked so very hard. . ." with his wife, who had now passed away. "And you have all those other businesses to help manage." Except that since he'd returned, Robert was acting like he was in charge of them. It seemed any time Sadie entered one of the Wellings' businesses, Robert was there speaking with the managers as if he owned the place.

He gave a curt laugh and faced her. "My mother-in-law, Jacqueline, God rest her soul, was an interfering and fearful person. She has left a mess by what she thought would be a method of keeping her family together."

Sadie had no idea what he meant, so she kept silent.

Mr. Welling went behind his desk and sank into his chair as if he had the weight of the world on his shoulders. "Tell me, Sadie, do you believe Maude could manage this inn? Or the other businesses we have?"

She frowned. "I really don't know. Did you and, um, Mrs. Welling prepare her for those responsibilities?" Sadie hadn't seen evidence of such. Usually, Maude kept busy running around the island taking care of whatever needs she saw. It truly was a gift that her friend had, in discerning a problem and making provision. "Maude talked about managing the inn with Greyson. I thought that was the plan."

He harrumphed. "But there's no Greyson. Well, there is but he's married to that interfering woman, Anna. I'd like to give her mother a piece of my mind."

Sadie cringed. "I think she's deceased, sir."

"Oh." Mr. Welling's face reddened. "Her father then. He's still running his rag of a newspaper."

"Sometimes children don't listen to their parents, though." Her sisters were giving her quite a taste of that truth.

"Ha! Jack gives full evidence of that. I told him to bring me that last apple from the bowl and where has he gone to?"

Sadie chuckled. "He's enjoying that apple very much, sir. It sounded quite crunchy, and it was very juicy judging from the way it dripped from his chin."

"That boy!" Welling slammed his hands on his desk.

Sadie took a step backward toward the door. As she did so, she cast a quick look at the tintype images of Maude's uncles, Robert's brothers. One wore a Union uniform while the other was attired in that of the Confederacy. A chubby-cheeked Robert, young enough to have been those men's son, looked so innocent. Amongst the picture of the three brothers, Eugenia Swaine Welling offered a tentative smile. She'd been so kind to Sadie. And to Ma. Tears threatened to flow, but Sadie willed them away.

The office door flew open. Jack ran in. "Maude's home! And I'm sure she's up to something."

Peter Welling wagged a finger at the boy. "You're the one up to something. I hear you've eaten that apple you were supposed to bring me."

Jack scowled at Sadie. "Aw, you're a tattletale, Sadie Duvall!"

Sadie cringed as Jack ran off. "If you'll excuse me, Mr. Welling, I'd like to go talk with Maude."

Mr. Welling waved a hand dismissively. "Certainly. You young ladies make sure Jack isn't eavesdropping."

"Yes, sir." She knew all too well how the boy could be as quiet as a mouse and then pop up just when she'd told Maude something of utmost secrecy.

She hurried upstairs to Maude's room and rapped on her door. Perhaps Jack was telling a fib and her friend had been home the whole while. Mr. Welling acted as if she was.

Jane, the family's maid, came alongside Sadie. "I thought I saw you, Miss Sadie."

"Hello. I came to see Maude."

Jane leaned in closer and whispered, "You'll find her around back getting a good scrub-down after her work at the Grand."

Sadie could scarcely believe the words. Yes, she'd heard that Maude had snuck out and taken a job at the hotel, but hearing the words come from Jane's mouth, she was well and truly shocked.

What in the world was her friend doing? Maybe Sadie could take Maude's job at the hotel and her friend could return to her normal life here at the inn.

"Follow me out back to the laundry room, Miss Sadie."

Why did this situation remind Sadie of the time she and Maude had dressed up like boys and taken a ferry to the mainland by themselves? How puffed up they'd been, so sure of themselves, so cocky over their success.

But Sadie had long ago run out of self-assurance. She'd need to lean hard upon God if she was going to find solutions to her situation.

Adelaide's spartan quarters perfectly suited her. No garish Victorian era reds, golds or greens—just the rusticity of wood and plain cream-colored linens and cottons. The former reminded her too much of recollections of her early life. And even though the plain surroundings were reminiscent of her times in the Poor House in Shepherd, Michigan, Adelaide still had fond memories. Memories that included young Peter Welling—the one true love of her life.

She patted the antique locket that she donned every evening after work. The small gold locket held a snippet of her birth mother's hair. The front was engraved in the French style—perhaps a gift from one of her mother's patrons.

Tonight, her head throbbed. This pretense, this position, was costing her dearly. And it was interfering with her management of her other businesses. She needed to accomplish her mission and then leave this job to someone who was actually suited to it and who needed it. She rubbed her forehead. Adelaide poured a packet of willow bark into her glass of water and stirred it. She took a long sip from the slim glass. How she hoped that the young researcher she'd recently sponsored, Dr. Felix Hoffman, would find solutions that would enable the company, Bayer, in which she was heavily invested, to produce a shelf-stable medication that could control headaches such as she experienced. Guilt often triggered an especially vicious attack. Tonight's pain was a mere annoyance.

At least all of her paychecks were being funneled back into training funds for the old-timey Sugar Plum Ladies catering group outside of Detroit. From there, Adelaide hoped to find her hotel replacement, come fall, for the following season. The post-Civil War group catered all of her events and she'd hired several workers from there for summer work in the Grands' kitchen. All of them kept her well-informed of any unusual situations.

She sipped the bitter solution. Maybe it wasn't guilt. Perhaps her current *mal a tete* wasn't from trying to avoid people and keep her identity secret. After all, of course, she'd known that there would be wealthy investors coming to the Grand Hotel. But Adelaide had not counted on there also being so many *other* issues. She was dealing with Mrs. Stillman, an assistant housekeeping director with a dodgy past, Peter's daughter, Maude, who was a nightmare as a maid. Then she'd discovered that the local Pinkerton agent, who was indeed somewhere in the area, refused to meet directly with her.

Before she could sleep, she must send out another directive, to her secretary Miss Reynolds, and instruct her to use all available means to secure the services of a Pinkerton who would answer only to her.

What good was money if you couldn't get what you wanted with it? And right now, Adelaide wanted answers.

Chapter Four

Robert turned the large brass key in the Island General Store's lock with a mix of both pleasure at having the means to open the building and discomfort, knowing that, rightfully, Peter Welling should be the one who had control of this structure.

Nothing I can do about it.

Wasn't there?

He relocked the door, went behind the walnut counter, and retrieved the inventory book. He opened it and scanned for the items he'd requested for the Duvall girls' upstairs apartment—*if* proud Sadie would give in and accept the space from him. But if Sadie knew the entire situation—of what his mother had done to limit her descendants—he doubted she'd accept his offer.

The door swung open, jingling the bell that his mother had placed there many years ago, when he was a young boy. When Jacqueline Cadotte Swaine had finally given up hope that one of her sons, lost in the Civil War on the opposing side, would walk through the door, something inside of her must have died. Even so, she'd determined to start over. What had his sister, Eugenia, thought? Did that daughter believe she wasn't "enough" for her mother—that she needed another son? child? That losing them had left a hole in her heart?

Robert had always known he was the *replacement* son, which made it all the easier to escape to the lakes, and all the harder when Mother had died. She'd loved those two brothers first. She'd loved them best. And Mother lost them both. Living in their shadows was an unhappy place to be.

And guilt was nobody's friend.

"Good morning, Robert." Leon Keane's droopy-lidded eyes widened as Robert removed his straw hat and set it on the corner hat rack.

Robert tapped the inventory list. "Is all of this upstairs?"

Lips puckering, Leon nodded, strands of his thinning auburn hair bouncing against his wide brow. "All set up. Right as rain."

"Good. And, of course, Sadie has an open tab here—anything she wants."

"Yes, sir." Leon scratched his forehead. "It's just that Peter—"

Robert raised a hand. "My brother-in-law has no say in the matter." Even if he wished it otherwise, as the will currently stood, Peter had no legitimate control over this business.

A muscle in the man's lean cheek twitched, but he nodded.

"I'm going upstairs. Let me know if Sadie Duvall comes in, would you?" Now that he'd told Bea about the available funds at the store, perhaps Sadie would stop by. When Bea had asked the same thing her older sister had—whether their father had left it there for them—Robert once again hadn't answered.

Was he lying by omission? *Father, forgive me.*

Robert went back outside and rounded the corner, to the side entrance, where a ladder hung from the side of the white-painted wooden structure, in the event of fires. The false front of the building gaped against the siding and appeared to be detaching. He'd send word to the carpenter to get it repaired. Now if only his fellow businessmen would repair their edifices as well. They all seemed to be distracted by the changeover of the National Park to a Michigan State Park, and too concerned with the legalities to focus on refurbishes.

He opened the exterior door and stepped into the entryway to the inside staircase, which smelled of fresh paint. Good, the painters finished. Light poured through the side window in the entryway and onto the stairwell. He opened the window to release some of the lingering paint fumes then mounted the steps and headed to the upstairs apartment. His brother-in-law hadn't wanted to be bothered with renting out the space, and his sister, God rest her soul, kept only some extra furnishings that she liked to rotate in and out of the inn.

He unlocked the solid oak-paneled door at the top of the stairs and entered. The scent of oil soap, beeswax, and lemon tickled his nose. Mary Meeker had done her job quite thoroughly, judging by the way the dusty, dank odor had been vanquished since he'd last stopped by. He should hire the industrious young woman to clean out the family cottage for him, up on the West Bluff.

Inside, the first room was about eight paces by eight, more like a large closet, and a good place for Sadie to store Bea's things, who was staying in the servants' quarters at the Winds of Mackinac Inn. In the main room, Keane had brought up a pastel, oval-shaped hooked rug

51

that covered most of the floor. The narrow divan, an overstuffed chair, and a table should all be comfortable for the Duvall girls.

He moved on to what he imagined would be Sadie's room, with lined Irish lace curtains at the windows, and a matelassé coverlet on the bed. A sturdy trunk and a bureau sat where he'd instructed Keane to place them as well as a substantial mirror over a small vanity table. This was a plain room but serviceable. The room for the other two sisters featured twin beds, side-by-side, with a small white wicker table between them. Hangers in the closet were empty. He smiled to himself. If it were up to him, he'd fill all the closets full to overflowing.

He removed his watch from his vest pocket and checked the time. Almost one o'clock. He'd go to the Grand for afternoon tea and speak with the lead housekeeper there. Knowing Maude and her ridiculous notions, no doubt his niece would follow through with her threat to obtain a position there if her father wouldn't let her run the Winds of Mackinac Inn. He blew out a puff of air and returned downstairs.

Inside the mercantile, customers clustered, bent over a display of yard goods.

The bell on the door rang. "Good morning, Mr. Keane." Sadie's breathy voice made his heartbeat accelerate.

Robert moved toward the back, hoping to avoid her and her sister, but to also catch a glimpse of Sadie.

"Miss Duvall," the clerk called out, his voice strained. "I'm so very sorry I failed to send word to you earlier about your line of credit here."

Robert felt like slapping his forehead and then that of the clerk's. No one would have extended a line of *credit* for Frank Duvall. *Only a dunce would.*

"Credit?" Sadie's thin voice sounded ready to break.

"No, so sorry—I meant you had funds here credited to you that you can draw from."

"Oh, I see." From her pinched expression, Sadie no doubt saw all too well.

Robert puffed out a breath.

Opal, Sadie's youngest sister, began heading toward the back of the store, where the books were, and directly toward Robert.

The little sandy-haired girl glanced at Robert briefly, then stood by a display of children's picture books.

He moved aside and pretended to be looking at a row of nautical books, while surreptitiously glancing at Sadie.

The child moved to his side and raised a book up to him. "Do you know what this cover says, mister?"

Treasure Island. He took the book in his hands, recalling days sprawled on the guest bed in Aunt Virgie's home, reading this book as a boy. How he'd loved Robert Louis Stevenson's enthralling story. "Ah, that is one of my favorites but I'm not sure a young lady such as yourself would enjoy it."

"I'm Opal, and I'm not a young lady—my pa says I'm a whelp. But I don't know what that means."

What kind of father called his child a whelp? *Frank Duvall would.* Robert inhaled slowly then exhaled. Unfortunately, there were a lot of Franks in the world.

"Opal?" Sadie moved toward them.

He fought the desire to run. He broke out in a full-blown sweat beneath his vest. It was as though he'd taken a good splash in a nor'easter.

"Robert?" Sadie's heart lurched. It really was him. Although Robert was only thirty years old, premature gray had streaked his temples while threads of white wove through the rest of his dark wavy hair. Small lines clustered only around his large hazel eyes, which focused intently upon her.

Too intently.

She pulled at her fingertips as though she had gloves on, which she didn't. Then Sadie hid her roughened hands behind her back.

"How are you doing this morning?" Twin dimples formed in his cheeks, complimenting his square jaw and cleft chin. With all that dark beard removed, there was no doubt Robert Swaine was a handsome man. The same fellow that as a youthful girl she'd pined after.

Robert clasped her hands between his. "You look like you've seen a ghost." At the contact of his hands, warmth sped through her like hot spiced cider on a cold winter's night.

Recollections flooded her mind—Robert roller skating with her and Maude, taking them for a ride in the carriage, hiking up to Arch

Rock, his comical attempt to teach her to ride a bicycle. His visits home were always the happiest times she'd known. A tiny sob threatened to well up. She shouldn't be so needy. She could take care of herself. She needed to do so and to offer her sisters a future off this island.

She didn't need to put her heart on the line. She was leaving this island to better herself.

Opal tugged on her elbow. "Sadie? That man wants to know when we're moving in upstairs."

Robert's cheeks flushed.

"Do you remember Mr. Swaine? He's my friend Maude's Uncle Robert."

Opal narrowed her eyes at him. "You look different. You're skinny and where's your beard at?"

Robert laughed. "It's still me."

"What do you mean about us moving in upstairs?" Sadie cocked her head at her little sister.

"There are, indeed, living quarters upstairs available to you, should you wish to occupy them." Robert's lips twitched.

Opal pulled again on her sleeve. "What's he sayin'?"

Dropping down on one knee, Robert looked Opal in the eye. "There are rooms over this shop where you and your sisters could live."

His gaze locked on Sadie. "If you want to."

"I do!" Opal clapped her hands and motioned for Robert to rise. "I want to live up there away from that mean landlady."

As he stood, he wiped at his knees. "Rather spartan accommodations, I'm afraid, but I hope you'll be comfortable."

Nothing could be more spartan than Miss Eleni's rooms. "I…" Pride grasped at her voice box, but hope shook it off, "…why that would be delightful." Maybe Pa had done something for them after all. And here, all this time, she'd thought he'd not given them a second thought. She'd give Leon Keane a piece of her mind when she was alone with him sometime.

Robert offered his arm, and she took it, a frisson of excitement startling her. "Would you like to go look first?"

His gentle voice, and the way he treated her like a queen and not the tavern girl who'd just *quit* the job that put food on the table, made Sadie a bit giddy. "Certainly, thank you."

They stopped at the register. "Mr. Keane, we have a few things for you to hold for us at the register, please."

"Certainly." Keane took their purchases but kept his gaze averted. Robert wished he liked the man better, but he'd always been so brusque with him. He'd been officious to Peter, though, and almost obsequious with Mother when she was alive.

"Come on with me and I'll show you." Robert extended his arm and Sadie took it.

Opal tugged on Robert's coat sleeve. "Is there a big cushion for me to sit on? My friend has one and she and I lie on it with her cat."

"Not right now." He winked at Opal. "But I imagine that can be arranged with Mr. Keane downstairs."

Sadie shook her head. "No. We need to use that money wisely and a floor cushion is a frippery right now."

"Aw, Sadie, you're no fun."

Robert shrugged. "I may have one at my house that you could use. I certainly won't be sprawling on a cushion on the floor."

"Why not?" Opal cocked her head. "Are you too old?"

Robert laughed but Sadie gaped at her sister. "Opal, I can't believe you just said that."

"It's all right. I'm sure I seem rather decrepit to your sister."

At the stairwell, he released her arm and Sadie felt the loss of his touch. But she needed to lift her skirts to mount the steps. Robert gestured her forward. Her head swam. Eight years older than herself, Robert had been an object of her fascination for years—her notion of the ideal man with his attentiveness, his humor, and kindness. She almost tripped over her skirt hem, and Robert caught her elbow.

"Careful, Sadie girl—I can't have you falling."

No, she couldn't fall. But it certainly felt like she might—just not as he meant.

She stepped inside. Fresh paint odors filled the entryway. At the top of the stairs, she opened an oak door carved with curlicues. Inside, lemon and beeswax scents comingled, and the wood furniture shone. They closed the door to the stairs.

A sturdy coat and umbrella rack stood nearby and what looked like a new rag rug covered the dark wood floor.

"It's a little warm up here." Robert crossed the room and raised a tall window. Lacy curtains were pushed back, allowing the breeze to filter inside.

Sounds of carriage wheels and horses' hooves carried up from the street and the scent of sugary sweetness from nearby candy shops, too. No odor of fish, ash, and moldering decay.

"This is very nice, Robert." She pressed a hand to her throat.

He blushed. "I thought that first tiny room would be perfect for storing Bea's belongings.

Sadie ducked her head inside as Opal pushed past her.

"She doesn't need a bed like Garnet and I do. I wanta see our room." Opal ran back out.

Robert laughed. "I think she's excited."

"If she'd got her very own bed to sleep in, I'm not sure she'll even calm down enough tonight to be manageable."

"Be prepared then." Robert swiveled around and Sadie followed him.

He opened the next door. "Your room, my dear."

Tears sprang up in her eyes. The bedroom reminded her of Maude's—decorated in a style she'd long admired and wondered if she'd ever have. When she'd imagined herself as Bernard's young officer's wife, she'd pictured something just like this. The delicate lavender paint on the walls and lacy curtains gave the room a feminine feel, while the bedding was cozy and substantial—ivory wool Hudson Bay blankets lay stacked in the closet for cool nights.

Suddenly lightheaded, she sat atop the trunk at the end of the bed as Robert held her elbow.

"I take it that you like the place, Sadie."

"This is so beautiful."

"Then don't say no—move you and the girls in."

"But the expense. I couldn't afford it."

He briefly raised his hands. "No one's using it. You and your sisters might as well."

She drew in a slow breath. "Let me think on it. And pray."

"Would you like to do that right now?"

"What?" Sadie stiffened. "Do you mean right here?"

"Why not? Doesn't God hear us anywhere?"

Opal skipped into the room. "Oooh, I like this room the best."

"Come join hands with us, Opal. We're going to pray." Robert motioned for her sister to join them.

The child gawked at them but then complied, slipping her tiny hand into Robert's much larger one.

Sadie took two steps closer and shyly extended her own hand, which Robert accepted.

He bowed his head and closed his eyes.

Sadie gave Opal the stink eye and her sister stuck her tongue out at her before lowering her head. Sadie drew her lids closed.

"Dear Lord, we thank you for your provision and kindness, we love you and we accept your mercies daily. Guide us dear God as we seek your will in all things. We ask this in Jesus's name. Amen."

"That's it?" Opal made a comical face.

"I think that's plenty." Sadie smiled at Robert. "I believe you got right to the point."

"Too bad Reverend McWithey doesn't keep his prayers short when we have coffee and muffins after church." Opal crinkled her pug nose.

"You're not supposed to have coffee anyways." Sadie wagged her finger.

"Pa says it won't hurt me none."

Pa. Where was he? Sadie caught the look of anguish on Opal's face just before she turned and ran out of the bedroom.

"I'm sorry, Sadie. I've got people looking into your father's whereabouts, but nothing yet." Robert exhaled loudly.

Sadie had to find him. Had to obtain a position where she could provide for all of them. For now, though, this was where she needed to be. "I think we'll move in here, if you're sure that's all right."

"Good."

And she felt peace about this decision.

Soon she and Opal departed, and Robert set off for the Grand Hotel to a business meeting with some railroad investors. He lived in such a different world from them.

Opal held hands with Sadie on their walk back and swung her arms back and forth with vigor. "Wait till old Mrs. Eleni hears about this!"

Nearby, an older lady gasped. "Will you look at what that boy is doing?"

Sadie turned to spy Jack Welling riding his bike with his arms raised high overhead.

"My oh my, some children simply don't use the sense that the good Lord gave them." The matron clucked to her friend.

Opal leaned in. "That lady is right about Jack, that's for sure."

"Opal, that's not nice."

"Yeah, but it's true." She swung her arms harder.

"You're going to tear my arms out of their sockets if you keep it up." She'd been reading an anatomy book at night when the girls were in bed. It was one of the books on the *Recommended Reading List* for nursing school applicants at the Newberry Asylum. Graduating that program could land her a job that would provide for all their needs.

Opal dropped Sadie's hand and ran off, darting between other pedestrians on the walkway.

"My, she's in a hurry." Mrs. Doud, the grocer's wife, pushed her tow-headed baby past in a stroller. "I think Opal could give Jack a good run for his money in a race."

"Maybe in a few years." Too bad girls couldn't run in the races. They all raced against one another at school but not in any organized community events.

"Humph, maybe in another lifetime when men let women have the vote and when we're out proving all we can do."

"Isn't that the truth?"

"You should join our Women's League group. We're supposed to hear from Mrs. Carrie Booth Moore this Saturday during our luncheon. She's speaking on finding one's purpose."

"I just might come by." Although what she could learn from a prominent socialite about finding her purpose Sadie wasn't sure.

"Come sit at my table with me. I'll probably have baby with me, though."

Sadie grinned down at the adorable little infant who was fast asleep. "Thanks for the invitation."

"We women have to stick together."

"Yes."

"I'll see you later."

Sadie continued on, a new lightness in her step. When she reached the boarding house, Opal was seated at the bottom of the stairs, crying.

She hurried to her baby sister. "What's wrong? Are you hurt?"

Opal shook her head and shoved a piece of paper with handwriting scrawled on it at her. "I think this says something bad."

"Where did you find it."

She hiccupped. "On the door."

Oh no. Sadie took the note and scanned it.

EVICTION NOTICE.

She sucked in a breath.

What if she'd been too proud to accept the free lodging over the store?

Opal sniffed. "What's it say?"

Get out. Be gone. "It says hooray—the Duvall girls are moving above the mercantile!"

"Really?"

"Yes, we're going to move to those beautiful new lodgings."

Opal scrunched up her face. "It looked like it said Evie ick shun. It looked like the note we got at our house."

Sadie crumpled up the paper into a ball. "What that note means is exactly what I said—we're getting ready to move to that place where you'll sleep in your very own bed. And you don't need to worry yourself about it—other than you need to start packing up your things tonight."

"Will you help me?"

"Of course." She tousled Opal's hair.

God willing, she'd help herself and her sisters in any way possible. Even if that meant leaving the island. First, though, she had to find employment that would pay for them to make that move to the mainland.

Chapter Five

Another morning waking up at the Grand instead of in his own home—but a place that reminded Robert that both his mother and now his sister were gone. When he stepped through that door for the first time, he wanted to be strong for the staff, and for himself.

Robert rose from bed, donned his robe and slippers, determined to get a good start on the day ahead. He must speak with Peter and open a dialogue with him. Robert cracked his door open and checked the hall, to retrieve his polished shoes. *Nothing.* Zebadiah, the shoeshine man, always did a fine job and started early, which meant Robert's broughams should have been returned by now.

Hushed voices carried down the hallway. Something rumbled and shoes tumbled from a cart and scattered across the floor, hitting with repeated thumps. One of the maids covered her mouth, stared at the mess, and then back at her empty cart. With quick but jerky movements she scooped up the footwear and placed it back on the cart. Something about her looked very familiar. He was sure it was an island girl. But who? The hotel didn't normally hire locals as maids.

Further down the hallway, another door opened. Attired in a silky-looking bedroom ensemble, Laura Williams strode toward the employee.

"May I help you, miss?" Laura, his old friend, began pairing up the shoes. "I'll check for room number tickets in each, too."

Robert closed the door and chuckled. Leave it to Laura to show up here and take charge. And once she realized that he was also present at the hotel, he'd likely have to add to his list of responsibilities where this lady was concerned. At least he could count on being entertained by Laura's stories of life as an actress. He'd see if she could take dinner with him one night soon.

A soft *thunk* sounded outside his door. Likely the shoes being placed there by the clumsy maid. He went to the armoire and laid out his clothes, then returned to the door and retrieved his buffed-to-a-shine shoes.

While he waited for someone to arrive to assist him with shaving, he'd catch up on some of his work. He took a seat at the desk and pulled out a wooden box full of items he must address.

Before long, someone rapped on Robert's hotel room door. He marked the place where'd he'd stopped reviewing statements that his accountant had sent from the mainland. He had to decide soon about ship replacements. He rose and moved closer to the door. "Come in."

A uniformed hotel staff member, whose visage looked somewhat familiar, opened the door. "Mrs. Fox suggested that you might need assistance, Captain Swaine."

Robert didn't have a manservant. This blasted daily shaving might have him rethinking that. He ran his hand along his prickly jawline. "I can manage most of my needs. But are you good at shaving?"

The man appeared to be about a decade older than Robert—perhaps forty. Presumably the man had mastered those skills.

"Yes, sir, but I didn't bring a kit up with me. Mrs. Fox said you preferred using your own."

Yet another inconvenience caused by deciding to become cleanshaven. "Yes, I've got my kit here." He pointed to the bureau.

"Fine, sir. I'll get everything ready."

Robert pulled a chair over by the table. "What's your name?"

"Trey is what I'm called but my full name is Shadrach Clark the third." A small smile tugged at the blond man's thin lips.

"Ah, Trey because you're the third?" Robert closed his eyes in concentration, recalling this man's father. Was he misremembering, or wasn't Sadie's mother a Clark? "You're an old-time islander and your father was a fisherman?"

The man grinned. "That's right."

"I think your family cabin is near my Aunt Virgine's."

The man laughed. "Virgie is a treasure."

"The Clarks and the Cadottes have some shared history, too. I've heard those stories."

Trey nodded. "Your mother's namesake was supposed to be the kidnapped infant of a French aristocrat."

"The commander at Fort Michilimackinac during the French-Indian Wars."

Trey set out the items in the shaving kit. "And my own namesake, Trey, and his wife, Mercy, took that little girl in as their own."

"And then one of my métis Cadotte ancestors visited the island and became love-struck."

"I've seen a painting of her, and I can see why." Trey inspected the shaving items.

"Oh, the stories Aunt Virgine has told me." Robert chuckled. "Including some frightening Ojibway tales that I had to shield my niece's ears from." Jack, on the other hand, delighted in the stories and would retell them with his own additional lurid details.

"I have no doubt of that." Trey grinned. "But I'd better get to helping you or Mrs. Fox will have my hide. I'm one of only a few islanders that she convinced management to hire this season."

"Well, Trey, I don't wish to cause you trouble. I could use a close shave, but I should be able to dress myself—that will spare you some time."

"As you wish, sir."

Soon Trey applied shaving soap to Robert's face with a deft hand. "I heard you are now a railroad man as well as a ship owner."

"That's true." He'd acquired his ships one by one and had made investments in railroads. "But I'm only able to manage ships—not trains."

Trey's eyes narrowed in concentration as he lifted the razor and examined Robert's face. "I knew your sister—she was a good lady."

"Yes, Eugenia truly was." He'd lost her, two ships with his closest friend and fellow captain aboard, and likely the goodwill of his brother-in-law. Was it any wonder that when Sadie seemed to doubt who Robert was that he couldn't manage any response? He *had* changed. His life had changed. His appearance had changed in response to all of these losses.

"Mrs. Welling gave my Ellie a position, a couple years back, when I broke my arm and couldn't work. It helped us keep our home in Harrisonville." Trey gave a curt laugh. "Don't be worrying—my arm is fine now."

"You read my mind." Robert looked up into the man's dancing blue eyes.

"I can give your hair a trim later in the week, if you'd like."

While one part of him wanted to let his hair grow out long and curl around his collar, he couldn't help wondering what Sadie would think about that. "Yes, that would be wonderful."

Trey soon cleaned Robert up and dealt with the shaving implements. "What brings you back to the island, Captain? If you don't mind me asking."

Robert was there to make things right within the family. Yet how did he do that? No doubt rumors were already flying as to the situation Peter had been left in because of Mother's codicil to her will. "Always good to see family." Even though he hadn't in the past year.

"That's good. Do you have a busy day, today?" With efficiency, Trey completed his tasks.

"I'm going to meet with my brother-in-law, Peter Welling." Then he'd move on to telegraphing his mainland friends to check on Sadie's father.

"Very good. He's seemed quite. . ." Trey's eyes widened slightly and then his lips clamped together.

"Go ahead, man. Finish your thought. We're both islanders."

The worker slowly shook his head. "He's been very out of sorts since his wife—your sister—died. Not that I blame him."

There was so much more than that going on in Peter's life, but Robert wasn't going to disclose anything more. "We're all missing her very much."

"My wife says the quilting group isn't quite the same without her and Mrs. Duvall. She was a distant Clark cousin."

Robert's heart clenched. Sadie was suffering, too. "They were both sweet ladies." And his sister had been like a second mother to him.

"They were." Trey slacked his hip. "Now that I think about it, since your mother's line was adopted into the Clark clan, doesn't that make you a distant relative of the Duvalls?"

He ran his hand over his jaw. How strange. The Clarks had rescued little Jacqueline and cared for her and thus Robert and his family were here. And from the Clark's biological lineage, Sadie and her family existed. "Seems so."

"I wish my wife and I were in a position to help Sadie and her sisters more than we have." Trey compressed his lips.

"Perhaps their distant cousin, by adoption, may be able to do so."

Trey's light eyes locked on his. "That would be a blessing to them." He smiled and departed.

Once he was attired, Robert headed down for a quick breakfast. As he strode through the lobby, he caught a glimpse of singer, Lily Swaine as she chatted with Dr. DuBlanc, the two looking thick as thieves. If he were a betting man, he'd lay odds that young Dr. DuBlanc was besotted with the songstress. Robert moved on and showed his hotel guest card to the maître d'. Breakfasts were notoriously lightly attended, since most guests were sleeping in after a long night of activities and parties. Today was no exception, with perhaps two dozen people in the massive room. Seated just inside the main dining salon sat Mrs. Lindsey and her daughter with the server setting steaming plates before them.

Robert waved to Friedrich König who was drinking coffee, a newspaper clutched in one hand and an apprehensive expression on his face. König nodded at Robert.

If he had time, he would chat with König, but Robert needed to get to the inn while he was sure Peter would be there.

"We've got a nice seat by the window, Mr. Swaine." One of the attendants beamed at him and gestured to the windows that offered a magnificent view of the Straits.

Robert dipped his chin and followed the young man.

"Coffee?"

"Yes, thank you. And I'd like to have some fruit and dry toast, please." His new habits died hard.

"Yes, sir."

Would he slip back into his habit of overindulging in sweets and breads now that he was back on the island? Would he have his driver take him by carriage to any destination under a half mile away? *No.*

An hour later, his now-dusty broughams took him to the Winds of Mackinac. He'd walked, instead of taking a carriage. Instead, he'd savored the fresh winds from the Straits that stirred his blood and urged him to stay home. Could those same gusts exhort him to set his anchor here—with Sadie? But hadn't Maude said that Sadie wanted nothing more than to be away from the island? That she felt trapped here.

The notion of Sadie feeling hemmed in on the island caused his ever-present low level of sorrow to swell into a moment of grief. If Robert honored his mother's wishes, that her heirs must remain on the island to retain their inheritance, and if Sadie. . . He shook his head. He wasn't going to ask, "what if." He was going to deal with what was.

Robert mounted the steps to the inn's broad covered porch and opened the massive oak door. Bea Duvall rose from behind the front desk, brushing wrinkles from her white apron. He'd heard from Cousin Stan, on his carriage ride home the previous night, that Peter had hired Bea, as a favor to Maude. Truthfully, with what he knew of the recalcitrant girl, he wasn't sure that was such a good idea.

"What are you doing here, Captain Swaine?" The girl's brusque tone set his teeth on edge.

This place technically belonged to him and his niece, until his nephew also came of age, yet he had to answer *why* he was there? Because Peter Welling wasn't accepting how things stood. This had been Robert's home for many years. And now he had to explain himself to Sadie's sister? "I'm here to speak with Mr. Welling."

"He and Jack are eating."

Robert had had enough of being treated like a stranger. "I'll join them." He strode down the hall, passing the family's maid, Jane, on his way.

"Why sir, it's good to see you. And you all clean-shaven, too!" Jane's cheeks grew rosy. "Are you joining the menfolk for breakfast?"

At least someone seemed happy to see him. "I am."

She bobbed a curtsey and headed off down the hall.

How many memories he had of this inn. Of this *home*. Of being welcomed graciously by his sister's open arms. Of her laugh and her love for the entire family. *God rest her soul.*

Robert straightened and adjusted his waistcoat. He took several steps forward until he stood in the doorway to the Winds of Mackinac's dining room. He opened the pocket doors and stepped inside. The heavenly scents of a family breakfast wafted toward him. Hunger stirred within him, something that hadn't happened at Virgie's or the hotel. But really the cravings he had were for family and reunification. That desire trumped all else.

His nephew, Jack, pushed back from the table. "Where's your beard, Uncle Robert?" He ran to him.

Robert scooped the boy into a bear hug, powerful emotions surging through him. When the child stepped back, Robert rubbed his knuckles over the boy's tawny head. Jack had certainly shot up in the past year. "I think you may soon surpass your father in height."

The boy's eyes widened.

Peter stood and cleared his throat. Not long ago, his brother-in-law welcomed him as a family member living under this very roof. Now Robert stood, awaiting an invitation to sit. Peter shot him an angry glance before he redirected his attention to his son. "Jack, take your seat."

"Aw." But the boy complied.

"Come in and sit, too, Robert. After all, this is your home, too." But Peter's voice implied otherwise.

Standing here now, to Robert it seemed that he'd always been away on a ship, out on the Great Lakes but his heart, his home, remained on this island. "Thank you. I believe this was my chair." Robert pulled out a well-used chair on the right side of the table, one that had a gash on the curved wooden back. "There's my Indian flint mark."

"I found an arrowhead last week up at the arch." Jack shoved a buttered piece of toasted bread in his mouth.

"We'll talk about all your running around unattended later, young man." Peter glared at Jack.

Virgie had written to Robert that Jack hadn't been given much supervision since his mother had died. And in their discussions since Robert had arrived, his aunt continued to urge him to offer supervision to the dear boy.

Robert settled into his chair. Hopefully Peter wouldn't ask about the Canary. "I won't stay long. I'll be up at the Grand, so no need to worry about me."

"I assure you, I won't." Peter's voice held a slew of frost, but Robert would not be deterred. "But since you look like you're not eating well, perhaps I *should* be concerned."

Robert quirked an eyebrow.

Jane, the Wellings' young Irish maid, entered. She set a familiar plate in front of Robert, as well as utensils and a golden yellow napkin—his sister had picked out the color because she enjoyed the cheerful color.

Robert met the kind young woman's concerned gaze. "Thank you, Jane."

"You're ever so welcome, Mr. Swaine."

Ah, he was *Mr. Swaine* now, not just plain old Robert.

His brother-in-law cast Jane a stern look and then pointed to sweet-smelling hot pancakes covered in butter and maple syrup, coddled eggs, and links of steaming sausage. "There's more than enough for you."

"Thanks, I think I'll have some." Robert reached for a plate of biscuits in the center of the table and grabbed two even as his conscience urged him to watch what he put in his mouth.

Peter made a noise that could have been construed as either gruff agreement or simply irritation.

"How have you been, Peter?" Robert took a bite of his biscuit. Delicious. No wonder he'd never been able to refuse food prepared by his sister's cook. But he needed to be careful. He didn't ever wish to be as sick, again, as he'd been the previous year. He set the biscuit back down. He tapped lightly on the table as he awaited his brother-in-law's response.

Peter's ashen complexion, the new lines in his face, and the stoop in his shoulders told of his heavy burden. "Might sell this place."

Robert flinched. It wasn't Peter's to sell. Sad, but legally true. This wasn't going to go well. And with Jack present, Robert had no intention of upsetting the boy. The child had no need to know that what should have been his father's property, instead would be divided between his sister and himself when he came of age.

"Let's talk about this privately, Peter."

"In my office, then." Peter swiped at his mouth with his napkin and then rose from his seat.

In the old days, Robert would have refused and finished his delicious breakfast. But now,

after giving Jack a smile and a wink, Robert followed Peter down the hall.

Stale cherry tobacco odor and the faint scent of brandy announced the inn's office as his brother-in-law's domain. *But it isn't.* Robert had to get Peter to realize that he didn't have the right to sell.

"Jack and I need to get away from here." Peter turned his back. "Away from the memories."

"Eugenia was gone too soon."

"Everywhere I turn, I see her. I wish my wife was here still."

"I know." Everywhere on the small island were reminders of Mother, Father, Grandmother, and now his beloved sister. At least out on the Great Lakes, he could escape the memories. Or so he'd thought.

"I imagine that's why you haven't been back to us in some while now."

"That's part of it." Robert laid the document from his attorney atop the teetering pile on what had been his sister's desk. "You should take a look at this information. At your convenience."

"And if I don't?" Peter arched one shaggy brow as though to challenge him.

Like the whipping currents in the Straits of Mackinac, Robert's temper flared. But like the good captain he was, he'd keep his eye on his destination. And coming here wasn't to push his beloved brother-in-law into another spell with his heart, if that indeed was what was causing his chest pain. Robert had his own fences to mend.

Truth be told, if it was Sadie they were discussing, Robert would feel as Peter did. He'd want to protect her, to cherish her, and give her every comfort that he could. But would she accept his offerings? "Sticking your head in the sand won't make this debacle of my mother's go away. We have to move forward."

"And have my children take what I've worked so hard for?" Peter shoved a broad hand through his silver-streaked hair. "To put Maude in charge here?"

"Where is Maude, anyway?"

A gentle knock at Adelaide's office door interrupted her review of the books for her hotel on the mainland, in Mackinaw City. The place was doing very well. Very well indeed. She smiled.

"You may enter," she called out as she closed the ledger book and slid it into her drawer and locked it.

Maude Welling, with dark circles under her eyes, entered the room. "I imagine Zeb might have gotten some complaints today, so I wanted to stop by."

Adelaide frowned. "No. He's not come by." She pointed to a chair and Maude sat.

"I knocked over the shoes on the cart this morning and I'm worried some of the shoes may have gotten scuffed."

"Did they look to be?" Adelaide steepled her fingers together. As much as this young woman was a sweet young lady, she was rapidly becoming a liability.

"Well, no. At least Miss Williams and I didn't think so."

"Miss Williams? The actress?"

"Yes."

Adelaide stifled the impulse to reach for her headache solution, instead simply eyed the mixture in the carafe nearby. "And how did Miss Williams get involved with the shoes?"

"She's my Uncle Robert's friend and she came and helped me."

Did Maude and her family know everyone on this island and everyone who visited? No, that was an irrational thought. But they did seem to have a spider's web worth of connections. "Well, that was very kind of her."

Maude nodded solemnly.

Adelaide rose. "But in the future, if a hotel guest should offer to assist you, then you'll decline. Am I clear?"

Maude stood. "Yes, ma'am. I'm sorry."

"As am I." Adelaide kept her voice low, "I'd like to try you at some work away from the guests."

She blinked rapidly. "Yes, ma'am."

Adelaide wished she could ask the young woman, who was reported to be a genius with bookkeeping, to review her own personal business books. "And if I were you, I'd continue doing bookkeeping for your relatives."

"Because you plan to let me. . . go?"

"Because it's an excellent skill. I may have you review some of our books here." One thing she wanted Maude to do was to go over every single employee shown in the entry book with every single person actually working. Something wasn't adding up right, and Adelaide was going to find out who was passing themselves off as an employee.

And she'd find out why. Were they here to expose her identity? Or was there someone here up to something more nefarious?

Sadie's arms ached from scrubbing and scouring every surface of their rented rooms. "We're almost done."

Opal set down her dusting rag and started to cry. "Why did Ma have to die?"

"And why can't Pa come back and help us?" Garnet flopped down into a chair.

Bea scrunched up her nose. "I work like this every day. Instead of acting like crybabies you ought to be thanking your lucky stars that Captain Swaine gave you a place to stay." She harrumphed as she stomped toward the wash basin.

Sadie finished wiping the nearby wall down then tossed her dirty rag into a pail. Might as well toss these out. "We're not going to give Mrs. Eleni any reason to complain about how we've taken care of these rooms."

Bea snorted. "This is likely the cleanest this place has ever been."

"Yup." Garnet got up and got in line for the wash basin. As she passed Opal, she jutted out her slim hip into her sister's side. "You, too, Oap-poe."

"Don't call me that." Opal rushed in front of Garnet and got behind Bea who was drying her hands.

"Do you want us to call you Nettie?" Bea swished the towel toward Garnet.

Sadie grabbed the towel and set it back by the basin. "Come on. Jerry will be here any time."

Bea's green eyes widened. "Jerry Meeker?"

"Yes."

Bea began patting at her hair. "You didn't tell me he was helping."

Sadie blew out an exasperated breath. "Robert arranged for Jerry to assist."

Garnet laughed. "Bea loves Jerry," she mocked in a sing-song voice as Opal joined in.

"Stop!" Sadie's nerves were already frayed. "He'll be here any moment."

"All right." Opal's face was full of contrition as she washed her hands. Garnet, though, smirked.

Sadie shook her head.

Sadie had known this moment was coming, but now, with Mrs. Eleni scanning the room, about to throw them out, the deep humiliation she'd *imagined* was replaced by gratitude. She had a grateful heart for Robert and for God's provision.

Her landlady marched through the apartment, like a colonel from the fort inspecting his troops. Sadie stiffened, wrapped her arm around Opal, and drew her little sister close to her.

Two times now they'd had to move in under a year. They'd lived in their little cabin all their lives until Pa had gone off and left them. Leaving their cabin for the boarding house had been far more traumatic for them than this change would be. With the way things were changing, soon most of the French–Canadian cabins on the island, such as they'd lived in, would disappear while inns catering to resort guests would be built to replace them.

Sadie bent down and whispered in Opal's ear, "It will be all right. Don't worry. We'll be in our new place soon."

Opal nodded several times in succession as if trying to convince herself of the veracity of Sadie's words.

Jerry Meeker, one of the draymen that Robert had sent, emerged from the bedroom. He lumbered past them, Sadie's dilapidated trunk in his arms. His overalls' straps drooped from his shoulders like Papa's often did, and Sadie resisted the urge to pull them up for him.

"This it, Miss Duvall?"

She nodded, her cheeks burning. Those meager possessions already carried downstairs and this trunk were all they had to move to their new apartment over the store.

Opal clutched her ragdoll to her chest, eyes wide, as Mrs. Eleni ran a finger over the mantel. Garnet crossed her arms across her skinny chest and glared.

The woman shrugged. "I guess the place looks all right, but with the many late payments you've made, I think I'm entitled to hold back the refund on your deposit."

Sadie had anticipated this response, had prayed about it, even had peace that God would work the situation out in her favor.

Someone cleared his throat, and Mrs. Eleni looked past Sadie and Opal to the doorway, her ruddy face turning a deeper shade of burgundy. "Mr. Swaine, how nice to see you." Her gruff voice left no doubt that she would prefer to not see him.

The tension in Sadie's body eased, even though her heartbeat kicked up a notch. "Robert, thank you for coming by."

Mrs. Eleni glanced between the two of them, as Robert moved to her side, then squeezed her hand and released it. "Are you ready, ladies?"

Opal's features bunched into a frown as she hugged her doll even tighter.

Trying to keep her voice calm, Sadie spoke as gently as she could, "I believe so."

"Why are you keeping Sadie's money?" Garnet asked Mrs. Eleni.

Her wrinkled face collapsed into a sneer. "I'm not—you impertinent child."

A muscle in Robert's jaw twitched. "I don't believe she's impertinent—rather she's observant and heard what you said as I arrived. You can send the Duvalls' deposit to them at the store."

He lifted his hat and gave her a brief bow, then turned them toward the door.

If Sadie never saw these rooms again, it would be too soon. They held the sourest of smells and the saddest of memories.

Robert lingered at the door, leaning in to speak with their landlady in a soft voice. "Mrs. Eleni, since when have you been so uncharitable?" His voice held disbelief.

"It's the leases, Robbie. I'm so afraid." Was that a withheld sob in her voice?

"With the transition? Is this not your own boarding house?"

"No, it's a lease from the National Parks."

"Oh." He sighed. "I'm hearing the same from others."

"My lease renewed right before the Michigan Parks took it over, but they're saying they won't honor it—that I'll be charged double on the lease. What will I do? I'll have to leave the island. It's the only life I've known, Robbie."

So, Mrs. Eleni was in a predicament not too far off from Sadie's own. Still, did she have to be so ornery to them?

Pride, too much pride, like your own. That still, soft voice pinned Sadie to the stairs.

She couldn't hear the rest of Robert's and the landlady's whispers. Soon he joined her on the stairs.

Looking up into his hazel eyes, she smiled in gratitude. "Thank you, Robert," she whispered as they descended the boarding house steps.

Several hours later, the dray had been unloaded and their belongings unpacked. Garnet lay across her bed reading.

Opal sat atop her own new bed, patting her doll's head. "It's gonna be all right."

Sadie bent and pressed a kiss to her sister's head. "Yes, I'm beginning to think it might be."

"I like this place."

Garnet looked up from her copy of *Little Women*. "I think Mr. Swaine might have fixed this place up for us."

The pink-tinged walls of the gathering room reminded her of sunsets over the west, over Lake Michigan, when she and Maude had watched with Robert and with Maude's parents. The light purple walls of her bedroom matched the color of her favorite lilacs. And the bedding and curtains were exactly like some she'd shown Maude, once, in a catalog. Had her friend told her uncle? Everything seemed brand new. And the scent of new paint indicated this apartment had only recently been made ready for them. Something didn't quite add up. She'd talk to the clerk on the morrow.

If Robert Swaine was the one sponsoring them... Her cheeks flamed. She could only imagine what the island wags would say. Sadie with no job. Robert home now. A line of purchase credit at the grocery.... She needed to find a job. And quickly.

If Maude could wander up to the Grand Hotel and be hired, perhaps she had a chance, too.

Sadie's pride was nearly gone. She'd beg her friend to help her. And she'd do anything extra that she could, to help fund her training.

She would support herself and her sisters and she'd not rely upon the kindness of others.

Her time for daydreams were gone. Her time to take actions that would get them out of the mess her father had left her in was now.

Somehow. Some way. There would be a better tomorrow for all of them. One which Sadie had some say and control over.

Chapter Six

A friend of Maude Welling's, you say?" Adelaide schooled her features into a mask of serenity as she gestured for the young woman to enter her office.

Although the pretty blond was dressed well enough, Adelaide's expert eye took in the slightly frayed hem on the skirt, the almost-perfectly darned hole in the plaid wool jacket and the worn heels on the leather pumps. A surge of emotion, unlike anything she'd experienced in years, flooded over Adelaide. She blinked back unaccustomed tears. This young woman appeared much as Adelaide had on her very first interview after finishing secretarial school. Adelaide had been so nervous. She'd known she hadn't had the pristine starched blouse worn by the other candidate in the waiting area and she'd not had an immaculate woolen skirt, but one handed down to her by Mrs. Welling before the woman had sent her off to school.

This girl, this woman, was not like Maude Welling. Oh no, Sadie was something else indeed, and likely in a situation much like Adelaide had found herself in thirty years earlier.

Adelaide drew in a steadying breath before she moved behind her desk. "My name is Ada Fox and you'll address me as Mrs. Fox. I'm the Housekeeping Manager here at the Grand Hotel," although hopefully not for long, "and I run a tight ship."

"Thank you for seeing me, Mrs. Fox." The woman's voice was barely more than a whisper and her hands trembled. "I'm Sadie Duvall and I'm accustomed to hard work."

Sadie's red and work-roughened hands, unadorned by gloves, gave testimony to her words.

"You'll find plenty of hard work here, Miss Duvall. I assure you of that fact."

"Yes, ma'am." Sadie dipped her chin.

"Have you worked as a maid before, in a hotel?"

"Yes, years ago, maybe about ten now, yes, I worked at Lilac Inn on the other side of town. Only a fraction of rooms compared to the Grand, but I believe I understand the basics of what might be expected."

Adelaide arched an eyebrow. "Good. Tell me more about your work experience."

Sadie's face reddened. "I want to tell you straight out I recently quit my job as a bar maid at Foster's. I was only there a short while. The conditions of employment didn't suit me." She cast a gaze at Adelaide that spoke volumes.

She raised her hand. "You don't have to explain. If you ever encounter difficulties with any of the male staff or guests here, you are to come directly to me and report it. Do you understand?"

"Yes, thank you, ma'am. That's a relief." Sadie clutched her hands in her lap. "Before that I had worked for four years for Mrs. Luce, an invalid, and she's given me a reference as well as Mr. Peter Welling, who paid for Mrs. Luce's care."

Heat shot up Adelaide's collar. "Mr. Welling did that?" The words had come out of her mouth before she could stop them. How like Peter to help others.

"Yes, Maude's father, he's a very kind man. Do you know him?"

Adelaide nodded. "I do know the owner of Winds of Mackinac." He was that and so much more. "And you provided care for Mrs. Luce only?"

"Oh no, I also did the housekeeping—while she slept. I also shopped for her, prepared her meals, and so on."

"I see." What Adelaide *saw* was a hard-working and beautiful young woman who'd have been married off years ago if she'd come from means and lived in a more populous region.

"Would you like to read the reference letters?" Sadie reached into her reticule and pulled out several sealed envelopes.

"Yes, let me take a look." Adelaide accepted the missives and scanned the one from Peter first.

To Whom It May Concern:
Sadie Duvall is a young lady of untarnished reputation who has been in my employ for four years, as the primary caregiver of a local woman who is confined to a wheelchair.

He hadn't typed it but had scrawled the recommendation in his familiar handwriting. Her heart lurched and her cheeks heated.

"Is anything wrong?"

"Oh no, this is high praise Miss Duvall. I'm trying to think where I should start you, given the experience you have."

"So. . . I have the job?"

"You do. Now—let's go over your duties and our expectations."

"Thank you, ma'am."

"One of your obligations will be to look after your friend, Maude."

"Oh?" Sadie arched one golden eyebrow.

"And also Friedrich König, one of our guests here."

The young woman's narrow nostrils twitched ever so slightly, but Adelaide had detected the "tell." Sadie knew something about the imposter.

But what did this young woman know?

Adelaide steepled her fingertips together. "Now Miss Duvall, do you possess great discretion?"

"I like to think so."

"Then obviously you must know her father doesn't care for her to be working here."

"Yes, ma'am."

"So if you're her good friend then you need to keep her job a secret and also help her stay out of difficulties."

"She's never worked a paying job before," Sadie almost whispered.

"I figured as much. But I think Miss Welling needs to learn some things about herself and how and what is needed to run an establishment such as this—especially if she intends to ever manage the Winds of Mackinac Inn."

Sadie looked skeptical. "I'm sure we can look out for each other."

Adelaide rose. "Follow me and we'll get you set up with your uniforms and your schedule."

"Already?" Sadie stood and smoothed out her skirt.

"There's no time like the present."

A rap sounded at the door.

"Come in."

One of the bellboys carried in an elaborate arrangement of lilies, roses, carnations, and ferns. "For you, Mrs. Fox."

"From whom?" She blurted out the question, in astonishment, before she could stop herself. Fatigue was definitely taking a toll on her ability to rein in her tongue.

"Mr. Welling."

Adelaide sat back down in her chair and watched as the young man set the tall bouquet in the middle of her desktop. They smelled heavenly. "Thank you."

"You're welcome." The employee departed and closed her door.

Sadie took two steps closer. "I think prayers are being answered."

"Oh?" Adelaide's tone came out sharper than she intended.

"We prayed at the Women's League just this past Saturday, for Mr. Welling to move past his grief. He's such a kind man and it hurts so many of us to see him so sad."

She didn't know why she wanted to share this information with a young woman she'd just met, but Adelaide nodded. "Peter Welling and I were dear friends when we were young. And we've both lost our spouses recently." Granted hers had died almost two years earlier.

"I'm sorry about the loss. But I'm happy he has a friend to comfort him. He's been all alone in his sadness, I'm afraid."

"I hope not anymore." And Adelaide meant it.

"How does he seem to you, ma'am?"

Adelaide gaped at the young woman.

She'd not confess that she'd been too afraid to reach out to him.

"I'm afraid I've been so very busy with my duties," *Liar, Liar* "that I've not been able to see him yet."

"Oh, Mrs. Fox, you need to remedy that. Please excuse me for saying so."

"I do, Miss Duvall. I believe yours are the words I needed to hear."

Sadie dipped her chin.

"Now, let me go over the rules and then I want you to get acquainted with the layout of the rooms here at the hotel."

Robert took Sadie's elbow and pulled her to the side as a trio of Grand Hotel guests strode down the hallway toward them. "You'll be working here at the hotel?" Robert wasn't sure if he should sigh in relief that Sadie would remain on the island or if he should panic at her being there where he was staying.

She nodded and cast a quick glance as the trio moved past.

He should set his pride and grief aside and return to his family home on the West Bluff. He knew it in his heart, but that cottage held so many memories. And pain.

"Yes, Mrs. Fox hired me." Sadie smiled up at him.

"She's much better than Mr. Foster."

Her pretty features tugged.

He leaned in. "I know you're fighting back an unladylike snort."

"You!" She swatted at his arm, and he threw his hands up.

"It's the truth. I've known you too long." Not long enough. He lowered his hands.

"I doubt there's anyone much worse than him."

He shook his head. "Oh, I assure you there are far worse behaved men than Foster."

She drew in a deep breath. "I believe you. Sometimes I think that living on the island has insulated me from the rest of the world and its realities."

Her brows drew together. The dark circles under her eyes, that he'd noticed since his return, didn't seem to be improving. He was tempted to caress her cheek, but he'd not do that in this busy hallway.

Two men, one wearing an expensive navy suit that Robert recognized as being from a Chicago tailor, and the other in ill-fitting brown jacket and trousers passed them from the other direction. The two kept their gazes fixed ahead. This may well be Mr. Butler and Mr. Parker, who'd come to fisticuffs at the hotel recently and weren't supposed to be on the premises. And Robert certainly didn't want them around Sadie.

"Keep to yourself, do your work, and listen to Mrs. Fox and you should be all right." But would it be? With thugs like Parker and his employer Butler visiting the hotel, he wasn't quite sure.

"You sound like me talking to Bea." She gave a curt laugh.

Again, Robert wanted to touch her. To take her hand and give it a gentle squeeze. But he couldn't do that. "Can I accompany you on your ride back home?"

She blushed. "I walked."

Of course she had. "Let's see if there's a buggy that we can take."

Sadie shook her head slowly. With her hair pinned up so severely, she looked much older than her twenty-two years and the dark circles beneath her eyes added to the effect. "I can't. The carriages are intended for guests and I'm an employee."

"But I'm a guest."

She compressed her lips, the color fading from them. "And I'm not, Robert. That's one of the many differences between us."

From behind him, Robert heard someone running toward them. He turned.

"Uncle Robert!" Jack grabbed his arm and tugged. "I need you to take me home."

Sadie frowned at the boy. "What are you doing here?"

Jack grabbed Sadie's hand, too, and pulled them toward the stairwell. "Come on. You promised me a ride home."

Robert and Sadie simultaneously exhaled a sigh. "Nephew, I promised you that if I ever caught you here at the hotel again that I would escort you back to your father."

Wide-eyed, the scamp looked up at him. "Yeah. Same thing."

"It's not," Sadie muttered.

Robert, with Jack pulling him, half-stumbled toward the stairs.

"The carriages are in front not back here." Robert pointed out the obvious.

"We can jump on the back of Stan's dray. He's waiting out back after dropping off a load of hotel provisions and he said I could catch a ride back if I didn't. . ." Jack released their hands and moved ahead of them to run down the stairs.

Two maids stepped aside as the boy rushed past.

Sadie arched a brow. "If he didn't *what?*" She took slow steps down the stairs, holding her skirts to the side. It didn't seem that long ago when she wore shorter skirts, sometimes well above her boot tops. But it had been over a decade, certainly. Eugenia had stepped in when Robert had mentioned that the girl needed more suitable garments. She'd ended up passing on some of Maude's belongings as well as giving Mrs. Duvall extra material that she had.

"I don't know what he meant. But we can ask Stan."

Sadie smiled at the two maids who passed them on the stairs, but the dark-skinned women averted their gazes. One he recognized as the shoeshine man, Zeb's, wife.

"We can ask him if that little devil hasn't simply run off or told Mr. Danner to drive away." Sadie gazed back at him, concern in her eyes. "Are you doing all right?"

He patted his cleanshaven face. "Since I have that weight of the beard off me, I find it much easier to run up and down stairs." In years past, his asthma and the extra bulk he'd carried would have had him wheezing by now.

Blue eyes gazed blankly at him but then she laughed. "Your beard's weight? Seriously?" She shook her head as she moved quickly down the stairs.

He caught up with her at the bottom. "Yes, I had to shave that heavy thing off so I could keep up with you now that I'm back. You're a good eight years younger than me."

Her shoulders stiffened. "I *feel* as though I'm a good deal older than *you*, now. I've got two sisters to raise—three if you count Bea. And I can assure you, that responsibility will age you quicker than you can say, 'Jack's pulled a fast one on us' and I mean that." She pointed to where Jack rode off on a bicycle that sported a tag identifying it as one belonging to the Grand Hotel.

Robert ran his hand back through his hair. "I'll have to talk with Peter about this."

She cocked her head. "About me seeming so much older, more matronly?"

He chuckled. "About his son."

Another headache. Adelaide and Lily had that in common. Adding to Adelaide's stress, the hotel's new singer claimed to be one of the heirs to the Swaines' estate—yet another person to steal some of Peter's rightful wealth from him. That last one wasn't exactly true. Lily Swaine hadn't asked to be included in the inheritance from Jacqueline Cadotte Swaine's estate—not yet anyway. Poor Peter. He'd been deprived of what was rightly his by that mother-in-law of his. The controlling woman's behavior reminded Adelaide of Peter's interfering mother. But if Mrs. Welling hadn't sent her off, Adelaide wouldn't be where she was today.

Right now, though, she needed to focus on managing her businesses from afar. Adelaide hadn't even been able to leave to check on her hotel in Mackinaw City yet. That was one investment she'd hoped she could utilize on her days off from the hotel. She shouldn't be complaining because now instead of leaving the island, she and Peter were visiting in her free time. She smiled.

The rapid knock on her door startled Adelaide. No one dared approach her in her private quarters. "Who is it?" She rose and went to the door.

"It's Mr. Costello."

She clasped her shawl around her shoulders. "It's after hours."

"I just wanted to convey how important it is—"

She unbolted and unlocked the door and pulled it slightly open. "Yes?" She arched an eyebrow.

Costello stood there in his ill-fitting brown suit. The man desperately needed a tailor. He looked like he'd borrowed a much bigger man's clothes.

"I'd forgotten to mention earlier that we have, indeed, booked the journalists' conference."

Adelaide stared at the hotel manager. More journalists? Wasn't Ben Steffan skulking about enough? She moistened her lower lip. "I appreciate you letting me know."

"Well, they can be so particular that you may need to rethink your staffing arrangements. I don't mean to interfere, but that one maid is an absolute disaster."

"Maude?" she whispered.

"That's the one." Costello heaved a sigh. "But the new girl from town, Miss Duvall, is first rate. I'd like you to put her on the same floor as the reporters."

Adelaide straightened. Sadie was a beautiful young woman. She didn't want her anywhere near those randy reporters. "As you mentioned, that would be my prerogative where my ladies are placed." She compressed her lips.

Her stern look had the desired effect because the manager averted his gaze. "Yes, well, I simply wanted to make sure you knew."

"Thank you, Mr. Costello." Her words came out just as clipped as she intended. Maybe more so, since she now would have to concern herself with not just Ben but his fellow newspapermen.

"You'd shared with me about Miss Duvall's concern over all the food being left out in the men's meeting room and because of that, the kitchen staff have significantly decreased the amount that is being sent down there during the psychiatrists' conference. She's saved me—saved the hotel—a tidy sum." Costello beamed in approval.

Some of the tension left Adelaide's shoulders. So, Mr. Costello wasn't trying to put Sadie in harm's way. "If I were you," she raised her free hand, "and perhaps it isn't my business to say so, but with the journalists I don't believe I'd bother to send down much more than sandwiches, coffee and tea, and cookie trays. Simple fare."

"I think you're exactly right." Costello actually smiled. "Oh, and Mr. Mark Twain or rather, Samuel Langhorne Clemens, has also confirmed his attendance."

That had Adelaide grinning, too. "I love his writing." And she'd met him on several occasions, granted always in one of her disguises.

"Don't we all?"

"Indeed." Jack Welling would be thrilled to hear that Mark Twain would be at the hotel. The boy loved his stories. Adelaide would have to procure a private moment for the child with the renowned humorist.

"And Mrs. Fox, please keep an eye on Mr. Christy."

"The craftsman? Whatever for?"

"No. Not him. The accompanist for our singer, Miss Lily Swaine. Clem Christy is his name. He's a relative of our own Mr. Garrett Christy."

Luckily the hallway held no guests, or Adelaide would have pulled the manager into her room. "Why do you need someone watching over the piano player?"

Costello leaned in. "He's taken up with a Chippewa woman in the encampment."

Adelaide shrugged. "Isn't that his private business?"

"Not if he brings her up to the hotel." He tugged at his waistcoat. "We have a great many guests who wouldn't look kindly on that."

The searing pain of her childhood had motivated so much of her behavior over the years. But was it really fair to herself to hold herself responsible for the prejudices of others?

What would hotel guests do if they knew Adelaide's past? Adelaide's secrets?

She needed to be free of this dread she'd carried with her from early childhood.

But how?

Chapter Seven

Wasn't that somethin' about those big boats wreckin' out yonder in the harbor?" Dessa patted Sadie's arm. "I don't think anyone's gonna get their work done right today after that." Just thinking about the two ships *sinking*, made Sadie shiver. "Thank God no one perished."

Dessa shook her head slowly. "If'n that new Round Island Lighthouse was done finished, maybe no collision would have happened at all." Sadie exhaled a long breath as she adjusted the lace-trimmed apron of her parlor maid's uniform. "It can't come soon enough to help prevent future crashes." But by then, she'd hopefully be accepted into a nursing program and away from here.

"Any of your friends help out with the rescue?" Was it selfish to be glad that Robert hadn't been anywhere near town when the two ships collided in the harbor? She'd been so relieved that Robert had taken Opal and Garnet on a horse ride despite the heavy fog, on trails through the island, that fateful day. And of course, islanders had risen to the occasion and helped those poor folks aboard. "Maude's father, Mr. Welling, rallied the islander forces behind the rescues. And of course, our hotel guest, Mr. König, swam out to save some families."

"He's a hero. They both heroes." Dessa raised her thick dark eyebrows.

"Yes." Bea had been inconsolable after the wreck until she'd heard Mr. Welling was all right. Sadie had no idea how her sister had become so attached to Mr. Welling. Bea confessed that Mr. Welling was her example of how a Pa *ought* to be—and the business owner had always been kind to her. Sadie no longer placed ads seeking information about her father's whereabouts. They'd have to trust in God to return their father to them, if Pa was still alive. Which he might not be. And they'd have to accept that—if such was Pa's fate.

"We best get our carts."

Sadie and Dessa greeted the other maids as they strode toward the carts that lined the end of the hallway on her floor of the Grand.

Time had passed quickly on this job. Too quickly. Sadie hadn't had time to send out her inquiries about nursing training yet. She exhaled a puff of discouragement. After ensuring the contents were in order, she maneuvered her pushcart toward the ladies' parlor, where she'd been given purview. She grabbed her feather duster and set to work on the cherry tables in the front corner.

"Mr. Swaine?" From nearby, Laura Williams's voice dripped with cherry-cordial sweetness.

Ceasing her chore, Sadie strained to hear the beautiful brunette actress's conversation with Robert.

"Good to see you. Excellent performance last night."

Was that the sound of him kissing her hand? Sadie gritted her teeth.

"Thank you. You know I always love to see your face in a crowd—even without your beard—which I miss, by the way." She giggled in a suggestive manner and Sadie fisted her hands.

"Oh Laura, come have afternoon tea with me, and let's talk."

He called the actress by her Christian name? He'd never shared with Sadie and Maude that he knew Miss Williams other than watching her theatrical performances. Obviously, Robert didn't disclose much about his personal relationships. Even more reason to be cautious around him. He wasn't a young islander whose whereabouts were known by everyone—he was a grown man, a shipping industry owner and captain. Who knew how many ladies he'd befriended in each port?

"Robert," Miss Williams' voice was hushed.

Sadie took two steps closer to the parlor to better hear, but the whispered words evaded her. This could not be jealousy coursing through her. Surely not. She had plans to take care of herself and her sisters. Plans that could take her away to Newberry if she could gain entry into the nursing program. She'd find a boarding house near the new hospital and training center, and she could put her sisters into the local school while she completed her studies.

I'm a woman, not a girl, and I'll not be a charity case.

A deep laugh accompanied Robert's voice. "I've been helping a friend and keeping busy."

Sadie cringed. She pressed against the plastered wall. *A friend.* That's all she'd ever be. She waited, tears burning at the corners of her eyes.

Robert's words reinforced her need to put her application for the nurses' training position into the mail on the morrow.

Lavender sachet scent preceded Mrs. Fox. The housekeeping manager's boxy heels clicked on the marble floor as she entered the salon and eyed her.

Like a ninny, Sadie stared blankly. Then, she lowered her eyes and bobbed a curtsey.

"Sadie, please attend to your duties." The command was said with a softness that Sadie hadn't heard—or perhaps noticed—before.

"Yes, ma'am." She began dusting a marble bust of Mrs. Carrie Booth Moore, a socialite who the brass plate noted was one of the benefactresses of the renowned Sugar Plum catering ladies from Detroit.

"Sadie?" Mrs. Fox eyed the figurehead.

"Yes, ma'am?"

"Miss Lindsey has requested you to serve as her lady's maid this week. Do you think you can help her?" Mrs. Fox took a step closer, narrowed her eyes, and seemed to be reading the plate on the statue. "They would compensate the hotel and you'd be given a temporary raise."

Enough to cover a trip to the mainland to look for Pa and to travel to Newberry for an interview? "Yes, ma'am. Thank you."

Mrs. Fox reverently touched the image's cheek. "This dear woman and Mrs., or rather now Lady, Gladstone, made life much easier for many widows after the Civil War. They made my life easier." Her last words trailed off in a whisper.

Shocked by her supervisor's disclosure of such personal information, Sadie waited, unsure of what to say. Had Mrs. Fox's father died in the war? Maude's uncles had both served, and died, and Sadie had lost an uncle, too. Ma said that was when Pa started drinking.

The petite woman blinked rapidly and then straightened. "Be sure you go to the Lindseys' room this afternoon before the next change of clothes."

It wasn't uncommon for the young ladies of the gilded class to change multiple times each day. "Yes, ma'am, I'll be there."

Two hours later, after completing her other chores, Sadie knocked on the Lindseys' door. Dawn opened it, grabbed Sadie's hand, and pulled her into the room. "Oh goody! I'm so glad you came."

Although they were about the same age, Dawn was the daughter of a Grand Rapids' textile manufacturer and had no doubt grown up in luxury.

"Mrs. Fox said you needed help."

"Unlike many of the young women of my set here at the hotel, I don't require five changes of clothing every day." Miss Lindsey took two steps toward the wardrobe and pointed to a satin and lace inset gown of heavy ecru linen. "But I do need help, particularly for dinner attire."

Robert had told Sadie that Miss Lindsey expected to spend time with Mr. Charles Bobay, a railroad magnate. But Sadie hadn't seen the two together, other than briefly in the hallways, and there, the young woman became dumbstruck around the intriguing man. Granted, Bobay had a strong presence and was frequently surrounded by his railroad cronies. But although he could be intimidating, the staff loved the gregarious man. The kitchen staff especially doted upon him because he had a well-known penchant for sweets, and they often designed desserts especially for him.

"I'm here to help however you need, miss."

"I thought I'd be engaging in more activities, but…" The pretty blond's light eyes shimmered with unshed tears. "I fear I have no invitations."

"What of your friend, Mr. Bobay?" Sadie sucked in a short breath, shocked at herself. How had those words slipped past her lips? She was a servant. She waited for the well-deserved reprimand, staring down at the boot tips peeking out from beneath her dark skirt.

"My friend? I would like him to be so much more!" The young lady's voice held a tremor.

How well Sadie understood those sentiments. But Robert had mentioned that Mr. Bobay was considering returning to Detroit early, presumably due to the lack of Miss Lindsey's interest. "Begging your pardon for my impertinence—"

"I don't stand on those silly rules. And you don't have to do so with me. And please call me Dawn."

"Yes, miss."

"Please call me Dawn, or I shall be upset."

"Yes, Dawn."

"Do you know Charles?"

"No." But seeing Dawn's disappointment, Sadie had to say something. "But I do know he came here specifically to spend time courting you—"

"What?" The young woman's shriek was a mix of joy and dismay.

"But he says you have shown no interest in him, and so he is returning to his business earlier than planned."

"No!" The shy woman Sadie had observed in the hallways seemed to have vanished.

The door opened and Mrs. Lindsey, a striking woman with rich golden-brown hair entered, dark eyebrows raised high. She quickly shut the door behind her. "What's going on here?

"Sadie says Charles came here to court me, like you thought, Mama."

Removing a long pearl-tipped pin from her elaborately feathered hat, Mrs. Lindsey sighed. "Then why isn't that happening? I've certainly given you enough time to be near him at all meals and on the porch in the evening."

"I think I can help." Sadie might not be able to do anything about Robert—*her friend*—but she could redirect the course of Miss Lindsey and Mr. Bobay, before it was too late.

It was *past* the time for Sadie to plan a future where she relied upon a man. No, she'd take matters into her own hands. But she would help this young lady who seemed determined to start a life as a wife and mother.

Peter Welling, Adelaide's dear friend, had been the hero of the shipwreck rescue. But he'd suffered some physical issues from his efforts. And she'd still not gone to him. That would be remedied forthwith. Soon she'd arrive at Peter's home and she could assess his health for herself.

As Adelaide's carriage stopped alongside the Winds of Mackinac Inn, she almost called out to the driver to continue on. Her nerves vibrated like a taut chandelier line, when lowered for the crystals to be cleaned.

I can do this. I need to do this.

A gust of wind tugged at Adelaide's wide-brimmed hat with pink velvet trim. Her gauzy cream and rose ensemble looked nothing like her attire at the Grand. And her hair almost looked like it's natural state, styled into a simple upsweep with curls trailing from the back.

A few years back she'd met Peter's wife in Shepherd, Michigan, at the general store. Adelaide had been struck by how much the woman physically resembled her. She'd even wondered if that was one of the reasons that he'd married the sweet-natured woman. But that might have been vanity speaking to Adelaide's hurt pride. Every so often she'd return to the town where she and Peter had lived—he on his family's farm and she at the Poor House. One of her favorite persons in that town was the young railroad man, Louis Smith Penwell, who now helped oversee the running of the Poor House with his wife, Sonja. Louis, like Adelaide, had spent part of his teen years at that very same Poor House.

In addition to donating money to the Poor House, Adelaide would pick someone to bless each time she traveled to Shepherd. Now Adelaide was the one in need of a blessing. She truly had been rescued by the hand of God, but her past kept interfering with where she should go next.

She needed to clear the air with Peter and to heal the hurts from all those early years. As she stepped out onto the boardwalk, a white-haired gardener looked up from where he was trimming a pink rosebush. His eyes widened before he lowered his head and resumed his task. Goodness, what was the man doing performing physical labor at his age? Adelaide just might have to add him to her list of people to bless—by hiring him and moving him to an easy job at one of her own businesses on the mainland. But perhaps the elderly man enjoyed his work.

Jack Welling burst out of the inn, the front door swinging back behind him as he jumped off the front porch. He waved. "Mrs. Fox! Whatcha doin' down here? Ain't ya gotta work today?"

To her surprise, the boy ran straight at her, arms wide. She opened hers to receive him as he almost slammed into her. Unbidden tears welled in her eyes as the boy clasped her tightly.

"You smell real good—like the flower gardens Mr. Chesnut takes care of for us." He gestured to the groundskeeper, but the man simply nodded and continued with his work.

Jack smiled at Adelaide, and she gently swept blond tendrils of hair away from his eyes. "I'm here to see your dad, Jack. Is he home? Is he all right?"

Since she'd sent a message to Peter, she'd be devastated if he wasn't there. But since he was still recovering, surely he'd be home.

"He's so excited. Said you were his bestest friend when you were kids. And was he surprised that I knew you."

Adelaide gave a curt laugh and held onto his arms. "I imagine so, since your sister said you're not supposed to be loitering at the Grand Hotel."

He crinkled his nose. "Yeah, well I like goin' up there to see Uncle Robert."

"Ada!" Although many strands of silver now laced his hair Peter still cut a dashing figure standing there on his porch. She saw no sign of any lingering effects from the daring rescue.

She gazed at him, a surge of longing and emotion bearing down on her like an express train headed for the station. They'd been so close. Knew each other's secrets. Planned a future together. "Peter! It's so good to see you, again."

Jack glanced between the two of them. "Um, I think I'm goin' for a bike ride. See ya."

Peter's son grabbed his bicycle and headed off as his father stepped down to join her. "How wonderful to see you, too."

Tears pricked her eyes. "I was so enthralled by the tales of your commanding the rescue of those shipwreck survivors. I'm so proud of you." She shouldn't have said those last words. She had no right to be gratified by his heroics.

His cheeks reddened. "I just did my civic duty."

"I heard you did far more than that, but you always were modest." She smiled at him. "How are you feeling now?"

"Fine as a fiddle—especially now that you're here to visit."

Her cheeks warmed. Did they both look like blushing young lovers, reunited?

He pointed to the side yard where a multitude of blossoms in a rainbow's array of colors beckoned. "Come, let me show you around our gardens. Not quite as posh as the Grand's but quite lovely. And I have a wonderful little nook where I've instructed Bea to come serve us tea."

Adelaide struggled to gain control over her feelings. To be with Peter again, she felt decades younger. "Do you remember how we'd select all the flowers that we'd put in our garden when we grew up?"

His cheeks reddened and he took her gloved hands. "I believe you'll find them all here, my dear."

Was it her imagination, or did she see a longing in his gaze, too? But so many years had passed by. Three husbands gone, for her, and an adult life full of experiences she and Peter could never have imagined. She'd been to Egypt, Istanbul, Paris, London, Japan, on safari in Africa, and more. But she'd never felt truly comfortable returning to her home country, where she kept herself in disguise most of the time to avoid the demands placed upon her as the wealthiest woman in America. Only a few people knew who she really was—and she wished to keep it that way. At least until. . .

"Ada? I asked if you'd like to see our lilies."

"Lilies?" She couldn't help but think of Lily Swaine. Their new songstress, from Kentucky, may have a connection to the Swaines of Mackinac, according to Adelaide's Pinkerton agent. The man had learned this after verifying that she was the daughter of a notorious mental asylum patient who'd burned down her sanitarium. Adelaide was keeping an eye on Lily. Adelaide's Pinkerton man was following up on the search to see if the young woman's background matched with that of a Swaine son who'd supposedly died in the Civil War. All evidence suggested that he'd married and had a child and survived the war, only to succumb later from injuries sustained. Adelaide could help Peter—if Lily Swaine also cut into the inheritance his children were supposed to receive. What good was all of Adelaide's money if she couldn't help those she cared about?

"Lilies. We have many. You used to like the daylilies that grew in my mother's garden."

"Oh yes, they were so pretty. And she always let me carry a few back to my room."

She linked her arm through Peter's, the warmth seeping through his jacket stirring something inside her.

"We have different varieties of lilies, including some of those fragrant white ones you adored."

She smiled. "I still love those."

"I think one day even those orange daylilies will have more varieties. Someone will no doubt figure a way to cultivate them one day."

"Do you remember we called them ditch lilies?"

"Yes, we'd find them by old, abandoned farms and in roadside ditches. They're certainly hardy."

Like she'd had to be, to survive. A memory of showy bouquets being carried up to the ladies "upstairs" in New Orleans skittered through her consciousness and she shivered.

"Come sit down with me and catch me up on your life since I last saw you."

Adelaide stiffened and she and Peter paused in their garden stroll. She couldn't tell him that she'd put three husbands in the grave, traveled the world many times over, possessed a fortune, ran many businesses, and yet lived a life in the shadows. "I'm. . .I'm the housekeeper up at the Grand, you know." That was true.

He patted her hand. "I've heard you were also Greyson's housekeeper, too, at his fraternity.

"Yes, I was. And I was so shocked—but delighted—to hear about you and your life through Greyson."

His quirked an eyebrow "I was delighted to hear that my dear friend Adelaide was well and living in lower Michigan. I'd hated losing track of you."

Adelaide stared at Peter. He'd been more than her dear friend. He'd been her lifesaver. He'd been the boy who'd made her life livable after her father and then her mother had died. He'd shown her kindness, while she lived in the Poor House in Shepherd, while almost no one else did. She'd offered him the first pure love that she'd ever felt in her heart. And she'd thought he'd reciprocated it. "I've missed you so much." Those words slipped out, accompanied by a lone tear that Peter swiped from her cheek.

"I've missed you, too, Ada-belle."

She laughed at his use of the pet nickname he'd given her. "I was certainly no belle then—neither am I now." She thought of the hideous images the newspapers had of how they believed Adelaide Bishop appeared—each new one more ghastly than the last.

He squeezed her hand. "You are even more beautiful now."

She gave a curt laugh. "It was hard to even look presentable—much less to look pretty—when I was underfed, overworked, and couldn't get adequate sleep at that miserable Poor House."

"True." Peter inhaled and exhaled slowly. "We worried so much about you."

His mother had a strange way of showing her concern—by sending Adelaide away from Peter to get training as a secretary.

"And I'm concerned about you now." She noted the dark circles under his eyes. "I imagine it's been difficult since your wife has passed."

He nodded. "She told me before she went on to glory, that she wanted me to be happy. That she knew she wouldn't make it. And she said she couldn't stand the thought of me suffering after she was gone. She made me promise that I'd try to keep on. . ."

Keep on living? Loving? "My husband was a gentle soul, a very kind man, and I've missed the comfort of his presence. He died suddenly but I believe he'd have shared the same sentiments." Especially since he'd known she'd been married before.

"How long were you married?"

"Not a very long time. I met him later in life." That was true. But she'd also had two other spouses before him. Not something she'd share with Peter just yet.

"I don't know if that's harder—having only more recently found love, or to have lost a spouse after so many years, like myself."

She resisted the urge to touch his cheek. "I suspect it's much harder, my dear friend, to have been married over twenty years and then to lose your wife."

Peter led her to a bench with a basketweave back and they sat.

Adelaide pressed her lips together. "But let's talk of happier things. I understand you have been blessed with two children."

"Yes. Jack is around here somewhere. He's quite a handful although Eugenia managed him beautifully. And Maude's usually off performing some kind of charitable work. Sometimes I believe that girl wants to be a saint."

Adelaide stifled the urge to laugh. She had a hard time imagining Maude Welling carrying out activities without injuring someone or something in the process. And *Jack*—that child trespassed at the Grand so frequently that she'd decided to assign him a chair in the corner in her office if he kept it up. "I'm sorry about your father passing away a few years back. I was in Shepherd right near that time—in 1891." She'd not disclose that she went there annually, usually when Peter was there with his beautiful dark-haired and dark-eyed wife and his children. And she'd absolutely not mention that she dressed almost as a specter when she was in Shepherd—in black mourning and with a black hat and veil. Sometimes, though, she'd donned some shabby cleaning woman's clothing and worked at the railroad station.

"Oh? Do you go back often?" His face lit up but his eyebrows drew together.

She smiled. "Yes, I do. I donate to the Poor House."

His eyes widened.

Oh no, she'd already slipped up. Had he ever noticed her there when he'd visited his father? "That is, I try to give back and help as best I can. And I also liked the train ride. It's very pretty and relaxing. Plus, all the good memories when I get there." Her heartbeat fluttered. Her good memories were all of Peter. But seeing the young couple she'd helped, Sonja and Louis, as they flourished, also pleased her.

He relaxed back onto the bench. "Do you remember all the chats we'd have by the fence?"

"Oh yes. Of all the things we'd do one day." That had never happened.

"The crops we'd grow." Peter clasped his hands in his lap.

"Yes. We'd intended to have the largest farm in the county." Even though Peter never seemed to grasp all the skills a farmer must possess to produce successful crops and sell them. They both had minds more suited to business.

"Ada, I'm seriously thinking of going home and living that dream."

Could she be part of that dream?

The way Peter smiled at her, she certainly hoped so. And God bless that lovely wife of his for encouraging him to be happy.

Chapter Eight

Robert offered his arm to Sadie as they entered Mission Church, the warmth of her touch so natural against his own. An older couple near the back, the sanctimonious owners of a feed store, turned and gawked. When Sadie stiffened, he pulled her closer. How many people on this island had belittled Frank Duvall and extended that prejudice towards his family? Sadie's sisters, hopefully oblivious to those two mean-spirited parishioner's hard stares, trailed behind them as he led the Duvalls to the Cadotte pew.

His niece, Maude, and her new friend Friedrich König, as well as Jack, and Peter occupied the left side of the aisle. Robert led the Duvall girls, *no* this was a lady, and her sisters, into the pew on the right side.

He couldn't help grinning. For Sadie's day off, he'd arranged for them to go on a picnic at Fairy Arch, after attending church. *Like a family would.* How proud he would be to call Sadie wife—if she'd allow it—and to care for her and her sisters. Maybe except Bea. The truculent girl brought up the rear with a scowl on her face as she cast a sideways glance toward the Wellings. Was it his imagination or did Bea especially stare at Mr. Welling, her employer? That man certainly cast a blind eye toward her behavior. Robert exhaled a quick breath.

They slid into the pew. As Robert released Sadie's arm, he resisted the urge to take her hand.

A few rows ahead of them sat pretty Mrs. McWithey with her children. What a happy family. Robert wanted that for himself. But what were those Bible verses about envy? The Lord wouldn't be happy about him sitting here and being jealous of what his brother-in-law had—especially since Peter had lost dear, sweet Eugenia.

The sermon, about finding joy and peace with God, rather than being rocked by the changes in life circumstances, resonated with Robert. And from Sadie's rapt attention, he hoped it touched her heart as well. Bea cast longing glances at Jerry Meeker, who was seated in his grandparents' pew ahead of them. Garnet chewed on her lower lip and kept tugging at her gloves. Opal smiled as she played with a tiny yarn-haired doll that Mrs. Christy had made for her. When she danced the stuffed cloth doll onto Garnet's lap, the item was taken from her by Bea.

Robert, almost holding his breath, leaned forward prepared to give Bea a stern look. To his amazement, the girl passed it back to her youngest sister and whispered something in Garnet's ear. Garnet then stuck her tongue out at Bea. Sadie, seemingly oblivious, sat stiff-backed beside him. But when the yellow-haired doll was tossed into Sadie's lap she readjusted its pink dress and white apron and handed it back to Opal.

"Count your blessings," Pastor McWithey advised. "And pay attention to those small things that make life full of joy."

Little Opal obviously knew how to get enjoyment from her toy. *But that's different. Peace and joy from the Lord satisfy deeply.* Robert recognized that conviction in his soul.

After the closing hymn and benediction, they all rose. When Jerry and his family turned to go, Bea smiled shyly at the dray driver. The cheeky boy winked at her. Robert narrowed his eyes at the boy, but his gaze was locked on Bea. Those two merited watching—especially since Garnet, too, harbored a soft spot for the islander.

Across the aisle, Peter seemed to be hurrying his group out. Was he trying to avoid them? Robert needed a resolution with his brother-in-law. And he needed his attorney to speed up his findings.

Sadie touched Robert's arm. "I told the girls that we're not going to the coffee *klatsch,* but can we at least offer them some of those cookies and a small cup of lemonade before we head out?"

"I don't see why not."

Opal leaned around Sadie. "Are there sugar cookies? Those are my favorites."

"I believe those are on top in a tin."

Opal clapped her hands.

As they exited down the aisle, Sadie whispered, "I don't believe that's what Rev. McWithey meant by small joys, is it?"

Robert grinned and shrugged. "I'll ask the pastor sometime if he has a special treatise on the merits of cookies," he whispered back.

She laughed.

He knew all too well the problem, though, with overindulging in cookies. He could write his own pamphlet on why one must indulge infrequently in such items.

When they stepped outside into the sun, a robin flew past and then alighted in a nearby maple tree. The girls raced over to where the carriage stood.

"Do you think they'll leave any cookies in the tin?" Robert kept his tone light, for he knew how sensitive Sadie was when teased about such things. The Duvall girls had existed in penury so long that he certainly wouldn't blame them if they wished for more than one cookie.

"I wish I could give them everything they'd ever need."

"I believe the pastor said we're to trust in God for what He believes we need."

"But we have to take steps to get in the Lord's will, too. We can't just get. . . stuck somewhere."

Was she talking about Mackinac? Hadn't Sadie always said she was worried she'd never get off the island? They continued on, soon joining the giggling girls at their conveyance.

"All right, finish up before we depart."

"Get your walking shoes from the back, too." Sadie pointed to the leather case. "And your clips and pins to hold your skirts out of the way for our hike."

He hoped this was a good idea taking them out for the afternoon. Peter often brought Jack because an afternoon of hiking the rough terrain to the beautiful arch, about a quarter mile away from Arch Rock, would wear the boy out for a bit. Maybe next time, Robert would bring his nephew along, too.

After the other parishioners who'd not remained for coffee drove off, or walked home, Robert's small group prepared to depart.

"You were right about wearing these old skirts under our church clothes, but I was hot." Bea pulled off her spring green skirt, revealing the brown woven one beneath.

Before Robert could stop them from undressing in public, they'd accomplished the deed.

Sadie shook her head. "At least no one is out here observing us." The others were in the church hall enjoying coffee and miniature Queen's cake or had returned home.

"Off we go." Robert gestured up to the carriage.

Riding with Sadie and the girls seemed as natural as walking the deck on one of his ships—perhaps more so, since he'd not sailed in a year. That desire he'd had to sail the Atlantic down around Cape Horn to the Pacific, still flickered in him like a candle that couldn't be extinguished. If he had a family, how could he justify engaging in such dangerous adventures?

Sadie tapped his knee. "You seem deep in thought."

He gave a short laugh. "Thinking about that big trip of mine that I'd always hoped to do." In his foolhardy youth, he'd even been crazy enough to think a bride would want to accompany him.

"Your Aunt Virgie still has those nautical maps of yours." She rolled her eyes.

"How did you know?" They were still there in the room he'd occupied.

"I lend her a hand with the bigger cleaning jobs—about twice a year."

He recalled what Trey Clark had said at the hotel, about the Clark and Cadotte families. "Has Aunt Virgine ever told you the story of our families' connectedness through my mother's namesake, Jacqueline?"

"I've seen her beautiful portrait in the museum in town. And yes, we've all heard the Clark legend of finding little Jacqueline on the island." Sadie's dry tone implied she'd heard the story more than once. "But I assist Virgie because I like her. And she's aided my family, too."

"I'm sure Aunt Virgine appreciates the help."

"Sometimes I think she simply wants the company. It's lonely living in the deep of the island."

"My cousins and their families return later this summer, and she'll find no quiet then."

"And has she enjoyed having you stay with her?"

"Definitely not. I make messes all over the house, eat all her food, and lock her out on occasion." He kept his eyes straight ahead on the curving road.

"I heard that." Bea leaned forward. "And that's really rude to do that to people."

"He's joking, Bea." Sadie sighed.

"Oh."

"I lock Garnet out if she's been mean to me." Opal's sweet voice was unusually serious.

Those two could get into some trouble very quickly if that type of behavior was going on. They needed more supervision.

"You'd better be joking." Sadie shook a finger at the little girl.

When Garnet and Opal giggled, Robert's shoulders relaxed.

Garnet straightened. "But I really do latch the door when Jerry Meeker tries to come see Bea, when she's there."

"Jerry comes to see Bea?" Sadie sat up straighter.

"He's just a friend." Bea's tone held a shipload of defiance.

"Jerry should not be visiting when I'm not home to supervise."

"I have no fun. I work all day and on my day off I want to visit with a friend. Is that so awful?"

"We'll talk about this later." Sadie's voice held a mixture of sadness and concern.

"You mean you'll talk at me." Bea harrumphed.

No good could come of Bea sneaking around with Jerry. A prickle of unease crept up Robert's spine.

"Can we take our shoes off now? My toes hurt." Garnet had been growing so quickly that perhaps she needed new church shoes.

"Yes, but don't step out of the carriage barefoot because there's all that stone there and dirt."

"We'll hand your shoes to you when we stop, girls." Robert injected his voice with some enthusiasm. They were almost there. This could be a lovely afternoon and a foretaste of days to come with Sadie and her sisters—even if it was overshadowed by concern about Bea and Jerry.

He slowed as they passed a group of older tourists, the women in wide brimmed hats and the men all using fancy hiking poles. The girls waved at them, and the walkers waved back.

Soon they'd turned onto the rutted lane that led to the footpath to Fairy Arch. Robert parked under the canopy of a wide oak tree. They changed out their shoes, and gathered their belongings for the hike to Fairy Arch.

"Chase you there!" Garnet called out and the three girls raced off—carrying nothing.

Sadie rolled her eyes. "I guess we'll bring the quilts and hamper."

"By 'we' I believe you mean that *I'll* carry the hamper and you'll bring the quilts."

"Exactly." Sadie laughed.

She took a step toward him and elbowed him.

"What's that for?"

"For old time's sake."

"In the old times, you and I would have clambered up that overgrown trail as quick as those girls, with Maude right beside us."

"Now we're the old folks carrying up the lunch."

"It was tin pails for us back then, no old folks here."

"Until I realized how young you were—even though you had all that early gray in your hair—I thought of you as someone very much older and more mature than us."

"More mature, maybe."

"Actually, I think it was your lack of maturity and general silliness that finally made me question Maude about your age."

"I'm shocked that the way my sister and her husband infantilized me didn't help you understand the differences in our ages." He scowled at the memory. "Eugenia was quite a bit older than me, and she made sure that I understood that fact."

"Perhaps losing her brothers, and then losing her first babies did that."

"You know about that?"

"She told my mother and Ma told me." Sadie shifted the quilts in her arms. "I think it's very sad."

"But she had Maude and Jack to care for."

"And a younger brother to treat as a child."

"I see what you mean." Truth was he'd not really tried to understand why Eugenia had acted so maternally toward him since he already had a mother who'd have liked nothing more than for Robert to have remained a young boy forever. It was his mother's fears that had driven him to seek life out on the water.

"We're almost there. I love this spot." A radiant smile and dancing eyes transformed Sadie's face into an even more beautiful visage than usual.

Robert's breath hitched. If only every day he could see Sadie so genuinely happy. "This is one of my favorite places." Especially since she was there with him now.

"Do you know I haven't been back here since we last came with Maude and Greyson?"

He wanted to ask if she'd never come with Elliott, but he bit his tongue. "I'm glad we're here now."

Sadie cast him a long look. "So am I."

Dappled sunlight filtered down through the trees, creating a lacy pattern on the path.

"And I'm glad that it's quiet out here. No tourists today."

"Yes. But that will no doubt change."

"Not now, though." He winked at her. "Let's enjoy it like the pastor said today."

"Yes."

A chipmunk raced across the trail and into the nearby bushes.

"I want to play some games." Little Opal called out. She clutched a red ball to her chest.

"Where did she get that?" Sadie frowned.

"Probably someone left it."

From a distance, a dog barked. Muffled laughter carried through the woods.

"Can you wait until after lunch?" Sadie called out as she inclined her head toward Robert. She shook out the first quilt.

Bea joined them and helped Sadie straightened the quilt.

"Can't I play?" Opal made a grumpy face.

Bea sniffed. "She's just a kid. She wants to have fun."

Robert snorted. "Aren't you just a kid still?"

The look Bea cast in his direction could have scorched his straw boater hat off.

Garnet ran up and helped with the second quilt. "Don't worry about her. Bea is mad about our dad being gone and she's not especially fond of boys."

Sadie gave a curt laugh. "Tell Jerry Meeker that."

Garnet wrinkled her nose. "Bea does like Mr. Welling very much, though. She thinks he's practically perfect."

Sadie shook her head. "Too bad he believes Maude is incapable of taking care of herself."

"My niece is turning out to be a real go-getter." He was so proud of Maude. "But I have to agree with Peter that I'm not sure she's ready to run the inn." At least from what he'd seen at the hotel.

"Pish posh. She's a lousy maid, but Maude understands business." Sadie arched an eyebrow as she smoothed out the second quilt. "She's kept the books for so many places that could have failed if she'd not stayed on top of things."

"Really?" Robert set the heavy basket down atop the quilt."

"Really. Cross my heart." Sadie made an *X* over her chest. "She's got a brain for business."

He laughed. "Eugenia had a real passion for the inn. For the people. And I do know that Maude loves taking care of folks and making sure they are looked after."

"Exactly." Sadie smiled up at him. "Reminds me of her uncle."

He grinned. "Yes, well, I enjoy taking care of certain people, too." Like Sadie and her sisters.

Sadie averted her gaze. "I enjoy taking care of sick people. And I'm good at it."

"Yes," Garnet agreed.

"I've heard from Mrs. Luce that you were a stellar nurse for her." Robert lifted the lid on the hamper.

She glared at him.

What was that all about? Robert flexed the sudden stiffness in his shoulders.

"I'm not a nurse yet. But I could be a good nurse if I got proper training." She frowned.

"I. . . I am sure you could." But what did that mean for them? Was there even a *them*?

"I miss Mrs. Luce so much. I took care of her for a long time. This maid's work is nothing like that."

"You could take care of a family." He tried to keep his tone nonchalant.

"I do take care of a family *now*."

But it wasn't her children, her husband. Still, Robert wasn't going to argue with her when they'd finally gotten to spend more time together. "I've really enjoyed spending these Sundays with you."

"I've enjoyed them, too." Sadie bent over the basket and began sorting the contents. "Look at all these goodies they sent."

Garnet joined her. "Oh my goodness. Bea! There's those little cheesecake squares you love. Opal! Come see the tiny tea sandwiches in here with chicken salad and cucumber."

"My cook has been beside herself with happiness at being able to put together all these delights for you." Robert winked at Garnet.

"I imagine she wondered if you were ever coming back here, Robert." Tears glistened in Sadie's eyes.

Had Sadie wondered if he'd ever return? Had he hurt her? Was that why she didn't trust him to care for her?

"I had a lot of things to take care of in my life before I. . ." Before he ended up like his sister. Eugenia's death had rattled him. He had to take care of his health. To end some bad habits.

Sadie sat down and motioned for him to do the same. "Opal, stop throwing that ball around and come serve Mr. Swaine and me. We've earned it, haven't we, Robert?"

He swiped his brow as the little girl tossed the ball aside and ran back toward them. He huffed a short laugh when she reached him. "Oh, yes, it's been such a trial ferrying you girls around the island while Sadie has been working. Especially this one." He patted the top of Opal's silky head. He had many friends with children about her age. Would he yet have his own family?

"Is that why you laugh a lot when you take us places?" Opal, hands on hips, cocked her head.

Garnet slumped down onto the blanket. "I think drinking phosphates at the soda shoppe is the hardest thing for Mr. Swaine to do with us."

"Oh, indeed, I imagine that's so taxing." Sadie leaned back, laid the back of her hand on her forehead--palm outward--and sighed dramatically.

Bea harrumphed. Only she, of the three younger siblings, began to serve. "If I have to hear one more time about the bike rides you've had, the whitefish you've eaten at Astor's, or the times you've been to the library with Mr. Swaine, I think I may scream." She scowled as she served sandwiches onto the plates. "I'm up at the inn, slaving away, in case you forgot. And now apparently I can't even spend time with Jerry when I do get time off."

"I'm sure Opal and Garnet appreciate the sacrifices we're making for them." Sadie shot Bea a warning glance as she passed out napkins.

"Too bad you're not here all the time, Captain." Garnet accepted a napkin from Sadie.

"Captain Swaine has an important job to do." Sadie's words sounded forced. He could imagine her adding, 'although that's not what he was doing last year—that's not why he left us.'

He would have to prove himself to her. *God help me.*

Chapter Nine

Would telling the complete truth about her life be as bitter as the headache solution Adelaide drank now? She rose from her desk and then departed from her office. She'd check in with Zebadiah and then see how Sadie was faring today. The young woman brought out Adelaide's maternal side more than any one she'd ever met. Almost as much as Jack Welling had. There was a boy who'd reminded her so much of young zestful Peter who'd made her days at the Poor House tolerable. He'd given her hope for the future—until his mother had nixed that.

Adelaide headed down the hallway, nodding at those maids who glanced up from their carts. They had a hard-working bunch of ladies on this floor, and she took pride in their efficiency. She'd be sure to praise them at their next weekly gathering.

"Mrs. Fox, how're you doing this blessed day?" Zeb stood at his stand, rubbing bootblack into the toe of a fine leather old-fashioned Hessian boot.

Ben Steffan might be taking his impersonation a bit too far—if those were his boots for his fake Friedrich König persona.

"I'm fine. Better than fine." But she rubbed the aching spot on the side of her head. *Liar.*

He laughed. "Gonna have to do better than that if you're gonna fool old Zeb, Mrs. Fox."

She grimaced. "You're right. Say, are there any more rumors about Mr. Parker and Mr. Butler? Those two concern me." Especially because her Pinkerton believed that her assistant manager of housekeeping, Mrs. Stillman, may have a connection to the two men. And they may be of the criminal sort.

"Yes ma'am. They're staying in town now, but they've made it known they believe it's their right to come back up to the Grand if they get a notion."

She exhaled loudly. "I've no doubt they believe that. But they'll find they get escorted right off the premises, again, if they do. We're not going to tolerate drunken brawling here."

"No, ma'am."

"And how's Sadie doing with her work?"

"Perfect. One hard-working gal."

"I thought she would be."

"Me and the bellman and a few others keep an eye out for anyone who tries to bother her." He raised his dark eyebrows.

"Thank you." Sadie was a beautiful young woman with an enviable figure. Adelaide understood well how debauched some men could be. Her first husband had freed her from a life of fending off unwanted interest. From what she'd seen of Robert and Sadie together, this could be the way Sadie could also be protected—by marrying the eligible, and wealthy, bachelor.

"Mrs. Fox, I don't know if you've seen them yet, but there's a slew of investors from the new railway line here. If you did benefit from overhearing any of their insider stories, you might want to keep yourself scarce." Zeb dipped his chin.

"Oh." He must have thought she'd been spying on the men when they'd had their board meetings in Detroit. She'd not disabuse him of that notion right now. She'd been there to hear the meetings but to not be seen. She didn't want anyone knowing that she was a shareholder and one of the wealthiest women in America.

"They probably never even looked at you, though, ma'am. Your hair was tinted a reddish color back then—and dressed as the cleaning woman."

Although not attired differently, when working at Detroit University, she'd kept henna on her hair. She'd not done so as Madame Patti, the renowned opera singer whom she'd heard in Paris, had done, to appear younger but to obscure her dark hair. "I assure you; I did nothing that caused illegal gain. That's all I can say right now about that. But thank you for your concern."

"Yes, ma'am." Zeb locked gazes with her. "I can't tell you how much that relieves my mind."

She bit her lip. "I had my reasons for being at those meetings, but I wasn't trying to overhear information for my financial gain."

He whispered, "You a Pinkerton gal, then? I've always wondered if that might be the case."

He looked so serious that Adelaide almost laughed. "Do you know any Pinkertons?"

"I've still been looking for who the Pinkerton is at this hotel, so I could tell you, but I keep come back to wondering if this is some kind of test."

"A test?"

"That you're the Pinkerton and just trying to see if I can find out." He compressed his lips.

She exhaled a long breath. "No, Zeb, I assure you I am not. And please keep seeing if you can learn who is our Pinkerton *man*." Although it certainly could be a woman.

Adelaide headed off toward the parlor without further ado. She needed to quickly send a message to Peter that she was able to meet with him that evening after work. But she spied some familiar people from her past, down the hallway, and panicked. She swiveled to face a wall of travel paintings. As usual, she carried a dust cloth with her in case she needed to blend into the woodwork herself. She pulled it from her pocket.

"My, isn't that painting of the Parthenon lovely? It's quite an accurate depiction, don't you think?" The familiar baritone voice caused the hair on Adelaide's neck to prickle. *Henry Michel*, one of her first husband's closest friends—bit older, rounder, and with less hair but possessing the same rich voice. Adelaide and her husband had traveled from Battle Creek to Athens, Greece, and had encountered Henry and his family there on holiday. They'd become friends. She and her first husband had a number of close friends. All that changed when he died, though. She'd learned who was simply interested in her money. She swiped at imaginary dust on a frame.

They moved down the hall toward her.

What should she say if he recognized her? Attired in her drab skirt and blouse, she clearly was staff, not a guest. But if he somehow realized who she was, should she acknowledge him? Ask him to keep her secret? Her head throbbed in pain.

"Now darling, you should know better than to ask an artist that question."

Adelaide exhaled in relief. He'd brought his wife with him. Mrs. Michel was a blue blood from New York and would never take notice of Adelaide. Not only that, but they'd not seen each other in over fifteen years.

This game of keeping her identity secret, out of fear, was getting far too difficult to bear up under. She needed Peter's advice. But not until after she was sure her full disclosure wouldn't impact his feelings toward her.

She must see Peter, again. Adelaide must summon up the courage to do what she'd come to Mackinac Island to do. She wiped at some dust on one of the images of Tibet, angling her body to ensure she could keep watch over the Michels.

"I say, aren't you Mr. Michel?" The cocky voice belonged to only one man—Dan Williams, a reporter, and a thorn in Adelaide's side.

The industrialist seemed to puff up. "Yes, I am, and this is my wife. She's an accomplished artist and was just remarking on this likeness of the Parthenon."

"Pretty painting." Williams' smile was as fake as a wooden nickel. "I believe you and your wife are friends with Adelaide Bishop."

Adelaide resisted the urge to close her eyes tightly shut and the competing desire to flee down the hall.

When Michel didn't respond, Williams continued, "I hear she's on the island looking to acquire another hotel."

"You don't say." The frost in Mrs. Michel's voice could have frozen the entirety of the geraniums lining the Grand Hotel's porch.

"Please excuse us." Mr. Michel took his wife's arm and led her away.

Adelaide continued to swipe at the frames of the paintings as she slowly moved away from Williams. She could hear him muttering as he strode off in the opposite direction.

Everything was coming to a head. She wiped perspiration from her brow.

"Hey! What's the matter with you?" Jack sprang up from where he was sitting cross-legged on the floor by a wide bench, his eyes red. "You ain't sick, too, are you?"

"Oh, Jack, you surprised me." Adelaide dropped her hand and reached for the boy. "I'm not sick, but who is?"

She pulled him into a hug as hot tears sprang to her eyes. She was not a crier. Wasn't that what she'd always professed? She patted the boy's head.

"My dad. I think his heart is getting worse."

Adelaide pulled away. "What do you mean?" After all this time, she couldn't lose dear Peter to a heart problem.

"I'm worried he's gonna die."

No.

Robert locked gazes with his brother-in-law, who sat rigid behind his desk. "I'm moving into the Canary—and I'm relieved to hear you've not rented it out this summer." Robert needed to be firm. He'd had a home here, at the Winds of Mackinac, for almost a decade—after his mother had died, but he'd spent much of his time aboard ship. And he no longer wished to impose upon his precious Aunt Virgie, who enjoyed her solitude, making her herbal potions. Nor did he intend to continue staying at the Grand Hotel when he owned a cottage on the bluff, only a stone's throw away.

Peter's face mottled and his nostrils flared. He looked for all the world like a bull about to charge. "I did not rent it out, because of my wife's death."

Robert cocked his head at his brother-in-law. "Good. Because I own that cottage and I intend to return to my home soon." He and Mother had lived in Cadotte cottage until her death. Father had preceded her, years before that.

"Are you intending to sweep in here and take my livelihood away?" Peter rested his hand on one of the piles of papers atop his desk.

"No. But if you'd come with me to see Attorney Hollingshead, maybe we could get started on fixing the problem my mother created." Mother had allowed fear to direct her path when she added that codicil.

Peter shook his head vigorously. "I've worked hard and I'm not about to be put out to pasture just because of what a piece of paper says. I'm going to sell this inn and then let's see what you do."

"You better not even *think* of trying that." Robert fisted his hand, but then relaxed it. "Maude will own this inn, shortly, per the law."

Peter blinked at him.

"I'll be taking occupancy of my home immediately and bringing the staff back on." And he'd given them his word.

"I don't even know where they are." Peter pushed his chair back.

"Thankfully, I do." Robert had kept the long-time handful of faithful servants on retainer, after Mr. Hastings sent him a message that they'd all been let go. He'd been furious that Peter had been so cavalier but extended grace, since Eugenia had just died—until now. "They deserved far more consideration than you gave them when you fired them."

"I didn't fire them," Peter sputtered, grasping the edge of his hideous Eastlake desk. "I just. . . I didn't know what to do."

"Well, I do. And I take care of my loyal workers." Which was why he simply had to acquire more ships and make decisions about where his business was heading. It wasn't fair to his manager to require so much of him and to continue to have his crews sail temporarily with other shipping lines.

"How are you going to manage under Jacqueline's terms in that codicil to the will?" Peter's eyebrows bunched together. "Do you really think you can reside on the island permanently?"

"I don't know. And we have the new issue of Lily Swaine to consider." For surely the new singer at the Grand must be his niece, too, despite appearing to be near his age. Yet another reminder that Robert was only on this earth because of his brothers' deaths in the Civil War.

Peter sank back into his seat. "This is what comes of trying to control adults, who are entitled to make their own decisions."

Robert couldn't stop the chuckle that escaped. What irony for Peter to protest such behavior.

"What's so funny?"

"Isn't that what you're trying to do with Maude?"

And wasn't that what Robert was aiming to do with Sadie? To influence her to choose a life with him on this island—or wherever his ships might take him next?

Maybe I'm more like my mother than I thought.

That thought cut deeply.

Chapter Ten

Adelaide arrived with Jack, at the Winds of Mackinac inn, just as the town physician, Dr. Cadotte, was leaving, carrying his medical bag. The local doctor was a relation of Peter's wife. Could the physician truly be objective? As the man passed, a large black Labrador Retriever pulled itself up with great effort from the porch.

"What's wrong with my dad?" Jack grabbed the doctor's free arm.

Cadotte shook Jack's arm loose. "I don't know. But go on in and give him a big hug—that should help."

Jack scowled at the doctor, even as he bent and rubbed the dog's head. Jack cast Adelaide a quick glance before he ran into his home.

"Come on Izzy." Cadotte strode off, his pet lumbering behind him, before Adelaide could even close her gaping mouth.

As the physician headed onto the boardwalk, Mr. Chesnut peered up from a boxwood hedge he was squaring. "Peter Welling's problems are all in his mind." He shook his head, his white hair glistening in the sun. "Mr. Roof, our handyman, and I both agree he's going crackers, as Jack would say."

Adelaide took a few steps closer to the man. "Why do you say that?"

She had learned over the years that employees often understood much about their employers. Certainly, her employee, Miss Florence Huntington, had urged Adelaide that she must take the position at the Grand, so she'd be closer to Peter, because Adelaide had become so distracted by her thoughts of checking in on him after his wife's death. Flo had also researched Mr. Costello and reported that he had a stellar reputation in hotel management.

"Peter has always been a fretter." Chesnut stood and brushed off his britches at the knee. "A bigger worrier I've never seen. And now he's got Mr. Roof checking his repairs two and three times before he's satisfied."

"He wasn't that way as a youngster." Adelaide bit her lip. Was that why Peter was always *there* when something happened? Always there to rescue her or others? "But he did always think about others and what they needed. I saw that often." *Too often.*

"Probably worrying about everyone else back then, too." The gardener set his clippers inside a clay pot filled with sand. "Like he did about his wife, God rest her soul—and look what good that did."

And now Peter may lose his entire livelihood. All he had left that was truly his own was the family farm in Shepherd. "I'm sure he's spoken with Rev. McWithey for guidance."

"Yup. But I'm thinking he needs more."

Dr. DuBlanc. The psychiatrist's name immediately came to mind. Perhaps he could assess Peter's mental state. "Thank you for speaking with me, Mr. Chesnut."

"I can tell you're the truest friend Peter has ever had." The man thumped his chest. "I've watched you with him and it does me good to see it."

She dipped her chin. "Thank you. That's high praise."

"If you've got any notions that might help him, now's the time."

Adelaide raised her eyebrows. "Indeed, I do." Now if only Peter wouldn't protest her suggestion.

Soon, she'd entered the building. Hopefully Jack had enough time alone with his father and would allow them a little privacy.

"Mrs. Fox?" An ashen faced Bea Duvall came from behind the desk. "Follow me. Mr. Welling has been asking for you."

She followed the girl into Peter's bed chamber. She'd expected a feminine retreat, for Eugenia and Peter's bedroom. But the space almost matched her own spartan quarters at the Grand. Perhaps Peter had removed all traces of Eugenia. Maybe too painful for him. She strode to the mahogany four-poster bed without a canopy. Adelaide bent and kissed Peter's forehead. When she raised her head, he grasped her wrist.

"Adabelle, I'm so glad you came."

"I told her she better come." Jack winked.

She shook a finger at the boy. "That's not true."

He crinkled his nose.

"But Jack did tell me he was. . ." she cast a quick glance at Peter's son, whose face looked stricken. "He told me he was worried about you."

Jack swiped his arm across his nose. "I'm gonna go get a doughnut from Mrs. Christy's shop. Old Friedrich calls them *olykoek*, doesn't that sound awful?"

"Oil cake? I guess that makes sense since the dough is fried in oil." Adelaide shrugged.

"Want one Dad? Miss Ada?"

"I don't think François would want me indulging in sweets, Son."

"Probably not. And I'll decline, too—but thank you." Adelaide mulled over what Dr. DuBlanc had shared with her recently—that his mentor, the renowned Dr. Alphonse Cardona, was coming to visit him. What if Dr. Cardona could give his opinion on Peter's heart problem?

"Jack, Ada and I are going to talk about the old days so give us some quiet time."

Jack scowled. "That's before my time, so I don't want to hear it anyways." He scampered off.

Adelaide laughed. "Before *his* time?" She sat in the chair beside the bed.

"He's a bit dramatic—like his sister." Peter took her hand.

"Not like us." They sat there like that for a moment, just holding hands.

"Do you remember the days of 'what if' and 'when we grow up' when you were at the Poor House?"

"That's all that got me through, Peter. Those dreams."

"We'd say, 'what if we had a farm of our own' and you'd smile." He gave her hand a gentle squeeze. "Like you're doing now."

"And I'd ask, 'when we are adults will we still like each other?' and you'd say—"

He cocked his head. "I'd say, 'Of course we will.' I was too shy to say I loved you."

They locked gazes.

"Life's too short, Adabelle, for those fears. The answer to that long ago question is that, 'when we are adults, Peter will love Ada just as he loved her then' and wanted to tell her so."

She blinked back tears. Adelaide leaned in and tenderly kissed Peter. And when he responded, he certainly didn't seem like a sick man. And those dreams from her younger years were watered and began to bloom even larger than she'd imagined.

When they finally stopped, he grinned. "Stay with me and let's talk about some new plans, my love."

Hours later, back at the hotel, she found Dr. DuBlanc lingering at the back entrance to the music hall. "Do you have a moment?"

From behind the wall, music from the piano and Lily's voice carried to the hallway.

"I'm waiting for Lily and Clem to finish. Then we're going for a walk."

"I only need a moment."

There was a pause in the music, and then loud applause erupted.

"What's on your mind, Mrs. Fox?"

"I wondered when Dr. Cardona arrives." She fingered the broach at her neck, a long-ago gift from Peter's mother. "I need a favor."

"Seeking a consultation?"

The manager, Mr. Costello, walked by with Mrs. Stillman, who glowered at them but continued down the hallway. *What's wrong with that woman?* Given her terrible demeanor, Adelaide could well believe the woman had a dark past.

"I'd like Dr. Cardona's opinion, and yours, on Peter Welling's condition."

One thick eyebrow lowered in question. "Which is?"

"He's been having what Dr. Cadotte initially thought were heart episodes but which he now believes are more of a. . ."

"An emotional nature?"

"Well, yes, maybe, I don't know. But I'm sure two psychiatrists could help us sort this." Especially since Mr. Roof and Mr. Chesnut weren't qualified medical professionals—but those two men surely knew their employer.

"I'm to meet my mentor in Mackinaw City tomorrow. Could you join us there?"

Another song began from within the music venue. It sounded like one of Stephen Foster's, a favorite of her father's—*Jeanie with the Light Brown Hair*. Adelaide stiffened and drew her petite form up to full height. Some of the composer's songs brought up early childhood memories too painful to contemplate, so she never listened to his music if she could help it.

"Yes, I can. I already planned to be there." To check on her hotel but DuBlanc didn't need to know that.

"Perfect. Bring Peter and we'll chat over lunch. Would that work? Or do you need more time? A private setting?"

The music continued and Adelaide's nerves jangled, and hands shook. She needed to get back to her own chambers. "Let's meet and if we need, I know a nearby inn where we can have some privacy." "Very good. We'll meet you at the place where dear Lily first performed. Are you familiar with that music venue?" "Yes, I am. Thank you." And she turned and hurried off away from the annoying music.

At least they weren't performing *Old Black Joe* or *Camptown Races*. Those two songs set her to grinding her teeth.

"Escaped slave from Charles City," the horrible man with crooked yellow teeth had said as he grabbed her mother. *"Even if she don't look like it."*

The staff food that Sadie was served had been wonderful, but more than that, she appreciated the new friendships she'd made around the table—and the encouragement she'd received from others even though she was an islander.

Sweet Dessa, Zeb's wife, leaned in at the servants' breakfast table as she passed the biscuits to Sadie. "I hear they talkin' about cuttin' back staff, Miss Sadie. But you keep on workin' hard like you do and you'll be all right." The woman's dark eyes held warmth but also a warning.

Sadie's hands shook as she accepted the blue and cream crock ware bowl. "I can't lose my job. I've got two sisters to support." And no other job prospects. And no matter how Robert hinted that he'd like to care for them, she'd seen him with Miss Williams too many times to believe that he cared for her as a future husband should. No. She was simply his charity case.

"Doc Cadotte, from town, tell Zeb you ought to go get you some trainin' to be a nurse. He say you do good work with Mrs. Luce and that new daughter-in-law of hers gonna put her in the grave, uh huh."

Sadie gasped. "I hope not. I love Mrs. Luce."

"I'm sure she love you, too. But Missy, you best think on gettin' you some trainin' outside of this place."

"Dr. Cadotte really said that?" She took a bite of her biscuit. Warm and flaky.

"Uh huh. And Dr. DuBlanc he say the same thing. Zeb was there when he told one of them psychiatrists from that Newberry Asylum—them fellas who are here for the conference."

Wouldn't that be something? *Accepted for training.* She could imagine her crisp nursing trainee uniform. Mrs. Fox had shown her a board clip device that a friend of hers was working to manufacture more widely. The wooden board had a clip at the top that held paper, for notetaking. She could almost feel the board in her hands as she took notes while they walked through the wards. "Thank you for telling me."

"Eat up. We ain't got much time left."

Sadie ate her fill. She tried to make this her only real meal of the day. She let her sisters eat most of the dinner food and she'd save a piece of fruit, usually an apple, for her evening snack. But what if she had no job with which to feed them? At the end of the season, she'd have to find employment elsewhere or start training.

Soon, she was off to her floor. She sought out Maude, who was picking up some sheets that had fallen from her cart. Sadie scooped them up and helped her to get them reorganized. "Maude, I heard from Dessa that some of the maids might be let go." She chewed her lip. "I was just hired. I'm afraid they'll release me."

"I think they'd let me go before you." Maude's amber eyes fixed on her. "After all, I'm only here part-time."

Sadie had been astonished, earlier, to hear that Maude was working a reduced schedule. "You seem to get along well with Mrs. Fox. Can you put in a good word for me?"

Maude patted her hair, which was pinned up with what looked like hundreds of pins. *That had to hurt.* Sadie kept hers in a simple bun or twisted braid with only a few long pins to secure it. She used several fancy shell pronged hair pins with scrollwork silver-plated tops. Mother had ordered them from the Montgomery Wards catalog, before she'd died—an extravagance, but they worked very well.

"Miss Welling?" Ada Fox strode down the hall toward them, her stiffly starched black skirt and puff-sleeved blouse making her look like a crow. That was an uncharitable thought.

God forgive me. Why did her manager dress so severely? If she loosened her hair and wore colors other than black, she could really be pretty.

"I'll see you later," Sadie whispered as she hurried on to retrieve her own work cart.

An hour later and several rooms thoroughly cleaned, Sadie spied Maude heading toward the maids' closet. She followed her there.

"I think I've just been sacked." Maude, slunk down onto the bench beside her.

"What do you mean?"

"Mrs. Fox said she felt this was not the place for me." Maude blinked back tears.

"I'm really sorry." Sorry—but not surprised. She gave her friend a little hug. "I believe your job may be safe, though."

Might be. Maybe. That was better than being let go.

But Sadie had to find something with more security. Dessa's words had encouraged her to do what had been on her heart.

Time to start planning for her future—as a nurse.

Through the paned window, outside the café where Adelaide sat with Peter, clouds bunched and wind shimmied the leaves of the maple trees that lined the street. How gorgeous those would look come autumn. She and her beau held hands, and he spoke to the two psychiatrists. They huddled in a booth that reminded her of some she'd sat in when on a trip to the Alps with her first husband, with sides that curved up around them.

Peter leaned forward. He still looked like the earnest boy who'd won her heart so many years earlier. "So, my fast heartbeat, and my flushed skin, and breathlessness—that's all in my mind?"

"Well, no, Mr. Welling. Those are real symptoms but not of a heart attack." Dr. Cardona, a handsome man with dark hair and flashing dark eyes tapped the wood tabletop. "Sometimes trauma, or severe stress, or even too much worrying about things—that can make real bodily symptoms that seem or feel like a heart attack."

"So, I'm working myself up and worrying everyone that I'm having a heart attack?" Peter cast Adelaide a quick glance and she squeezed his hand.

"What about recommended treatment, Doctors?" Adelaide cocked her head.

"Mr. Welling needs to learn some new ways to deal with these very real stressful things that are going on in his life." Dr. DuBlanc knew something about that, since he clearly was pursuing Lily Swaine, who may have some rights to inherit some of what should have been Peter's property.

"It's likely I'd have chest pain, myself," Dr. Cardona patted his chest, "if I'd learned someone had claimed the efforts of my business—my psychiatric practice—as their own. And if I'd lost my wife."

Peter's stiff shoulders relaxed, and his arm pressed into hers. "I say hallelujah that this isn't from a true heart disorder. I'd rather be working myself up into a false episode than having real heart trouble."

"Amen," Adelaide agreed.

The two psychiatrists exchanged a long look. Dr. DuBlanc's lips twitched.

Cardona cleared his throat. "I've not had any of my patients thank me for telling me that their medical condition was really caused by their mental processes."

"You need to locate a situation where you find life less stressful." Dr. DuBlanc, despite being young, had a very nice professional air about him that Adelaide hadn't truly realized before now.

"I know a place where you weren't tense, Peter." Adelaide smiled at her sweetheart.

"I do, too." He pulled his watch from his waistcoat pocket. "But right now, I believe we three fellows best catch the ferry back or we'll all be quite anxious."

The doctors carefully slid from the booth. Dr. Cardona stood and then bent to look out the window. "Looks like a bit of stormy weather coming."

Peter stood and kissed her. "I'll see you tomorrow. And thank you for your help."

"You're not returning with us, Mrs. Fox?" Dr. DuBlanc frowned.

"No, I have business here in Mackinaw City and I've procured a hotel room for the night." Never mind that it was her own hotel. That was information she was keeping to herself for now.

"Best wishes." Dr. Cardona, who came across as a true gentleman, extended his hand to Peter, and then took Adelaide's and bent over it, and in Old World-style brushed a kiss against her hand.

If only today's young whippersnappers possessed such manners.

"Thank you," Peter splayed his hand across his navy and green plaid waistcoat. "You've relieved my fears, gentlemen."

Adelaide smiled at the psychiatrists, who'd just offered her the best hope she'd had in ages.

A weight seemed to lift from her. A giddiness threatened to make her laugh, skip, or even jump with joy. If she was wearing her satin pumps she would. Maybe tonight, alone in her rooms, she'd spin around and around, as she'd done as a child, when her adoptive father had returned from sea.

When Peter turned his back to leave, Adelaide slipped an envelope into Dr. Cardona's hand. "Thank you, Doctor."

"You're welcome. I didn't expect to see any patients while I was here but I'm happy for the consultation."

"You have no idea how happy you've made two people today." When he saw the amount she'd written the check for, he'd be quite pleased, too.

Adelaide exited the building with the men but then separated from them at the street. Peter gave her a quick, but warm hug, and a kiss on her cheek.

"I'll see you tomorrow, my sweet Adabelle."

"Yes, and for many, many more days after that." She threw a kiss to him as he crossed the street to head to the ferry.

She had a few hours before she'd meet with Ben. Zeb and Sadie had both confirmed what she already knew—that he was a journalist there at the hotel for a story, as was Danny Williams, but at least Williams was honest about his work. Ben was focusing on gold-diggers and their motives and so, apparently was Williams. He had a story planned that could devastate both the Wellings, with the focus on Maude working at the Grand, and on her ex-fiancé's wife, Anna, the daughter of a wealthy newspaper owner—the rival to Ben's newspaper. The island, Adelaide had quickly learned, was a tight knit community. For such a story to be published, so many people would be badly hurt.

But she had a plan.

Adelaide still couldn't believe Peter's daughter had fallen in love with the journalist. Ben Steffan had seemed to her to be someone who had his own heavy bag of secrets that weighed him down. Adelaide had prayed long and hard before deciding to share that she was

Adelaide Bishop and that she would give him the story of his career if he'd not publish the one he was planning.

She'd shared much with Ben. It had, however, been a slight falsehood to say that her parents had died of typhoid. Only Mother had. Her adoptive father had gone down with one of his ships on a trip to the Caribbean--a trip that he wasn't supposed to have been on. After that, they'd discovered that Father had left them deeply in debt. They'd relocated from Massachusetts to lower Michigan, outside of Detroit. The Sugarplum Ladies Catering group had offered Mother work. But when she became ill, and then died, Adelaide had been sent on to the Poor House in Shepherd.

Adelaide hurried down the boardwalk, past a bakery, a tobacconist, and a shoemaker's shops until she reached her hotel. She drew in a deep breath of pleasure. A fresh coat of paint, that spring, had livened up the dull edifice. And the flowers now bloomed in the front garden without any weeds. The wooden benches had been replaced with beautiful wrought iron ones and trellises with climbing vines fronted either side of the stairs to the wide porch.

That night, at her hotel in Mackinaw City, Adelaide shared a little more with Ben about her life.

"I'm not a skinflint like those rags try to make me out to be. Rather, I live a careful life, living simply in small homes and purchasing just what I need. No luxuries other than some exquisite teas here and there. Never have kept a horse." She couldn't. Her birth father had owned a horse farm in Virginia and having them around, even being responsible for the creatures, reminded her of what she'd lost.

"So, is it true that you lived in what they called 'hovels' in poor neighborhoods?"

Adelaide frowned. "If you call a simple wood-sided building, well-tended, with a little garden in the working-class part of town a hovel then I'm sure you'd offend your readers."

"*Touché. Nein.* I would not."

"But Mr. Steffan, I did travel quite a bit. I would say that was one of my guilty pleasures of spending."

"Oh? Where to?"

"I've traveled the world."

"Truly?"

"Yes." She sipped her tea.

One of her favorite trips was when she'd purchased the brothel, where she and her mother had been taken to, in New Orleans and traveled there to watch it being knocked down. That was one of the best trips she'd ever made. There was satisfaction in wiping out the blight of evil.

"You look deep in thought."

"Ah, I was thinking about how some trips are more pleasurable than others." But wiping away the building hadn't removed her memories.

She and Ben spent the next hour talking about her life—at least that which she was willing to reveal to him.

But she'd not share her most terrible memory—when she and Ma were taken from her father and their farm in Virginia.

Ladysmith. The name suddenly came to her. She'd tried for years to remember the name.

"Ladysmith?"

She locked eyes with Ben, not realizing she'd spoken aloud.

"Oh, it's a pretty area between Richmond and Fredericksburg, Virginia. Lots of farms." She picked up her teacup, but it was empty. "My late husband loved traveling to the south." He had, but that wasn't how she knew Ladysmith.

Ben yawned. "Sorry. It's been a long day."

"Well, I feel the same way about my story—it's a big yawn. I don't know why people have had to make up all these things about me over the years."

"You're a recluse, supposedly, and the wealthiest woman in the world. There are all these myths that have sprung up about you."

She frowned and raised her hand. "Well, now you have the truth." Or at least part of it. "Now, off to bed with you."

Ben gave her a boyish grin, but there was hesitation in his eyes as he left her.

Adelaide sat with her memories, sipping her tea, a tiny quilt pulled across her lap. That quilt was one of the few things she possessed from her early childhood. Ma's name, Satilde, was stitched in a heart shape on one square. Pa had taught Ma to read. But Ma had pulled his name from the interlocking heart with her name when they'd been carried off to New Orleans. Adelaide had never forgiven him. And Adelaide had never found the words to explain to her mother that those bad men told Pa they'd kill Adelaide if he didn't let them both go. They'd also said they'd burn his house, barn, crops, horses and Pa, too. In the end, they'd carried Ma off, kicking and screaming, and Adelaide crying as she stared at her father, who'd fallen to his knees and wept.

She got up and set about her evening ablutions and in no time had settled into bed for the night. Why couldn't she remember Pa's name? She'd been so young. Or was it because of her anger toward him?

She knelt beside the bed, on a circular wool rug, and prayed. "Lord, help me recall."

Adelaide stood and pulled her thick curtains shut, to keep out the last rays of summer's lingering sunshine. She got into bed and pulled her Pacific-patterned comforter, with its deep blues and turquoise colors, up high. What a day it had been. She sank into slumber.

Solomon—that was Father's name. The image of him, attired in farmer's clothing, talking with Ma, woke her from sleep. Solomon, Ma had called him. *Solomon Lightfoot.* If he was yet alive, he knew Ma's and her secret. She'd send the Pinkerton Agency a telegram to see if Solomon Lightfoot might still be alive. He'd be about seventy now, if he was yet living. The War had taken many men, though. A shiver sliced through her. She couldn't imagine Pa fighting on behalf of the Confederacy—not with what had happened to him—to them.

She returned to sleep, troubled by disturbing dreams until she awoke and rose. She donned her French cashmere, heliotrope-colored, Henrietta fabric robe, which she kept there in her personal suite. Such a luxury—but the purple color was too much a reminder of the periods of half-mourning that she'd already endured. Time to replace this garment.

Someone knocked on her door. "Mrs. Fox?"

Adelaide moved closer to the door. "Yes?"

"We've brought your breakfast up as you requested."

"Ah, thank you." She opened the door and allowed the worker inside with the cart.

The young woman wheeled the delicious smelling contents over to the window. She pulled back the curtains. Outside, carriages passed by, filled with well-dressed people no doubt heading out to church. Ladies' hats sported satin ribbons, tied beneath their chins—a smart notion since the Straits were often so windy. Adelaide, felt that she, as a woman in her forties, was much too mature for ribbons. Maybe she'd try it and see. She did love wearing an ostrich plumed hat, though. "Do you still wish for the porter to come up for your belongings in an hour?"

"Yes. Thank you." Time to get back to the island.

Soon, she'd finished the outstanding breakfast of fresh strawberries, waffle, clotted cream and a pot of exceptional black tea and had then gotten dressed and packed her clothing and personal items. Adelaide descended the polished oak stairs, said her goodbyes to her staff, and stepped out into the street. She'd have no privacy whatsoever after Ben Steffan, also known as Friedrich König, published her story, so she might as well enjoy today's anonymity.

Adelaide smiled as she prepared to cross the street to the docks. She waited as a man driving a dray stacked with hay drove past. She froze. The man in the seat was her father. It was Solomon Lightfoot. She raised a hand to her throat and watched as he passed by. *Straight posture. Red hair and beard. Pale complexion. Compact but sturdy build. High cheekbones and flashing green eyes.* She gaped and the driver glanced in her direction, then continued on.

No. Don't be ridiculous. This man was in his thirties perhaps. Not seventies. She drew in a deep breath and then exhaled. All this thinking about Ma and Pa and what had really happened to her—it was taking a toll. Maybe if she spoke with Peter about it, she'd feel better.

But she couldn't tell him. Not everything.

She had to share with someone, though. Soon.

Chapter Eleven

The two little spies, Opal and Garnet, reconnoitered with Robert two tables away from Mr. Charles Bobay. The wealthy gent slowly finished his bowl of ice cream topped with whipped cream and a cherry on top. Both Duvalls eyed the distinguished looking man. These girls would be Robert's sisters-in-law if Sadie were to ever marry him. Given the mixed messages she'd been sending him, that might never be. Still, he didn't mind squiring them around the island and often they offered insight into some of their big sister's behavior. Today, he'd brought them to Al's Soda Shop because Sadie's "ladies" as he called them, the Lindseys, were wanting to know what the gentleman was doing that day.

"Are we really spying on Mr. Bobay?" Garnet pressed one eye closed and leaned in toward Robert from across the table. "For Sadie?"

He crinkled his nose as if in distaste. "That's an accusation none of us should confirm nor deny." He waved toward the proprietor to come over to their booth.

Uncle Al joined them, his sleeves pushed up with black arm garters and his red bow tie slightly askew. "Don't tell me these dainty Duvall girls want another bowl of ice cream. Or another phosphate?"

"Where would they put it?" Robert winked at Opal.

Opal made a tiny circle with her index fingers and thumbs and placed it over her upper stomach. "I have room right here."

They were children. He truly felt more paternal toward them than as a brother might feel. Just the opposite of how he'd felt with Sadie and Maude, where he'd always felt more a brother than an uncle to his niece and her friend. "You saved room for only that much?"

"Me, too, I saved room right here." Garnet formed a bigger circle over her stomach.

Robert laughed. "Better leave space there for dinner at Maria's Cafe later."

"Is Bea coming to Maria's with us?" Garnet patted her mouth with her green and white gingham napkin.

I hope not. Was it uncharitable to hope the outspoken, and often cranky, girl would still be at work as he'd been told? "Sadie and Bea are working a tad late today—thus, I have the privilege of escorting you this fine evening."

"I'll save half of my dinner for Bea," Garnet offered.

Opal nodded solemnly. "And I'll save half of mine for Sadie."

If he kept up these food outings with the girls, he'd end up back where he'd started with his health regimen. "No need for that. I'll have Matilda pack up a couple of tins with dinner for them." If he began entertaining at the Canary, he'd require a chef or cook. For now, he'd retained only Matilda and Hastings and the gardeners, and he'd begun the search for the kitchen staff. In recent years the house was rented out in the summertime and some guests brought in their own cooks.

"We can keep our extras in our new ice box." Opal's gamin face showed pride.

Garnet met his gaze. "We've never had one of those before."

"I love it." Little Opal clapped her hands.

"I'm glad." He grinned at the two.

Amazing how so small an item could bring these children such happiness. His sister had made sure Jack and Maude were grateful for God's mercies, too. How he missed Eugenia. A gentle soul and gone too soon.

"Your eyes are leaking."

He swiped the moisture away.

"I was crying over my Ma and Pa this morning. That's why I have puffy eyes." Garnet pointed to her eyelids.

He'd not even noticed. He'd been too busy trying to occupy them with a carriage ride to the beach near Arch Rock, wading through the water which was still very cold, a picnic lunch, and now this ice cream parlor trip.

Opal stretched and Garnet yawned.

"Would you like to take a nap before dinner? We'll be walking to Astor's later." He'd brought the carriage back to his cousin Stan's stable and they'd taken a taxi to Al's.

"We'd better."

The shop proprietor shook his head. "Put this all on your bill, Nephew? Or should I call you Captain?"

Robert gave his uncle what Jack called 'the stink eye' and then opened his wallet and paid for their treats.

Hours later, Robert was the one who'd napped. He awoke to the sound of giggles. The Duvall girls had wrapped several rolls of brightly colored satin ribbon around him in the Victorian balloon chair. "What's this?" He hollered in his best take command voice. "Someone will be walking the plank!"

"They don't do that on the Great Lakes' ships." Garnet crossed her arms and squinted at him.

"How do you know? Have you ever been on such a vessel?" Robert cast her what he hoped was his best stern face. Now probably wasn't the time to mention that he hoped to purchase some ocean-going ships in the coming year. If things didn't work out, or possibly even if they did, he intended to sail around the coast of South America.

The girl huffed a sigh. "All right. Opal, untie the pink satin bow first and remove the ribbon."

Footsteps sounded in the nearby stairwell and the door opened. Sadie entered. She removed the white glass-headed pins from her unadorned, brown, sailor hat. She set the long pins in a shallow saucer on the small table beneath the hat rack. "Oh dear. What shall we do?" She winked as she hung her hat beside the girls'.

He should be humiliated, but a surge of warmth flowed through him.

Opal ran to Sadie and slung herself into her older sister's arms. "We made the captain a present for you."

"She means we wrapped Captain Swaine up like a present."

"For you," Opal insisted.

A delightful blush spread across Sadie's high cheekbones. "You can't give a person as a present."

But oh, how Robert wished they could and that the woman he loved would accept him as a highly wanted treasure—returned from the sea.

Opal stood, arms akimbo. "Yes, we can. He said there's no gift like spending time in the present. So in case he thought of leaving while we napped, we kept him here. He's in the present. He's the gift."

Robert shook his head. "I think that's called circular reasoning."

"Yes. We wrapped him all in a circle of ribbons. I like the purple one best. Mr. Keane gave us that one free. He said it was too God-dee, but how can something be too God-dee? God is good."

Sadie laughed as she set her work satchel down on the table. "I think he meant *gaudy*, which is a word different from the divine. It means something is way too overdone. Like you've tried to overdo your wrapping of Captain Swaine and with all those different colors." Robert looked adorable stuck there tied to the chair. She had the overwhelming desire to go and kiss his flushed cheek. But she'd need a bath before she got anywhere near him after her long workday.

"For heaven's sake, come and rescue me, Sadie." Sun streaming through the window lit the multiple colors in his wide hazel eyes.

"I don't know." She tapped her foot then cringed from the pain caused by standing all day and then walking the two miles home. "I mean—I'm not really supposed to be here right now. So maybe I shouldn't interfere. Maybe this was something you and my sisters set up as some kind of game. I know how you love games."

How many board games, card games, pantomimes, and outdoor sporting games had she and Maude and Jack played with Robert over the years?

"This is mutiny! There'll be penalties to any of my crew who fail to release me. No bread, no dessert, and entrée with your dinner—only thin broth and no crackers."

All three of them straightened. A pang pierced Sadie's heart. Surely, he didn't know that they'd had many a meal of just that—thin broth—since her mother's death and her father's disappearance. If it hadn't been for her position with Mrs. Luce, that would have been all they'd had.

Garnet and Opal rushed toward Robert and rapidly released his bonds. He cast each a slow, appraising look. He must have noticed the change in their demeanor. Even now, both Garnet and Opal trembled in fear.

"No need to fret." He swiped at his arms, releasing some of the wrinkles on his jacket, then stood. "I'll restore all your ship's privileges as crew, as long as you'll allow me to escort all of you lovelies to dinner."

"Hooray!" Opal grabbed a burgundy fringed pillow and tossed it at Garnet.

Sadie raised her hands. "I'm not going anywhere until I've washed up and changed. And that could take a bit." Thankfully, serving as a personal maid to the Lindseys wasn't as taxing as performing regular maid's duties—otherwise she'd require a full bath.

"Aw. Can we go by *ourselves* with Mr. Swaine?"

Garnet elbowed Opal. "That's rude."

Opal shrugged. "Why? I'm hungry and I don't want to wait."

"Sadie, I have some word of Mr. Bobay, for you, too." Robert stretched.

"Wonderful. I hope it's good news."

He cocked an eyebrow at her. "You'll have to wait until after dinner to hear."

"Well, I am especially glad I was given this evening off then. And I hope I'll be able to reward the Lindseys' generosity with a bit of cheer."

"Patience, my dear." Robert's teasing tone made her smile.

"Let me get out of these clothes."

His features tugged and his lips compressed but he didn't say anything. Surely, he didn't think she'd wear her maid's uniform to Maria's Cafe. Or were Robert's thoughts going where they oughtn't?

Her cheeks heated. "It will only take me a few minutes to change but I'll need to wash up."

"Oh! We want to put our new dresses on, too!" Garnet grabbed Opal's hand and sped past Sadie to their bedroom.

"New dresses?" She couldn't keep the frustration from her voice. They must take care with appearances, especially now that they were being housed over the store.

Robert pulled at his collar. "Keane said they hadn't sold."

"Pre-made dresses?" Those were an extravagance most islanders couldn't afford. And summer visitors no doubt had their own tailors and dressmakers. So perhaps this was true.

"Yes. I hope they fit." Robert shrugged.

"If not, I can take them in." She'd sewn her own clothing for years as had Bea. Garnet had just started learning to follow and alter a pattern before Ma died.

"Well, thank you." She went to her room. There on the bed lay a white blouse with lace at the collar and a black ribbon to tie at the neckline. There was also a dove gray skirt. A blue-gray linen vest, in a modern style, lay beside it. She could not accept these gifts. Maude had just sent over some of her outgrown clothes that were serviceable and pretty. Accepting this clothing, as a grown woman, could imply some things to their fellow islanders. But if it was true that the items weren't selling. . .

Sadie slumped onto the bed and removed her work boots. She should say something to Robert. But she'd just thanked him—for the girls' clothing. She removed the envelope from her pocket and opened it again and removed the letter. She re-read the message. If she were accepted to the nurses' training program in Newberry, then she could eventually support her sisters. She could hold her head high—no longer a charity case. But if she remained on the island after the season ended, what would she do?

She rose and returned to the parlor. Robert looked up like a penitent child. She placed one hand on his shoulder. "While it was very thoughtful of you to buy clothing for me, too, I am an adult. Have you thought about what other people would believe if they heard you'd bought me clothing?" Her cheeks flamed at the thought of tongues wagging.

He pressed his hand over hers. "I assure you Mr. Keane shoved these items at me, all in a box, and claimed they are simply too pricey for the store. Peter, that is Mr. *Welling,* had advised him to order them on a trial basis."

"Oh." Embarrassment clenched her gut. "I'm sorry I made assumptions."

He kept his hand over hers. "Would it be so wrong, Sadie, if I did want to buy things for you and your sisters?"

What he was asking her seemed like so much more. He was a mature man, not a young buck. Who knew what other ladies he'd loved since Miriam had jilted him? Clearly Laura Williams was more than simply an actress he enjoyed watching on stage. Sadie swallowed hard. She would not touch the topic of Robert's love interests. She was not a young girl fantasizing about what a life with handsome young Captain Swaine would be like.

She pulled her hand free. "I think you should—"

"Look at us!" Opal ran into the room, shoeless, swallowed by a loose blue floral dress with several layers of flounces.

The dress indeed would need altering. "Bring that pink ribbon over here and let's tie that waist a little tighter."

"I love mine. Thank you." Garnet, wearing a pale apricot skirt topped by a yellow blouse, appeared almost grown up.

The sight made Sadie's breath catch in her throat.

Garnet pointed to the hem. "If we add some lace to the bottom, it will be long enough. But I can wear my boots with it tonight, and it will work fine."

"I'll let Mr. Keane know that the garments will get good use." Robert's tight smile didn't fool her. He was upset with her.

"Thank you, Robert. I know you were only trying to be helpful." What was wrong with someone trying to be helpful?

The problem was that she'd spent her life feeling like a charity case. Ma had worked so hard for them so they could keep their heads held up. Although she'd always been grateful for help from others when they'd truly needed it, Sadie knew it had cost her mother something.

Was the cost of pride worth what Sadie planned to do?

She shivered and rubbed her arms as though she could chase away the pain that haunted her.

Insistent sharp raps on Adelaide's office door startled her and water sloshed onto the white pintucked shirtfront of her balloon-sleeved blouse. She swiped at it with her hand as the chill soaked to her skin. "Enter."

Lily Swaine opened the door and stepped inside. The girl was pretty as a picture, but some of her flamboyant costumes, when she sang, set Adelaide's teeth on edge. Granted, most were "inherited" from Miss Ivy Sterling, who had broken her singing contract and run off with a wealthy gentleman, leaving her wardrobe behind. Miss Sterling's fancy frocks, one of peacock silk velvet and another a mottled silk plush cardinal with cream accents and jet beads, reminded Adelaide somewhat of the silks and satins Ma and other women had worn in New Orleans, before the war.

She rubbed the side of her head. "How can I help you, Miss Swaine?"

The singer, who was a little past thirty, swiped at her modest reseda-colored skirt, the gray-green a color Adelaide found soothing. "I hate to trouble you, ma'am, but I'm having some difficulties with the assistant housekeeping manager on my floor."

Adelaide forced herself to hold back from saying that she, too, had grave concerns about Mrs. Stillman. "Oh? What exactly is happening?" She remained standing. She didn't want Miss Swaine to have to deal with her bustle when lowering into the office seat. And frankly she didn't want the conversation to be overlong.

"We seem to disagree over my maid, Alice, and her smoking." Lily nibbled her lower lip. "And I suspect someone has been coming into my chambers, but Mrs. Stillman treats me as though I'm a criminal for complaining to her."

Adelaide couldn't stop her features from pulling in shock, at the woman's rude accusation. She briefly closed her eyes and schooled her face into a mask of composure. "Miss Swaine, I assure you that I will look into these matters."

"Thank you."

"Your maid should not be smoking. For one thing, she's too young, and for another that definitely shouldn't be happening during work hours."

Lily tugged at her tan jersey gloves. "I. . . the smell of smoke bothers me something fierce." The woman's Appalachian accent was stronger than Adelaide had heard before. And her inflections were different from the Virginia drawl that Adelaide had come to recognize was one of the first accents her young ears had ever heard.

"I understand. I wish we didn't allow the men's smoking room, too. It's one of the places from which we can never quite rid the odor."

Her father, or rather the man who had her call him "Father", didn't smoke. Called it a "Filthy, dirty habit."

Well, he should have known—didn't he have some of the same, himself? On the other hand, if he'd not indulged his evil habit in New Orleans, what would have happened to Adelaide?

He'd saved her.

And he'd given her, as a daughter, to a woman who never really had accepted Adelaide as her own—even as hard as she tried.

"Mrs. Fox?"

"Oh, I'm sorry. I quite lost myself in thought for a minute." Adelaide forced a thin smile.

"With all you have to do, ma'am, it's no wonder."

Never in all of Adelaide's business ventures had she been bothered by the various and sundry demands. But now, with Peter so near, it felt as though her emotions were bubbling up and threatening to overflow. They'd met three times so far—once on her day off and twice after she'd finished work. And with each encounter, her emotional attachment to her old beau flamed anew.

"Miss Swaine, I shall follow up on this for you. I'm sorry you're having these difficulties." She inclined her head toward her. "You did the right thing in coming to me."

"Thank you, ma'am."

Only another month or so till this charade is all over.

Could Adelaide hang on until then? Her stint as a house mother at the fraternity had been difficult, but short lived. Her normal work involved her meeting with her very limited staff in a nondescript office building. There, Miss Florence Huntington kept watch over Adelaide's investments. And her long-time accountant, Anthony Zandi, now engaged to Miss Huntington, kept the books for all of her businesses. Periodically, Adelaide, Florence, or Anthony would make site visits. They also sought out worthy candidates for sponsorship—either in business, education, or church related.

What had made Adelaide think she could manage the staff of a large hotel? Owning them wasn't the same. She'd gained a new respect for the men and women who managed her properties. They'd all be receiving generous bonuses this year.

Why hadn't she come up with a better idea of how to be nearer to Peter? Conviction hit her. She hadn't trusted. She had not reached out for God's plan. She'd made her own.

She sensed in her gut, though, that something awful was going to happen on her watch.

You can't control everything. Was that the lesson that God continued to whisper to her soul?

Chapter Twelve

The Grand Hotel buzzed with activity since more of the journalists had arrived on the island that morning, in anticipation of Mark Twain's visit. Sadie knocked on the Lindseys' door and was soon allowed entrance. Miss Lindsey, attired in her night shift, stood by the tall armoire, one that hotel craftsman Garrett Christy had designed just for this room, with roses artfully carved into the oak front. She'd miss Mr. and Mrs. Christy when she left the island as she eventually must do.

"Do you have any word for me, Sadie?" Dawn clasped her hands at her waist.

"Indeed, I do." She grinned at the young woman. "He takes ice cream by himself almost every afternoon. No lady involved."

Mrs. Lindsey giggled like a schoolgirl. "How perfectly delightful. Let's pray that is my daughter's only competition for his attention."

"Yes ma'am. And this afternoon, Mr. Bobay is playing croquet with the investors. All of their wives will be there and their children, as well. So you'll need…" Sadie opened the armoire and pulled out a watered silk, mint green ensemble with a wide satin sash adorned with embroidered lilies. "This should be appropriate for the activity."

Mrs. Lindsey nodded her approval as Sadie laid the beautiful clothing on the bed. She returned to the closet and located ivory kid pumps and a matching satin clutch. "I think Mr. Bobay would like you to wear that cream-colored hat with the emerald feathers on it. You said he'd complimented you on it the other afternoon during tea."

"Yes, he did. I heard him." Mrs. Lindsey agreed.

"I looked right back into his eyes last night, just like you told me to do, Sadie, and he gave me such a delicious smile." Dawn sighed.

Mrs. Lindsey rolled her eyes. "A smile isn't delicious."

Stifling a laugh, Sadie removed matching hooked kid gloves from a drawer in the armoire.

"Aren't we presuming a lot if we just show up at the match?" Dawn twisted her linen handkerchief into a wrinkled mess.

Her mother sniffed. "It's open to the public, darling."

"Still…" Dawn raised her arms upward in a stretch.

Someone knocked on the door but before anyone could answer, a note was slid beneath it.

Dawn hurried to retrieve it, opened and read it—then squealed in delight. "You've done it, Sadie! Charles requested our presence at the match today."

Mrs. Lindsey clapped her hands. "Praise God for answering your father's and my prayers."

Sadie had no mother anymore to pray for her, and her father was nowhere to be found. Her heart ached to think she might never see Pa again.

You have a heavenly Father.

She stilled, almost expecting to see someone else in the room with them. She went to the armoire to retrieve some stockings.

Another knock on the door sounded as mother and daughter exchanged a quick embrace. Mrs. Lindsey straightened the linen skirt of her afternoon gown and strode across the carpet to the door.

Robert Swaine stood framed in the doorway, immaculately attired in a dark navy-blue worsted wool cutaway suit. Sadie's heart lurched.

"I wondered if I could have a quick word with Miss Duvall?"

As she turned to face Sadie, the matron's eyes widened. "Captain Swaine wishes to speak with you."

Sadie curtseyed, and eyes down, left the room. What was so urgent that he needed to converse with her now?

Outside in the hallway, hazel eyes locked on hers and her knees weakened. "What is it?"

"Could you and the girls come up to the Canary tomorrow night?"

One of the other maids strode past them, arms stacked high with fresh towels.

"I have to work."

Robert grasped her shoulders, the warmth of his hands seeping through the coarse fabric.

He grinned down at her. "You don't have to work so hard, Sadie. I wish you'd let me help you."

Sadie pulled free from him. She couldn't keep relying on the help from her friends. She needed a permanent job when this seasonal position ended. She opened her mouth, but no words formed. She clamped her lips back together.

"I'm trying to free up your time tomorrow, if you'll allow it." His handsome face was so close, she could reach up and stroke his cheek if she dared.

Why was she indulging in allowing this infatuation to reignite?

"I need assistance."

"What is this for?"

"I'll take you home later and tell you all about it." The warmth of his voice and of his breath on her cheek as he leaned in unnerved her. "But might I have permission to request Mrs. Fox give you early leave?"

She needed her earnings. But Robert had done so much for them. She dipped her chin.

"Wonderful. I'll meet you in the lobby then?"

She'd certainly not meet him, in his fine attire and her in shabby maid's clothing where guests could gawk at them. "No. Meet me behind the building." Mrs. Fox would have apoplexy if she viewed one of her girls leaving from the lobby with a hotel guest.

"All right." He cocked his head at her, his eyes lowering to half-mast, as if he might...

Sadie took a step away and reentered the Lindseys' room.

Now, two hours later, Sadie stood outside in the back of the hotel, near her co-workers, palms damp, awaiting Robert's arrival. She needed a bath, and her clothes required a good scrubbing. She must tend to her sisters' needs, also. First, she'd hear Robert's request.

"Hey, Sadie!" Jerry Meeker unloaded boxes from his dray behind the hotel. He inclined his head toward the street. "Captain Swaine is down there looking for you."

"Thanks." *Lovely, now all the workers knew. At least he's an islander—or had been one.*

All eyes followed her as she lifted her skirt and hurried toward the hilly street. Granted, she'd spent years being escorted around the island by Robert. Now, though, it felt like she was doing something wrong. She was taking advantage of his generosity. That morning, Mr. Keane had let it slip that Robert was indeed funding both their apartment and their purchases at the store. Even now, when she'd tried to use her first paycheck for groceries, Mr. Keane had refused to take her money. This could not continue.

As she neared the carriage parked on the side of the street, Robert waved at her. After another dray loaded with crates turned into the back drive, she crossed the street, dodging horse droppings in the hard-packed dirt street to join him.

"There you are." Robert assisted her up into the one-horse carriage, a smaller gig than he normally drove. "Glad Mrs. Fox let you off early."

Truth be told, she was relieved, too. That bone weariness she battled every day kept threatening to overwhelm her. But here now, with Robert, a surge of energy rushed through her.

When his hands lingered at her waist, Sadie held her breath. He was so close, his dark hair curling around his brow, his hazel eyes so serious. She could reach out and touch the cleft in his chin. She could lean her head down and kiss him and tell him how much he meant to her. But to allow such feelings would get in the way of her taking care of herself and her sisters, like she needed to do. Hadn't she learned well that you could absolutely not count on anyone else?

"Make way!" Someone whistled loudly behind them, and the heavy sound of Belgian horses' hooves carried on the packed dirt as a drayman passed them in the street.

Robert set her in her seat, and Sadie felt his absence as he strode around to the other side, and then took his place. Loneliness, even in this busy summer place, lingered in the breech. This was an emptiness in her heart that only Robert had ever fully filled.

There had always been something about him that had made the world seem more promising, more filled with hope of good things to come.

Was she making a mistake in planning to make those good things come from her work?

She couldn't take a chance in not pursuing her options.

Ben Steffan had done the right thing, and he'd made Adelaide proud. He'd not published her story and he'd procured himself work so that he could remain on the island with Maude. She would be Maude's stepmother, soon, too—she was sure of it. Would that make Ben her step-son-in-law? Standing here, on the lawn behind the Cadotte-Swaine cottage, she pressed a hand to her chest, imagining what a wedding there might look like. For now, though, she tried to stay out of the way of Maude's precious friend who worked hard to ensure this evening would be magical.

"Coming through," Robert called out as he carried a huge crate of glass jars to the setting for tonight's proposal.

Adelaide moved aside, and watched, with a feeling of reverence for romance that she'd never possessed before, as Sadie and Robert decorated the "Canary"—such a vulgar name for such a beautiful house and grounds. Never had Adelaide enjoyed a female friendship like Sadie and Maude had where someone would go to such lengths for her. The closest to that would be her friendship with Peter. Florence Huntington, who was keeping excellent correspondence both business and personal with her, could become that true and devoted friend to Adelaide.

Sadie Duvall brought in another tray of smaller glass jars and arranged them. When filled with candles they would make the most enchanted fairyland setting for an engagement that had ever been planned. Although Adelaide did what she could to assist, Robert and Sadie had the decorating well in hand.

Adelaide returned inside and inspected the rooms. All were clean. Adelaide sat down at the kitchen table and began polishing more of the silver for the dinner that night. When she was done, she rinsed them, dried them, and then assisted in setting the table.

Sadie set a bountiful bouquet of Queen Anne's lace, ferns, roses and other flowers in the center of the dining table. "What do you think so far?" She swiped the back of her hand across her pale forehead, a strand of blond hair breaking free from her upswept hair.

Adelaide shook her head slowly. "I am simply in awe of all you've accomplished. I truly am. You're a marvel."

The young woman's cheeks turned the same shade as the rosy peonies in the arrangement. "Thank you so much."

Robert carried in a matching bouquet. "Where should I set this?"

Sadie pointed farther down the table. "Right there."

From the way Robert Swaine looked at Sadie, it was clear he was smitten with her. Yet Sadie seemed almost indifferent to his attentions. Maybe not immune to them but wary. Was Sadie like Adelaide had always been? Intent upon making sure she could take care of herself because she'd never trust anyone else to do so? Perhaps—for Adelaide had been astonished to receive a letter of inquiry from the Newberry asylum requesting a character reference. Of course, she'd supplied it. But weren't Sadie and Robert on their way toward marriage?

"You look lost in thought, my dear." Peter cupped her elbow.

"Oh, you've arrived." She leaned into him. "I'm standing here doing nothing—like a ninny."

Peter bent and kissed her cheek and Adelaide was sure she must be blushing. His eyes lit up. "You're a beautiful adornment for the room."

She couldn't resist giving him a playful swat like she did when they were youngsters. "Peter Welling, you flatterer!"

He raised his hands and laughed. "Simply stating the truth."

Sadie raised her eyebrows. "Now you two, I have lots to accomplish here so let's start filling these jars with the candles for outside in the back."

"Aye, aye, captain." Peter saluted Sadie.

Robert smirked and looked like he was holding back a retort. After all, he was the real captain. Those two men needed to settle their differences. When she and Peter had dinner recently, Adelaide hinted that she'd saved quite a bit of money over the years. Someday soon, she'd tell him more.

Peter leaned in. "They make a nice-looking couple. I don't know what Robert is waiting for—he's getting more silver in his hair every time I see him."

"It would certainly stop tongues from wagging." She resisted the urge to cover her mouth.

Peter turned her toward him and leaned in. "Are people talking about them?"

Adelaide shrugged. "I'm sorry. I shouldn't have said that. You know the Grand Hotel is a hotbed of gossip."

"They've already gotten Lily and Stephen married, expecting a child, and having secretly lived in Kentucky together is what I've heard." Her sweetheart shook his head.

Adelaide rolled her eyes heavenward. "Oh, and I'm sure you must know her cousin, Clem, is a bank robber in hiding and a polygamist with wives all over the place."

"Hadn't heard about the bank heist thing but yes, they say that strapping pianist has several wives and intends to marry his Chippewa sweetheart, Marie, so he can go into hiding amongst the tribe members."

"The only truth in all of that would be that yes, if he really wanted to slip away, the tribe members would keep him well hidden." Adelaide certainly knew all about hiding.

"I can't believe we're standing here gossiping." Peter took her hand and pulled her closer. "Let's give them something to gossip about."

He kissed her so long and so soundly that Adelaide began to feel a little light-headed. Then the clapping started.

When Peter released her, every eye was on them.

And she didn't mind. Not one bit.

What a success Maude and Ben's party had been. Sadie couldn't stop smiling, even two days later. Bent over a utility cart at the Grand Hotel, Sadie recalled the beautiful family gathering. Dressed in an apricot ensemble borrowed from sweet Dawn, and with her sisters Opal, Garnet, and Bea attired in finery that Robert had somehow procured, the evening of her dear friend Maude's engagement had been magical. She'd never forget it.

She and Robert had made the garden a fairyland for Maude and Ben and their special moment, by placing hundreds of candles, nestled in glass jars, in the garden. What a gift Maude had been given in having her dream come true…of the proposal she and Sadie had discussed when they were younger. A dream of a prince pledging his troth in a fairy garden—a fantasy Maude had, and Sadie had nurtured. What a delight to help make that dream come true. Now, though, Sadie had to get her head out of the clouds and back to work.

She was still a maid, and she had chores, so she pushed her cart down toward the parlor. At the party, she'd eaten fine fare from Cadotte family china and used Swaine family silver and drank from crystal glasses that Sadie had feared her sisters would destroy. Today she'd not eaten with the staff. Instead, she'd eaten her liverwurst sandwich from her tin pail and tried to be glad for it. Once she was off at school, she'd have to get used to beans every day, again.

"Sadie?" She looked up to find her supervisor casting her a quizzical look.

"Yes, ma'am?" Last night Mrs. Fox and Mr. Welling revealed themselves as an official couple. Poor Mr. Welling—he deserved a little happiness. But was this austere woman, a friend from his past, capable of bringing that about? Ada Fox was so different from Maude's mother, although she did strongly resemble Mrs. Welling. Or had it been that Eugenia had resembled Peter Welling's friend, Ada, and that had been what attracted him to her? Mrs. Welling had dark hair, as Mrs. Fox, too, did. Mrs. Welling was the descendant of an Ojibway princess. Perhaps Mrs. Fox, too, had native blood.

Mrs. Fox offered a gentle smile. "You've proven yourself, Miss Duvall, despite my misgivings."

What did she mean? Was she referring to her work or to her ability to step in as hostess alongside of Robert? "Thank you, ma'am."

"You looked perfectly at home in the Cadotte cottage last night." Was that admiration or disdain Sadie heard in the woman's voice? She'd always been supportive at work, albeit stern.

The *Canary*, as Robert and his family called the yellow home on the bluff, was more of a mansion than a cottage. "No, ma'am, I'm an islander and a family friend and have visited before, but I'd never presume to make myself at home there."

Ada Fox arched an eyebrow at her. "Is that so?"

"Yes, ma'am." Sadie's cheeks heated and she stared down at her booted toes. "I hope people aren't making presumptions."

"Such as?" There was an edge in the housekeeping manager's voice.

"That Robert…" She couldn't say the words.

"People will talk, my dear. They always do." The older woman adjusted the chatelaine dangling from her waist. "The question is what shall you say if tongues do wag?"

Sadie lifted her head. "I can't lose my job over this, ma'am."

"I understand." She sighed. "But do you care for him, my dear?"

Sadie sucked in a shallow breath. She dared not answer this question. "I best get back to work, ma'am." When another servant passed by, Sadie grasped the handles of her cart, her mop bucket slopping ammonia-scented water. Would she forever toil and clean the slops of folks who traveled far to view the Straits of Mackinac, where the waters of Lake Michigan and Lake Huron met and mingled and churned, where romances bloomed like the abundance of flowers that covered the town? But could she somehow get to Newberry and interview in person for that nursing training spot?

Laughter carried from inside a nearby room, its door left ajar.

"Did you see how the captain looked at me over lunch?"

Was the occupant speaking of Robert? But many ship and military captains stayed at the hotel.

"Why, he looked like he positively wanted to scoop you up with his teaspoon!" The woman's heavy Southern drawl, and the room, identified her as the Texas matron about whom the other maids were complaining because of her verbal abuse.

"If it weren't for that maid, he'd be mine."

Maid? Were they speaking about her? Sadie pushed against the wall.

"We've gotten rid of other maids, we'll send that blond packing, too."

If only Sadie could take her cart, turn around, and run, but she couldn't.

The two women emerged from their room. The matron narrowed her eyes at Sadie and surveyed her head to toe. Just two nights earlier, Sadie had been bedecked in an apricot silk gown and beautiful jewelry and had presided with Robert over a dinner for Maude and Ben. Now, she was back in uniform.

"You were eavesdropping, weren't you, you nosy creature?"

"No. The door was open, ma'am."

Footfall from behind her announced Mrs. Fox, who must have lingered in the hallway. "Mrs. Chandler and Miss Peacock, how do you do today?"

"Fine." Miss Peacock sniffed.

"But we'd be better if your staff didn't sneak up on people and listen in on private conversations." Mrs. Chandler's eyes could have bored holes in Sadie.

Mrs. Fox cocked her head. "I walked by earlier and your door was open. So, I'm sure you said nothing you wouldn't *want* our staff to hear."

Both women assumed a sour expression.

The supervisor looked pointedly at Sadie. "And anything heard here by our staff is not repeated. Am I right, Miss Duvall?"

Sadie bobbed a curtsey, and Mrs. Fox waved her to move on.

As she passed the other rooms, Sadie blinked back tears. She had to find other work. Before everything went awry. She had to get to the mainland, on a train, and over to the hospital. It was such a booming town—maybe someone there had heard something of her father, too.

Sadie scurried down the corridor to the main rooms near the porch. In a large alcove near the registration desk, she paused to watch Zeb, the shoeshine man, work. A ruddy-faced man was seated in the chair.

"Yahsir." The black man polished the businessman's shoes, his long nose buried in a paper, yet he kept up a litany of comments.

"Yahsir," the bootblack repeated.

When the hotel guest left the shoeshine chair, he pressed some coins into the worker's hand.

"Thank you, sir."

As soon as the hotel guest rounded the corner, Zeb sighed. "Cheapskate." He rubbed the two coins together. "Won't barely cover the cost of my supplies."

"I know." She'd had to purchase shoe care items herself. "I'm sorry."

"Sorry ain't gonna do me no good, Miss Duvall."

"For me, neither. I've got to find another job, Zeb, before one of these guests tries to get me run off."

He chuckled and she stiffened.

"I ain't laughin' at you, but at those society gals all jealous about your captain."

"He's not my captain." But her insides warred and insisted that she'd like Robert to be hers. What would they call her though? Sadie Duvall, the charity case and gold digger?

"You better tell him that then, miss." He jerked a thumb toward the concierge's desk, where Robert stood, his back to her, as he engaged in an animated conversation with the theater star, Laura Williams. The beautiful woman was about his age—and reported to be unmarried.

Was she one of his sweethearts? Someone in the men's smoking parlor the previous night had jested that Robert, "Likely has a lady friend in every port city on the Great Lakes." All the men had laughed in agreement. None of them noticed her at all. She was just the maid carrying out the detritus that they'd accumulated in the room.

"He looks pretty taken with Miss Williams."

Zeb returned his supplies to their proper places and then wiped his hand on a cloth hanging from his waist. "Nah, she's not for him."

How Zeb knew this, she didn't dare inquire.

"Seems to me if you want a job to take you away from the captain, you gonna have to get to the mainland, like you been talkin' about." The shoeshine man eyed her skeptically. "That man whose shoes I just shined done told me somethin' that might help you, miss."

"What's that?"

"They definitely hirin' nurse trainees and all manner of young women to help at that hospital, over there in Newberry. So's if'n you can get yerself there, I'm thinkin' it'll be a done deal."

"Really?" She swallowed hard.

"Frantically searching, he said they was."

What if her determined quest for nursing training and her despairing search for her father could both yield results?

That would be the answer to her prayers.

Chapter Thirteen

*A*delaide Bishop Succumbs to TB in Her One-room Tenement in *New York City*, read the headline. Although Ben, God bless him, hadn't shared Adelaide's story with his employer, the *Chicago World* now proclaimed her *dead*—which truly surprised her. Perhaps she should blow a breath on her looking glass to make sure she hadn't shuffled off this mortal coil yet—as Shakespeare put it. She gave a curt laugh as she set the newspaper down atop her desk. Adelaide Bishop was neither dead nor missing—she was right here on Mackinac Island. Granted, some considered this place heaven on earth—a peaceful escape from the demands of city life. The flower gardens, which thrived in the island's climate, certainly bloomed in heavenly profusions.

The Grand's large rose garden had been her favorite place to visit in her limited off-hours before she'd begun spending her time with Peter. Oh, dear Peter. He had a right to know who he planned to marry. Since journalist Ben Steffan hadn't submitted his article, which would have exposed her to the world, maybe it was time to reveal her true identity on her own terms. But certainly not to everyone.

And there were many people at this hotel who were in hiding. There wouldn't be a Pinkerton hidden amongst them if there wasn't something afoot. Gus Parker, who'd gotten into an altercation, was a thug from Chicago. And since his associate was Mr. Butler, a supposed businessman, Adelaide had to assume he, too, had some criminal associations. The sensation of something awful being just around the corner tugged at her spirit.

Adelaide's office door burst open and Jack came through—more disheveled than usual. Maternal love warmed her heart, despite the interruption. "Jack? What's the matter?"

"Hey, Miss Ada, ya got any bandages in here?"

Bright red blood dripped onto her wool rug. She rose and rushed to him, pointing to a nearby chair. "Sit."

She pulled a handkerchief from her pocket and wet it with the water from her desk carafe. Adelaide bent and gently wiped the boy's knee.

"Ow!"

"Hold that on top and let me find a bandage."

Someone rapped on the open door.

Dr. DuBlanc joined them. "I followed the patient and his trail of blood down the hallway."

Adelaide sucked in a breath. They'd need to wipe that right away before it set in the wool, but first things first.

"It ain't nothin', Doc." Jack shrank back in his seat.

Sadie strode in, holding a bottle of antiseptic, gauze, and tape. "I saw the accident and figured Jack would come here."

"As Jack knows, he's not supposed to be here at the Grand Hotel." Adelaide arched an eyebrow. "I can only imagine he must have fallen in the street nearby as he was practicing his running skills."

From the quick glances exchanged by the doctor, the maid, and Jack—and their lack of response—no doubt Jack was disobeying his father's orders, again.

Dr. DuBlanc gestured for Adelaide to remove the handkerchief and she complied. "Let's have Miss Duvall bandage Jack's injury." He swiveled toward Sadie. "I've heard of your skills with Mrs. Luce."

Sadie had shared with Adelaide that she'd wished to become a nurse. Here was a chance for Sadie to prove herself. So instead of sending Sadie, in her capacity as maid, down to wipe up the blood, Adelaide said, "Yes, let Sadie bandage our dear boy and I'll have one of our other girls clean that up." She nodded curtly to the doctor. Adelaide then went to locate a maid for the main floor.

She found a young Irish servant already down on her hands and knees with a bottle of seltzer water and white cotton towels blotting up Jack's blood.

Adelaide breathed a sigh of relief "Thank you very much."

"'Tis my job, ma'am." Her lyrical voice made Adelaide smile.

"Come see me at the end of your shift. I believe in rewarding initiative."

The young woman's light eyes widened. "Oh. . . I'm just doin' my work, ma'am. Nothing special."

"Still. Stop by later."

"Yes, ma'am."

A stout middle-aged couple, the woman sporting popular princess-style faux curly hair bangs, stepped around the area, the woman's large nose wrinkling in distaste.

Adelaide hurried to her office to find Sadie and the doctor in conversation.

"There's a great deal of *lagrippe* going around on the mainland, I've heard." Sadie sounded half-dismayed half-fascinated as she finished cleaning Jack's wound.

"Yes, on both sides. We're hoping we don't have an outbreak here on the island," Dr. DuBlanc replied.

"What have you found to be the best treatments?"

"Well, I haven't got any old lagrippe and I just want to get back outside." Jack crossed his arms and glared at Adelaide. He reminded her so much of old Mr. Welling, Peter's father, that she almost laughed. He really looked like a grumpy old man right now with almost the same expression that farmer wore when he was irritated. *Still, old Mr. Welling was a kind and generous man, God rest his soul.*

"Be glad you're not sick, young man." Adelaide tried to give him a serious look, but when he stuck his tongue out at her she had to turn away to keep from snorting at his impudence. There was Peter Welling all over again. He'd jump from the hay mow at his family's farm and hit something beneath. Once he'd almost landed on a pitchfork that his father had forgotten to put away and that had put the fear of God in Peter once and for all. But best not to share those anecdotes of Peter with Jack right now—her beau probably wouldn't appreciate it.

She removed a taffy candy from the covered bowl on her desk and turned to hand it to Jack. The boy had a sweet tooth just like Peter had.

"Thanks." Jack sniffed. "I'm glad but how long's it gonna take to get a scab on this so I can keep practicing my running?"

Dr. DuBlanc cocked his head. "I'd estimate three days, four hours, and fifty seconds. What do you think, Nurse Sadie?"

Sadie looked up from wrapping the scraped knee, her lips twitching in amusement. "I like the sound of that. But maybe only twenty seconds not fifty."

The adults chuckled but Jack ignored them.

"*Nurse* Sadie sounds like an old fuddy duddy. I don't like the sound of that. I like Aunt Sadie much better." Jack shot Sadie a harsh look, but she ignored him instead returning her focus to his bandage.

"Why couldn't she be both Nurse Sadie and Aunt Sadie?" Those words slipped so freely over Adelaide's tongue, that she felt as though she'd had no control over them.

When all three of them looked up at her, Adelaide clasped her hands at her waist, feeling contrite. It wasn't her business to comment or be telling Sadie what she could or couldn't do, not even if her growing fondness for the young woman made her want to take her in hand.

"You act like you were born a generation ago." DuBlanc patted Jack's head. "Young women are beginning to want both a meaningful occupation and a family. There was a lady doctor in my graduating class."

"Call me old fashioned then—like my dad." Jack lifted his chin and scrunched his eyes closed, looking a bit like a Parisian gargoyle in that instant.

What about Peter? Once he learned of all of Adelaide's business responsibilities, would he insist she end them? She enjoyed the intricacies of investment and business management.

Time to put her cards on the table.

A hint of woodsmoke greeted Sadie's nostrils as she exited the back of the Grand Hotel. She wrinkled her nose. It wasn't cool enough today for most fireplaces to be lit during the daytime but there were always elderly or infirm people, like Mrs. Luce, who were known to keep the fires going at all hours.

She walked past a cluster of employees, several who were smoking. One was Miss Lily Swaine's maid—a young maid who certainly didn't look old enough for that bad habit. Alice was talking with one of Mr. Christy's workmen. The fellow looked much more like a guest rather than a worker, with his tailored clothing and a hat from a haberdashery and not one plucked from a General Merchandise store. That little maid was going to get herself in trouble with Miss Lily if she caught a whiff of cigarettes on her. The singer had been overheard fussing at the girl several days earlier about her smelling of smoke.

"Have a good evening, Miss Duvall," One of the other maids called out to Sadie.

She waved back.

Once she was away from the group of smokers, the odor was less intense.

Sadie focused her attention back on the past several days. She'd coached Miss Lindsey about displaying more attention to Mr. Charles Bobay and their romance was blossoming. That happy thought was chased by another that was less joyful. Unfortunately, she'd also suspected Robert and Miss Williams's interest was increasing. Sadie had spotted the two everywhere together. And as much as it hurt her, she knew Robert and Laura had much more in common than she and he ever would. Laura Williams was a refined lady. Sadie was suited to become a nurse, taking care of people and working day in day out. She'd be attired in a uniform that could stand up to the wear and tear it would take whereas the actress would be garbed in silk, chiffon, and beautiful delicate fabrics that would suit her life of ease.

Sadie exhaled hard as she headed down the hill. Why should she be jealous? Robert had never promised her anything. He'd been nothing but kind to her and her sisters. Yet it stuck in her craw that today, Robert had taken Opal and Garnet along up to old Fort Holmes to hike and picnic. And he'd brought along Miss Williams. Was he simply showing off his charity cases to impress the beautiful woman? Not wanting to see them all together, when she'd returned after work, Sadie had stayed later.

For her last task, Sadie had fixed Miss Lindsey's hair into a golden coif. The upswept style made her look like an angel and had earned Sadie a hug.

Soon Mr. Bobay was sure to make his intentions clear. Was Robert doing the same with Miss Williams? And right in front of her sisters? By now, though, her sisters should be back home, preparing dinner. And Robert and Laura should be *gone*. Maybe they would take a romantic ride alone or go out to dinner and there he'd produce a box, with an engagement ring, and propose to the actress.

A muscle jumped in her cheek, and she relaxed her tense jaw. Her imagination was getting the better of her.

Sadie eyed the bicycles parked by the hotel as she walked down the hill. With only a word, she could request a bicycle, or two or three, and Robert would procure them. But that would be wrong to impose any further upon him. She walked on, under her own power—as she'd have to do if and when Robert finally married.

Something was making her eyes water. Sadie bowed her head, the chill wind blustering that smoke-scented breeze her way. She rounded the corner and glanced out into the furious blue straits, where whitecaps danced like malevolent sprites across the high waves.

Few people were in their yards today, but she did spy a matron watering her begonias on her front veranda. What must that be like to have servants perform all the chores and to be left with only the task of watering the porch flowers? Sadie might never know but she could at least dream of a day when she'd have a tiny cottage and perhaps a window box of begonias or daisies to call her own. She'd work hard as a nurse and come home to her little home and be grateful for work well done.

The scent of smoke grew stronger as Sadie neared the Winds of Mackinac. Jack Welling rode down the side alley so fast that he looked like he'd fly from his bicycle. Sadie froze.

The boy slowed and then jumped from his Sterling, which had no brakes, and threw it into the grass. He ran to her, blood oozing through his bandage, and grabbed her arm. "Come on, Sadie! The General Store is on fire!"

"What?" *What's he saying?*

"Your place is ablaze!"

"No!" The apartment had become a home. Their refuge. Were the girls there, inside? Had Robert left them and went off with the actress?

"Did you see my sisters?"

"No." He ran toward the inn, calling over his shoulder, "I gotta tell Dad and get some help."

No! Oh Lord, be my ever-present help. I can't lose them, too.

Stan Danner drove his dray team past, water barrels strapped in back. "Make way!" he called to the carriage ahead of him in the street. "There's a fire! Make way!"

Sadie hurried past people clustered on the boardwalk. Her sisters. She had to get to them. Tears pricked her eyes. If she'd gotten home earlier instead of remaining at work longer, she'd have been able to help them. Her jealousy could cost them their lives.

The fire crew carriage rolled by, with Greyson Luce clanging a bell as they went. Fear and determination were etched in his features. As upset with him as she'd been for throwing Maude over, Sadie was grateful for his assistance now. *Lord keep them safe. Keep my sisters safe.*

All along the street, islander men vacated their workplaces and streamed into the street, many carrying buckets of sand. Sadie continued on, trying to catch her breath. The pain over losing her mother opened up like a fresh wound, gushing sorrow within her. Her chest ached with grief she'd never fully released.

She had to do something.

Arriving at the store, Sadie rushed toward the side entry door. She pushed past the crowd gathered near the fire wagons. She had to get to her sisters. She looked up at the side window. Opal's doll seemed to be waving down at her. Opal would *not* have left her doll behind. Sadie choked back a sob and worked to open the door, but it was jammed. She pushed harder but it wouldn't give.

The fire brigade volunteers began setting up, preparing to pump water. A queue of islanders passed buckets. The air thickened with smoke.

She had to get to them. She would.

Greyson stepped out from the group. "Get back, Sadie!"

She shot him a glare.

In a flash, she pulled her skirts aside and climbed onto the ladder mounted to the side of the building.

"What's she doing?" a voice called out.

Sadie ignored everything and continued upward.

One precarious step at a time as smoke billowed around her.

Robert pulled the carriage up beside the docks, secured the brakes, and handed Laura the reins. He jumped down and patted the horses' heads to reassure the whinnying creatures.

"That's Sadie up there!" Garnet stood in the carriage, pointing toward the building, but Laura quickly got the child to sit, and wrapped an arm around her.

Sure enough, Sadie was climbing the ladder on the side of the store. He cupped his hands around his mouth. "Sadie!" he called out, but she didn't respond.

Lord, we need some help here. From shore, a water bucket brigade urgently worked. The fire carriages surrounded the building.

The earlier breeze ceased, holding an eerie stillness. Thank God for that small mercy—for wind was surely fire's closest friend. An evil friend.

Robert ran across the street. *Oh God, don't let her die up there. I can't live without her.* He was almost to the building when a band of iron seemed to wrap around his upper arm.

"Stop. It's not safe." Greyson grabbed his arm, but Robert broke loose from his grip.

He pushed through the crowd until he got to the boardwalk, the smoke nearly overpowering him. He loved this woman, he needed her. Forever. He couldn't lose her now. Not like this. Not ever. "Sadie!"

Almost to the second floor, she looked down at him.

"I've got the girls with me. Come down!"

A powerful explosion split the air and Sadie screamed. Fire rained down on him, scorching Robert's clothing but he stepped in, bracing himself as Sadie hurtled toward him. He caught her in his arms and fell hard to one knee, wrapping his arms around her as all around them, gasps, coughs, and cries created a hellish cacophony of noise. He shielded her with his body as she clung to him.

Water poured down on them. First from the volunteer firemen blasting the wooden structure with their hoses and then from above as the heavens broke loose. Sadie shivered but he held her there—he in his sodden tweed jacket, and she in her maid's uniform.

"I love you, Sadie," he whispered. But he had to get her away from the building.

She pulled away; lips slightly parted. She looked terrified. Was it his words that inspired that emotion or the fire? She stood and he rose and wrapped his arm around her. He pulled her toward his carriage, which Laura had moved down the street away from the burning building. Opal and Garnet waved to them from the back.

"I thought they were in there." Sadie choked back a sob, looking back at the inferno. "My sisters. They're all I have."

She had him, too, he wanted to say. Robert took her hand, led her across to the harborside, and then continued up the boardwalk, following the carriage.

Thunder boomed overhead.

"I can't believe it." Robert tipped his head back. An enormous black cloud, not uncommon in the Straits, moved quickly in their direction yet without an accompanying wind—as if the hand of God moved it there.

Thank you, Lord. Robert's arms trembled with emotion.

Sadie, her face streaked with black soot, had never looked so lovely. Other than singed hair and clothing, she should be fine.

He could resist. He should. But Robert bent and covered her mouth with his, right there in the street, as the clouds opened up and poured down chill rain by the bucketsful. Nothing had felt more right than her in his arms, his lips covering hers.

When he pulled away, she still looked up at him with distress in her blue eyes.

She didn't care for him—not as he did for her.

Shame washed over him with the pouring rain. His instincts were right. He shouldn't have kissed her. And as a gentleman, he'd greatly overstepped.

Forgive me.

If Adelaide couldn't get these recurring tears to stop, she didn't know what she'd do. She pulled another clean handkerchief from her desk drawer and slid the damp one inside. Sadie Duvall's calamity had struck Adelaide with such an emotional force that she vowed she'd do everything she could to help the young woman. Sadie was just as lost as Adelaide had been at her age and her fondness for her was making her feel more. . . well. . . motherly. Between the love she felt for Jack, who would soon be her stepson, and the affinity she felt for Sadie, Adelaide's emotional balance had been disrupted. Was this really what she'd been missing out on all these years? On emotional upset over one's children? No wonder so many sermons were aimed at the parishioners who were parents struggling to raise their children.

And what about Maude? Her future stepdaughter was a young adult. But she, too, could use some help—if she'd allow Adelaide to do so. But overhelping was something Adelaide was struggling to overcome. It wasn't a good thing—unless God had put it on her heart to assist. She truly was trying to be more in tune with the Holy Spirit's guidance. The sooner she could step down from this position, the better.

The staccato triple rap followed by two slow ones announced Robert Swaine. The door slowly opened, and he peered around it. Then he produced a vase full of roses, geraniums, and Queen Anne's lace.

"For you, madam."

"Those are beautiful. Thank you." Adelaide's eyes widened at the large arrangement, held in what she recognized as one of the ceramic vases from the captain's home.

"My brother-in-law asked the girls if they'd make you up something for your office."

"They did a wonderful job." As he set the bouquet down atop a crocheted doily, she touched one of the silky red roses.

"I agree."

"Have they settled in at your home? I know Peter would have taken them in if the inn wasn't booked all through high season."

"Yes. The only one who seems unhappy about it is. . ." Pink tinged his high cheekbones.

"Sadie?" Adelaide really shouldn't interfere. Today, she would bite her tongue and not share her opinion about what Robert should do.

He huffed a sigh. "Yes, but she's settled in a room that Maude has often used."

"Peter said that Maude sent clothing over for her."

"We're replacing their belongings with items from other stores we own."

"And I'd like to bring them something, too—maybe some new toys and books from the mainland—something we can't find here."

"I'm sure they'd appreciate that."

Adelaide shook her head and swiped a tear from her eye.

Robert cocked his head. "Are you all right?"

"It was a shock, wasn't it, with the fire?" Her voice hitched. She had deliberately burnt down a building, in New Orleans, where so many people had been harmed by evil, not by fire. But there were those who'd know hell fire if they never repented.

"I've never been so terrified in all of my life."

"Love will do that to you. When you see a loved one in danger." An image of Ma crying in her window, waving a Turkish red scarf flashed through her mind. Then someone had grabbed Ma away, she screamed, as Adelaide's new father covered her eyes and carried her to his ship.

"I've lost my parents, my sister, and my ships. But until yesterday, I didn't understand how much my life would change if Sadie was gone—and the unendurable pain I'd feel."

The scent of the flowers wafted toward her. "You've got another chance. Just like Peter and I have."

And she'd not waste her opportunity. She prayed Robert also looked hard at his behavior and stopped squiring Miss Williams about. But now wasn't the time to say so.

Chapter Fourteen

Sadie stood in the middle of the salon and rubbed her fingers over her lips, recalling the pressure of Robert's firm kiss. Bernard's kisses had never affected her like this one had. But she had to stop remembering the thrill she'd had when Robert had been so bold.

Still—men made absolutely no sense. Sadie pushed a lock of blond hair from her brow then began dusting the piano in the ladies' parlor.

If Robert loved her, and had kissed her so thoroughly right in front of everyone, then why did he still escort Laura Williams around the island while Sadie was working? The only thing that made sense was that he was toying with *both* of their affections. All her sisters cared about was that Robert had moved them all into his mansion on the West Bluff. And of course, Jack hadn't been happy that Opal had selected the room he'd normally used. Sadie had similar feelings. She wasn't comfortable taking over rooms that had belonged to Robert's family members. It didn't seem right. Maude, though, had encouraged her to take her normal room. She was such a good friend. She'd made sure Sadie had clothing, shoes, and everything she needed for now. How could Sadie ever make it up to her?

Two matrons entered the salon and eyed her. Sadie stiffened and quickly averted her eyes. Normally, guests took no notice of the servants. It was as though they were nonexistent. Although this was not open parlor hours, Sadie held her tongue. The two ladies, one dressed in an unflattering Zouave set, took seats opposite one another at a round walnut tea table.

One of the waitstaff wheeled in a small tea cart piled with cookies, scones, and muffins, and with a teapot nestled in a cozy. When Sadie sent the young man a quick questioning glance, he simply raised his eyebrows in response.

"Thank you, young man." The older of the two women, with a pouf of silver hair framing her sharp features, nodded curtly.

"We'll pour our own, thank you." When the waiter left, the lady with auburn curls did indeed pour tea for the two.

Sadie continued to dust and shine the furniture as the two women chatted about the weather.

"And my, wasn't that something about the fire the other day?"

"The whole village might have burned."

The way fire leapt between wooden structures; indeed it could have. But the firemen and God put the inferno out quickly.

"And Laura Williams—abandoned in her carriage while Captain Swaine dashed off to save some island girl." The woman tugged at her lace collar, secured with an amethyst broach.

"Shocking. I heard the silly creature was climbing into the inferno."

Of course, Sadie was trying to climb up. She wanted to rescue her sisters. She clenched and unclenched her fists.

The older woman sipped her tea, then set the cup down with a clink. "I should think Dr. DuBlanc should refer her to the asylum in Newberry. I've heard rumor that our singer, Miss Lily, may possibly have set her cap for the good doctor. Can you imagine? A Southern singer marrying such an educated man?"

"Indeed. It's quite shocking but then again, she's on the shelf and likely feels she must throw herself at him."

"As that maid is surely doing with Captain Swaine."

"Tut, tut."

How dare these ladies sit and judge her and Lily? Sadie's heartbeat kicked up, pumping heat to her face, as she spread lemon oil over the surface of a lamp table and rubbed it vigorously against the grain.

"Poor Laura. How humiliating to have her beau seen embracing another woman."

Her beau?

"Her beau?" The older woman repeated Sadie's own thoughts. "There's to be an announcement at the ball, after her last performance, and I believe he's to become her fiancé."

No. That can't be. Robert had tended to Sadie's burns, had made sure she and the girls were housed again. Had brought her and the girls up to the Canary to stay.

"Yet he apparently keeps this other woman put up elsewhere."

"Scandalous."

"Once they're engaged, Laura will put a stop to that. Mark my words."

"A *kept woman* on this island?" The elder matron pulled a lorgnette from her handbag. "No doubt all these islanders know about it."

"She'll be drummed out of here."

"You'll see."

When the two pointedly glanced in her direction, Sadie turned and fled the room.

She was a third of the way down the hallway when a strongly built man backed out of a workroom. Garrett Christy, master craftsman and family friend, pulled an elaborately carved console table into the hallway. Apples, deer, and pine trees covered its large, rounded legs. He released the piece and locked gazes with her.

"Sadie, you're just the person I've wanted to see."

"Yes?"

His expressive features tugged and pulled. "I've got something to tell you."

"What is it?"

Although she shouldn't be listening in on private conversations, Adelaide stood there in the alcove, with Mr. Williford, whom she suspected of being an undercover police officer, when she overheard Garrett Christy's deep voice. What did he want to share with sweet Sadie? All of her protective, maternal instincts jumped into play.

"Sadie, there's a man in Newberry, at the hospital, who might be your father. My brother told me about this fella—an injured lumberjack."

"What? Really? Who?"

"We're not sure but some new men at the next camp over from my brother's said a fella matchin' your pa's description, was taken up to the hospital after an accident. And he's not come back in about a year."

"Oh, I hope it's him. But did they say about the injury?"

"No, only that a tree had come down on him."

"Oh no. But he—that is this man—he's alive?"

"Someone saw him on the grounds at the asylum."

"That's where I've applied for my nursing training."

"My brother, Richard, says he'll get you over to that hospital to see if'n that man is your pa. And you could knock out two birds with one stone if'n you've got an interview lined up."

"I should hear something very soon."

"My Rebecca Jane says I can travel with you, to see if that's your pa, and to see my kin over there."

"Oh, thank you."

"My brother will take time off from the camp and pick us up at the train station and carry you up the hill to the asylum. It's a fair way from the tracks in town."

"Oh, this is wonderful news. I would appreciate that very much."

Adelaide's heart warmed to hear how Mr. Christy was helping this dear girl. But poor Robert if Sadie did land a position in the nursing training program. Could he give the woman, who he clearly loved, room enough to test her dreams? Or not? He had finally slowed his attentions to Miss Williams, which was a relief.

Mr. Williford cleared his throat. "Did you hear me, Mrs. Fox? I report only to Mr. Costello. I don't want to be contentious, but you, madam, are *not* my employer."

Her cheeks heated. Neither was the Grand Hotel Williford's employer, as she'd recently discovered when Maude had reviewed the books, before she'd been let go at the hotel. There was no employee record on file for Mr. Williford. And it worried Adelaide that often she'd found him somewhere near their singer, Lily Swaine, who genuinely appeared to be Robert's cousin. If one listened to Jack, he'd claim he'd always known the lady was his relation—because she looked like his grandmother.

Williford strode from the dark paneled alcove and out into the hallway.

If only her Pinkerton agent could come up with better answers for her. She would put Williford on the list for him to investigate next.

Adelaide closed her eyes. *Dear God, maybe I really am better off to be alone in my home and offices back downstate. Maybe You aren't the One who sent me to the university and now here. Maybe that was all me.*

Both the fraternity house position and now this one at the Grand had turned out to be far more difficult than many of her dealings in business. But if she hadn't done that little jaunt at the college, after her third husband had died, she'd not learned about Peter and his family. And if she'd not come here, she'd have not rekindled her relationship with Peter. Finally, healing was happening in her soul.

"Mrs. Fox?" Sadie's voice interrupted Adelaide's reverie. "Is something wrong?"

She opened her eyes. "No, *my dear*, I'm fine."

The young woman's eyes widened.

Adelaide's face heated. She'd never used a term of endearment with Sadie before. She'd called Maude that, though, and more than once. Life was short. You should bless people when you could. Show affection when you were able. And not regret taking a new path.

"I'll get back to work, then."

"Wait." Adelaide gently grasped Sadie's forearm. "Someone should tell you what a good worker you are. How patient you are with some of our most difficult patrons. And how you are loyal to your friends and devoted to your siblings." The words tumbled out like dice rolled at a European casino table.

Sadie blinked rapidly and then swiped at her cheeks as her blue eyes overflowed.

"I didn't mean to make you cry." But Adelaide wasn't done yet. "You do a job thoroughly—not looking for praise but for a job well done. You don't give up, don't give in, but you persist. You, my dear, are an example of womanly excellence—and you need to hear that from someone."

Adelaide took the maid into her arms for a quick hug. She didn't care who saw her. "Never, ever believe that you aren't worthy. You are. And if I could have a daughter just like you, I couldn't be prouder."

Pulling a handkerchief from her pocket, Sadie sniffed. "Thank you."

If Sadie did not marry Robert, then Adelaide would take this young woman under her wing and make sure she understood how to take care of herself and her sisters, financially. As Adelaide had done, over the years, she'd bring this young woman into the little "family" she'd made in the business world.

"There's a whole wide world out there just waiting for you, Sadie," with Robert she hoped, but that was for those two to determine. "And I can't wait to see what wonderful things you do. What marvelous things you see in the years ahead."

"I want to be useful, but I want to make a difference in peoples' lives, too." Sadie squared her shoulders. "I believe I could do that as a nurse—and it suits me."

"Well, I'll pray in agreement with you that God will direct you on your path." Adelaide repeated the words that Rev. McWithey had spoken in church recently. And she found she truly believed them.

Sadie smiled. "I think He has."

Adelaide would help any way she could.

Birdsong and a mourning dove's plaintive calls stirred Sadie from her slumber. She pushed aside the heavy bedcoverings on the tall bed, bringing alive the scent of dried lavender. She and Maude had slept in this bed on occasion when Mrs. Swaine had invited them up to her home. Light shown from alongside the curtains.

Oh no. She was going to be late to work.

Wrapping a robe around her, Sadie peeked into the halls. Robert's laugh carried up from downstairs. She padded downstairs, barefoot, as the grandfather clock softly chimed the hour. Six. My, that was terribly late. She strode toward the dining room.

"Sadie? Is that you?" Robert sat at the grand long dining table, smiling up at her as natural as could be, from behind a *Detroit Free Press* newspaper. In front of him lay a silver tray of pastries. Lemon poppyseed muffins, cinnamon rolls, and almond twists covered the tray, crowding one another out. "They've started recording the weather. Can you believe it? It's about time we got more scientific about keeping track of these things."

She laughed. "I've known islanders with rheumatism who could predict the weather with their joint pain. So, I don't know how helpful that will all be."

He pushed back his chair, rose, and gestured to the chair beside him, as he pulled it out. "I can tell you that as a mariner, that national and international weather information, over time, could be very useful for planning."

"True." She remained standing.

Would this be what mornings could be like if she were Robert's wife? They'd take breakfast together as he read the paper. They'd discuss the news. And their children. . . *Stop!*

She raised a hand. "No, I can't sit. I have to get ready for work. I'm going to be very late."

Robert continued to hold the chair for her. A cool breeze gusted through the open window and rustled the lace dining room curtains. "Have no worry, I sent word to Mrs. Fox that you required some rest." Her mouth went dry. "I need to work, Robert." She needed that paycheck. She needed to find another place for her sisters and her to live. But she sat in the proffered chair and allowed him to adjust it for her.

"Any word on Mr. Keane?" Dr. Cadotte, Robert's cousin, had attended the shopkeeper, who'd suffered burns and inhaled smoke.

"François says he'll be fine." Robert took his seat adjacent hers. Although Mr. Keane's unattended pipe had caused the fire, which could have killed Sadie and her sisters had they been upstairs, she wished him no ill. "I'm glad to hear that. And we should pray for him and his family." How would he manage without employment? She understood that desperation all too well.

"I'll do that." He poured more creamer into his coffee. "And I've already requested my cousin to give him a position at the mercantile."

"No smoking allowed, I presume."

"Indeed." A smile tugged at Robert's lips. "I almost feel like I need to thank him, though, for bringing you here. You brighten the place by your presence."

And when Miss Williams found out, what then? "Is that so?"

"We need to get you settled in here for the long haul."

A rush of emotions surely shown on her face as she blinked in shock, clenched her teeth in anger, and sighed in frustration. For she and her sisters to officially take up residence here would make it look like she was Robert's kept woman, like those horrid women at the hotel had said. Her cheeks heated. She couldn't manage to make her protest. She used the silver tongs to choose an almond pastry that looked as twisted as her insides felt.

"We can't live here, Robert." She took a small bite of the flaky baked good.

"Why not?" Robert frowned and avoided looking at her. "You're Maude's friend, and I've known you for years."

So, she was just his niece's friend and a charity case. That was all she was to him. She opened her napkin and shook it out before placing it on her lap. "But people will still talk."

Rosy circles bloomed on his high cheekbones. "Let them talk. I've nothing to hide."

"It wouldn't be your reputation that was tattered." She pushed the almond twist aside, her appetite fleeing.

Maybe the girls could stay, and she could go to the mainland and get a job. Find out if that man at the asylum might be Papa. With her not in residence at the Canary, then perhaps the rumors wouldn't go far. Sadie nibbled on her lower lip. "Could the girls stay here while I go to the mainland?"

"Certainly. I'd gladly accompany you to Newberry to see if that patient might be your father." He covered her hand with his, sending warmth through her. "Gretchen will watch the girls. And Aunt Virgie will be coming by, too."

"That would help." Especially if she was hired on and had to save up money for a few months to bring the girls to the mainland.

He quirked a dark eyebrow at her, making her stomach do funny things. "I'd be glad to let Mrs. Fox know that I'll accompany you."

No, she would do this on her own. She was going to Newberry to see if that man was Pa, and to inquire about the nursing program. "Imagine how that would look. You and I going off on a boat, and then a train, together."

What about Laura Williams? What would she think?

Chapter Fifteen

M rs. Moore, the wife of a wealthy Chicago industrialist, recognized Adelaide—she was sure of it, from the glint in her beady eyes. This had been a mistake coming out onto the porch, in search of Lily Swaine.

"Don't I know you?" The matron locked gazes on her, but Adelaide offered an enigmatic smile and shook her head. *Lord forgive me, that headshake means I don't wish to speak with her.*

"You do look so familiar." Moore's voice trailed after her as Adelaide hurried off after Lily.

Why had the wealthy socialite noticed a housekeeping director at all? If Adelaide hadn't approached Lily outside, if she'd stayed in her private office, then she'd have avoided the Moores, who were seated with their son on the porch, breakfasting.

Adelaide could make up an explanation of why she was there if Mrs. Moore realized that she had once been the wife of their wealthy industrialist friend. That had been over two decades earlier, though, and people changed. Adelaide would work on her voice a little more. *Make it lower.* But if she was indeed recognized then she'd need a plausible story. One that didn't niggle at her conscience. She could say she'd lost most of her money in the previous year's economic crash— not true, though. Could say everyone had a doppelganger. She could do like she'd been doing—keeping to herself.

She'd almost caught up with Miss Swaine when she spotted the singer with her maid. Alice raised her voice and Adelaide stopped in her tracks. Certainly grounds for dismissal—but the girl was so young. And Mrs. Stillman insisted on managing Alice. Adelaide huffed a sigh. She'd be ending this farce in a short time, and she'd not waste precious energy on someone else's charge.

When Alice stormed off, Adelaide caught up with Lily. "Miss Swaine, I wanted to remind you about the family gathering coming up. Will you be able to join everyone at Cadotte cottage?"

"Yes. I'll be there." Lily pressed her hand against her decorative yoke, which matched her beaded stomacher—both covered in jet beads.

"Very good."

"I'm off to see Stephen, that is Dr. DuBlanc, now."

"And I'm actually departing the hotel for some free time." Adelaide inclined her head toward the door, turned and headed off in her own direction.

Time to head down to Peter's to discuss their plans for Jack's training. That boy had unbelievable athletic skills and could become their nation's fastest runner—she was sure of it. After all, as a twelve-year-old he was the fastest runner in Michigan. Adelaide went to her room, grabbed her parasol, her hat, and her shawl and headed out the back of the hotel.

As she reached the hallway to the hotel's dress shop, she spied Robert Swaine gazing at the mannequin in the window. She turned and went down the hall to join him.

She sensed that someone else followed her down the passageway and she turned to see Miss Lindsey and her mother. The two were engaged in animated conversation.

Adelaide continued on until she reached the captain.

"Good day, Mrs. Fox." Robert offered her a charming smile. He gestured toward the window. "This beautiful dress is almost the exact color of my dearest's eyes."

"Is that so?" Adelaide cocked her head at him. Indeed, the blue matched Sadie's pretty, but often sad, eyes.

Mrs. Lindsey stepped alongside Robert. "It's a Worth gown. I recognize it from a shop I frequent."

The captain shoved his hands in his jacket pocket. "Worth is the designer I prefer when I order something for my niece. Their work is excellent."

Miss Lindsey giggled, even though she was a mite too old for that. "And any woman who wears a Worth gown is transformed by its beauty."

Adelaide's lips began to twitch. "It's perfectly appropriate for Captain Swaine to gift his niece with a gown but of course an unmarried man *never* buys such a personal item for a woman." But she could. She could be like the fairy godmother in the *Cinderella* book by Charles Perrault.

"Oh no, I wasn't intending to purchase." Robert gave her a tight smile and nodded to the other two women.

"Of course not." Adelaide hoped she'd not upset him. Robert had been too obviously generous with Sadie Duvall already and was on the precipice of destroying her reputation. Adelaide wouldn't allow him this impropriety.

Robert took two steps closer as he moved to exit the hallway. As he passed, he leaned in. "I would love to order it. But you are right—I cannot. Thank you. When my sweet one agrees to wed me, then—but I don't know if that is to be." He dipped his chin at her and left them.

Miss Lindsey clasped her laced and hooked kid-gloved hands together. "Let's go inside and look."

"The accessories are gorgeous," her mother gushed. "Join us Mrs. Fox."

The matching sapphire necklace, bracelet, and earrings alone were likely the sum of her annual salary here, but a pittance compared to her actual wealth. "I'm sorry but I'm on my way into town."

"Have a good afternoon."

"Thank you. And you as well." Adelaide headed off. She'd find a way for the items to be purchased. She'd done that many times without anyone linking it back to herself. She'd send a message to Miss Huntington, her secretary, who was also rapidly learning the ropes of business management.

When she stepped out of the hotel and into the sunshine, Alice Smith, Lily's maid, and Mr. Diener, the new craftsman with impeccable manners, again stood together chatting. Adelaide wasn't sure which of the two was more out of place—the young maid who'd no doubt lied about her age or the circumspect artisan, perhaps just shy of thirty but with the world-weary air of a much older man.

Adelaide kept her head down as she passed by.

"I don't care what that Miss Lily wants! I am fed up with this place." Gone was Alice's Irish accent, replaced by a stronger northern Midwestern one—Wisconsin if Adelaide was correct. She cringed. With Maude Welling pretending to be a maid, Ben Steffan a wealthy industrialist, Adelaide the housekeeping manager—why should it surprise her that yet one more person wasn't who they were supposed to be?

"You just need to calm down. Stay away from them as much as you can." Mr. Diener's reassuring voice sounded much like that of a father figure. Or older brother. How did he know Alice? Jack had been concerned about the young girl meeting outside with him.

"How can I be calm after all that has happened to me because of that horrid Mrs. Moore? It's her fault." The girl began to sob.

From the corner of her eye, Adelaide spotted Mr. Diener taking the maid into his arms. *Oh my.* Adelaide would have to follow up on what she'd overheard today. But for now, she needed to get to Peter's. She strode down the hillside in her sturdy low boots, parasol raised overhead.

A memory accompanied her. "You've got to keep out of the sun, Adelaide. You know what happened last summer when you were out in the garden too long." Mother hadn't wanted Adelaide's skin to get dark. She always wore a hat and gloves and carried a parasol to protect her skin. Mother wanted to keep Adelaide's complexion light. To not give their neighbors any more reason to talk about the young child who had mysteriously shown up with her husband, the ship captain, one day.

The waves on Lake Huron danced like tiny ballerinas in gauzy white skirts as the sun glittered over the tops of the waves like tiaras. How Adelaide had loved going to ballet recitals and to the opera with her first husband. He'd been a good man. He wasn't Peter, the one she wanted to be with, but he was kind, generous, handsome, and completely smitten with her. In a way he'd rescued her from secretarial school much as Father had liberated her from the house of ill repute in New Orleans. And he'd tried to save Ma, too—by buying Adelaide from her and then smuggling her out and aboard his ship. Later they'd learned that Ma had paid the ultimate sacrifice in order for Adelaide to get free.

She sniffed and wiped away the warm moisture on her cheek as a gust of wind threatened to tear her parasol away. Adelaide lowered it and tucked the umbrella under her arm. Soon she was at Winds of Mackinac Inn, the cheery yellow building inviting her inside.

Sadie's sister, Bea, a taciturn girl, almost grunted at Adelaide as she entered the inn. "A good day to you, too, Miss Duvall."

"I didn't say that." Bea crinkled her nose.

"Well, you should have, young lady." Adelaide's voice sounded snappish, but the girl deserved the implicit scold. Bea's personality and behavior often seemed almost the opposite of her sister, Sadie's.

The girl's green eyes widened. "Why?"

"Because that's good manners."

Her face reddened. "Good day to you, Mrs. Fox."

Adelaide offered a tight smile. "Much better."

Peter opened his office door and motioned for her to join him. "So glad you could come, Adelaide. Bea, could you please ask Cook to make us tea?"

"Yes, sir." At least the girl made an effort for Peter, her employer.

Adelaide went to her sweetheart, and they clasped hands. Then he kissed her cheek. She felt the warmth of his lips as they sent a spiral of emotion through her. A longing for a simple life. The wish for family. The loss of what could have been between them. But now they had the future ahead.

She really needed to quit the Grand as soon as was possible. But when?

"Come in and sit down." Peter kept her one hand in his and led her into the office. "You said you wanted to talk with me about something."

"Yes." She set her parasol on the rack and removed her shawl. "I wanted to let you know that I made some contacts, and we have sponsors for Jack for his training." Granted, Adelaide was the main sponsor for the boy, who aspired to become an Olympic runner one day. He was the fastest runner his age, in the state of Michigan.

"That's very exciting." Peter sat down next to her. "I got a letter from the Wenhams, who've leased the land. And I've learned that my family's old farm is in better shape than I thought."

"I'm so glad." Adelaide had paid some workers to go in and make repairs.

"Because you know I want us to live there."

She knew that marriage was what he'd been hinting at since he'd had his last spell with his heart. Which had, however, turned out to be cause by anxiety. "I know you're concerned about this mess with your mother-in-law's estate—"

Peter blew out a breath. "I may only have the farm, Adabelle, but we could still have a good life together."

"Yes, and I also want you to know. . ." *That I'm the wealthiest woman in America. That I have more money than you can imagine. That I cannot allow my secret to get out because then who knows who will come crawling out of the woodwork to seek money from me. And*

with all that publicity how long would it be until the truth of my birth.
The truth of my background come out. "My first husband left me very
well situated, as did my second—may they rest in peace."

"That doesn't seem right, accepting money from my wife—my
future wife that is." He kissed her knuckles and she could feel the
warmth through her jersey gloves.

"I am very happy to share what I have. What's mine truly can be
yours."

"But when we get things straightened out with this mess that
Jacqueline created, then I'll be more than able to care for all of us.
And to make the farm successful."

"Peter?"

He locked eyes on her. "What is it?"

"You needn't worry about us. I'm a wealthy woman."

His eyes widened. "You are?"

She squeezed his hand. "I'm a very wealthy woman, in fact."

Peter blinked at her. "But you're only the housekeeping manager
at the Grand—and a fraternity house before that.

"That's true. But I also have enough savings, shares, bonds, and
stocks to allow us to live a very comfortable life—even if you never
receive a penny of the money you deserve for working your heart out
for these businesses of your mother-in-law's and your wife's."

"Were your husbands so well off?" He pressed his back into the
cushion. "What are you saying?"

"You don't need to worry any more about this problem. Let it go.
Let us begin anew—without this hanging over our heads." Adelaide
leaned in and kissed his cheek. "If you want, I can share with you
some of the bank statements so you can see that I'm speaking the
truth."

He raised one hand. "No, no, that's not necessary. But why are
you working at the Grand then?"

"I'm asking myself the same thing." She dipped her chin. "I
guess you know I wanted to be near you. And I wanted to be useful."

Useful—that was something that Sadie liked to say. She wanted
to be doing something that counted.

"Submit your resignation. Let's get married. We've wasted so
much time already. And honestly, even if your money isn't worth the
paper it is printed on, we've got the farm in Shepherd and we've got
each other."

He pulled her into his embrace, the scent of cherry tobacco faint on his wool jacket.

"I think you'd be real useful as my mom." Jack's loud voice startled Adelaide and she sat up straight.

"Great Jehoshaphat! Jack Welling what are you doing in here?" Peter's voice boomed in her ear.

Jack crawled out from beneath his father's large desk. "I was trying to sneak some candy out of your bowl and then you came back in here with Miss Ada, so I hid under there. Then you started canoodling."

"We were not canoodling, young man." Peter's cheeks flamed red.

"Jack, you can't be listening in on other people's conversations. It's not polite," Adelaide chastised. But she'd been known to do the same, herself.

"Yes, but then I wouldn't know nothing—like that there's police officers staying here at the inn, and they are working in secret."

And why didn't her investigator know that?

"I think Cousin Lily might be in trouble."

Chapter Sixteen

Mackinac Island

Robert shielded his eyes from the morning sun and watched from his porch as the boat departed for the mainland—Sadie upon it, without him. The craft moved out into the startling blue of the Straits of Mackinac and then slowly disappeared from view. He raised his cup of coffee to his lips and sipped. Lukewarm. He swallowed it anyway. Was that how Sadie's affections were for him?

She's really done it. Sadie had left without him. She'd not given him an opportunity to help. But it seemed she had been getting assistance from someone else and not just Garrett.

Hastings stepped out onto the porch. "Can I fetch you anything, sir? Some breakfast?"

"No thank you. I'm off to the hotel in a moment."

"Let me get your hat and jacket ready."

"Thank you. My broadcloth cap, please." If it made the elderly butler happy to dust off his jacket and hat, so be it.

Soon he headed off with jacket and his braided, navy, yacht cap on his head. His gardening crew arrived just as he stepped onto the walkway.

"Good morning, sir."

"Good morning. I'm glad to see that new one looks a little more manageable." He pointed to the lawn mowing machine, which was indeed sleeker and more lightweight.

"Yes, sir. Just as advertised." His head gardener grinned.

"Let me know if you need anything else replaced."

"Yes, sir. Thank you."

The two other gardeners headed to the boxwood bushes, trimmers in hand.

Robert walked to the hotel, the sun warm on his dark cap and jacket. Seagulls swooped by the boardwalk, on the opposite side of the street. The Straits gleamed a hard mineral blue today, with few waves.

Soon he'd reached his destination and strode down the hallway at the Grand Hotel, intent on locating Ada.

The scent of late-blooming roses wafted from a crystal decanter on a console table nearby.

"Mornin' Mr. Swaine." Zeb dipped his chin as Robert passed the shoeshine station.

"Good morning." He paused.

Zeb's client kept his nose buried in the *Detroit News*.

"Have you seen Mrs. Fox?"

The man shook his head. "Not this morning, sir."

"Thanks." Robert continued on to the office and entered the outer antechamber.

To his surprise, Ada's inner office door was open. Jack stood over Ada. He handed her a rose that looked exactly like the ones from the hallway. *Scamp.*

"How lovely, Jack." Ada cast the boy a knowing look. "Would you mind placing that back in the vase with the others on that table down the hall?"

She squeezed the boy's hand and actually gave a girlish laugh.

"See ya later, Miss Ada." Jack hurried past Robert without an acknowledgement. Was he angry about something? Or just embarrassed about the flower?

"Good morning, Robert. How may I help you?" She motioned him forward as she rose from her desk chair.

He entered the room. "I think maybe you help a little too much."

She arched an eyebrow at him and then she closed the door. "How so?"

"With Sadie, for one." This office was rather spare in its furnishings, but it seemed to fit the woman.

Ada gestured to a seat, but he remained standing.

"This won't take me long."

"Oh? And can you explain yourself?"

"I know you bought that gown for Sadie."

"Can you prove it?"

He gave a curt laugh. "That's what a villain always says when he's—or in this case she's—the culprit."

"And you believe me to be a villain or I guess a villainess?"

Robert shifted his weight. "I know you gave her a glowing recommendation for the nursing school."

"And why wouldn't I?" The petite woman definitely sounded offended. She crossed her arms over her chest.

He averted his gaze. "I don't know."

What he did know was that the attorney had explained it could possibly be many years before they could unravel the mess his mother had made in the codicil to her will that had left Peter out in the cold. And he knew that Sadie, *his Sadie*, was gone from the island. And he'd never felt so alone. Even with the Duvall girls in the house and family nearby and all the friends he had did not take the place that Sadie now occupied in his life.

"Do you even *understand* her, Robert?"

He looked up to see Ada appraising him with cold eyes.

She sat behind her desk, but he remained standing.

Ada steepled her fingers together in front of her. "You have no idea what it's like to be impoverished. To depend upon the help of others to simply subsist. To feel you have no control over what your family members do that directly impacts your life."

She didn't ask it as a question.

"That's true. But I like to think I'm a modern man and attuned to the sensibilities of others."

The woman snorted. And in a most unladylike way. "You have no idea how Sadie needs to feel she can take care of herself and not depend on others. That she must prove herself capable or she'll never feel she can be your equal in a marriage. And she must feel her worth or she'll never be happy."

"My love alone cannot fill that void?" Had he been arrogant to think it could?

"No. And you can't keep giving her things and always helping her when she needs to feel able of handling things herself." She frowned.

"Aren't you the pot calling the kettle black?"

Her face drained of color, and she tugged at her stiff white collar. "What do you mean?"

"That old expression. You're saying I'm trying to sway her through my generosity? Isn't that what you're doing? Helping Sadie so she'll go on the path that you believe is best for her? Did someone make you God?"

Ada gaped at him.

Robert's face heated as embarrassment over his outburst set in. "I'm sorry."

She reached for a glass of water on her desk and took a sip. "I'm upset. I shouldn't have said those things."

Ada locked her gaze on him. "And the kettle calls the pot black, also."

Conviction hit him. He was the one thinking he could make everything easy for Sadie and her family. He'd pushed past her resistance. Now Sadie was gone. "You're right."

"And now what do we do about the error of *our* ways?"

"I think we'd better ask God to enable us to let Him do his job. What do you think?"

"Agreed."

"And then as he convicts Sadie—and us," he gestured between himself and Ada, "then we'd better get on board with His plan, not ours."

Ada rose and came back around the desk, her face still pale. She touched his arm gently. "And perhaps, if we're fortunate, God's plans will align with ours."

And if not? God would have to help him let go.

That didn't sit well with him.

St. Ignace, Michigan

Garrett Christy hoisted his tan leather satchel, filled with carving implements and a bag of his sister, Jo's, goodies, as he followed her onto the train and Sadie's worn carpetbag, which held several items for the overnight journey. Bea had found the bag cast-off in a bin and had cleaned it up and offered it to her sister for the trip. Sometimes Bea really did surprise Sadie.

Sadie's hands shook as she climbed about the train, the locomotive engine indiscriminately belching smoke into the air. "I've never been aboard a train before, Mr. Christy." She coughed.

"You and most of the locals up here." He chuckled as he followed her down the narrow aisle. "It won't be fancy, like I hear the trains between Detroit and Chicago are, but we'll be all right on our little journey."

She hoped so. "Thank you so much for accompanying me to Newberry."

"Pleased to do so. Gonna see my brother, too, and sister-in-law, too." He scratched his cheek. "Rebecca Jane and I couldn't let you go on your own."

They took their seat. "You and Rebecca have been such good friends to my family. We're so glad you moved to the island."

"We're mighty glad Rebecca Jane could set up shop on the island."

Sadie was grateful, too, because the Christys had often shared their items with her family—sometimes being the difference between whether her sisters would go to bed hungry or not.

Soon they were underway. The train rocked and swayed and Sadie grabbed the edge of her seat. "I'm not sure about this train."

Garrett laughed. "I'm used to trains used for haulin' logs out of the lumber camps. And right now, I'm feeling a bit like a big, old, felled white pine that's gettin' ready to fall off the back of my train car."

"At least it will be much quicker than traveling rutted roads by wagon." She chewed her lower lip, recalling her family's journey North in a covered wagon that creaked and groaned constantly.

He nodded. "Many a time, it would take us an hour to walk from town, in Mackinaw City, out to my family's camp."

The train seemed to settle into a groove, because now there was simply the vibration beneath her feet and less of the tilting sensation. "Was it hard for you, with all that skill you have as a craftsman, to have to work as a lumberjack?"

One dark eyebrow rose. "I reckon I got a little afraid I might harm my hands—if'n I got cut or if a tree came down on 'em."

Sadie nodded. "One bad strike and all that gorgeous furniture you've designed for the Grand Hotel would never have come to be."

His cheeks reddened. "Thank you for your kind words. I'm right pleased with the work the Lord has given me."

"You do it well. I'd always been amazed at your designs for your tea shop, but your pieces at the hotel are so. . ." She had a hard time thinking of the words. "I think they are the kind of thing to last a lifetime—maybe more." She wanted to make a difference, too, by saving people's lives or at least helping them recover from sickness or injury. She wanted to matter in this world.

"Mostly I guess I fretted 'cause I didn't want to upset my Pa." He blew out a breath. "Ya see, he owned the camps we lived in. Was the boss man. Didn't want to disappoint him."

She didn't want to disappoint Robert, either—but if she didn't at least try to pursue her dream, how could she ever feel like she'd obeyed that call that God put on her heart?

Garrett pulled a chunk of wood, a knife, and a piece of flannel cloth from his bag, which he set on his lap.

As the train gently continued on, Sadie looked out the window at the thick woods and the blue sky. She was possibly headed toward her future. And Pa might be at that hospital, if Richard Christy's suspicions were correct.

"What are you whittling, Mr. Christy?" Some kind of animal was coming to life in the craftsman's hands.

Garrett laughed, stopped carving, and rubbed his thumb against his thickly bearded jaw. "It hasn't told me yet."

Just like Robert failed to answer her question about Laura. His vague reference that it wasn't his place to say as far as Laura's personal business, had irritated her to no end and had stoked the fire to send her on this journey.

The craftsman dug his knife tip into the wood to make eyes. "I need to carve the mouth, and maybe then he'll talk."

"What?" She laughed. No wonder the Christy's adopted children were always teasing each other. If only she knew how to make Robert spill the beans. He'd always held his secrets close to his vest, much like Maude could do.

He bent his dark head over the piece of oak and continued to carve. "I think it might be a lumberjack."

"Not a bear?" The scent of coal dust and light smoke filtered through the cabin as the train rumbled on.

"Maybe a Moose." He chuckled as he expertly dug out a chunk at the base of the wood. "That would be his big feet."

"Only two feet?" She cocked her head to the side, the flickering light from the train windows illuminating the long narrow form. "Or are they called hooves?"

"That's my younger brother, Moose, who'll accompany you to the hospital."

"I thought his name was Richard."

"Wait till you see him at the station and you decide which name best suits." He smiled and continued to shave portions off until its arms began to emerge. "He'll have to take you to that asylum because he knows his way around there. I've got a bushel and a peck of visitin' to do at the lumber camp while you two figger out whether the unidentified lumberjack might be your father."

How would it be, having a stranger accompany her? Maybe she should have allowed Robert to bring her. "Your brother thinks that poor injured man is my pa?"

"Wasn't sure, but he thought you might want to come see for yourself." A shadow passed over his face. "My own pa has had some narrow misses, too, with some trees wantin' to come down on his noggin. Don't know what I'd do if he'd ended up such a place."

She'd never been to an asylum. Dr. DuBlanc made the modern treatments sound promising, though. Water therapies and so on seemed to help some patients. Still, many never returned home. Sadie chewed on her lip.

"Want some Beeman's?"

Sadie accepted the offered chewing gum. She'd spare her lip from further abuse. "Thanks."

Outside the windows, the forest began to thicken with massive pines, maples, and oaks, stealing away some of the fading sunlight. Garrett tucked his carving tools away, inside his leather satchel, and set it on the floor.

"I wish Richard had written you more information." The vibration from the rails caused her seat to shake slightly.

"He's a Christy. He doesn't usually say much."

Whereas Robert Swaine had always been a talker. He loved to spin a good tale. That was one of his traits that had caused her to fall in love with him when she was so young. Too young to marry. And then Miriam had caught his eye, and then crushed his spirit. "I thought Rebecca said Richard is a big reader."

"He is, but he lets that librarian wife of his do the talking for both of them."

"I think Robert would do the talking for both of us if I let him." Yet he was remarkably closed-mouthed about Laura.

The conductor ambled through, rocking side to side, eying each of the passengers on either side of the rumbling train. He nodded at them; his wire-rimmed glasses so low on his nose that they looked like they'd slide off.

"You know the captain has your best interests at heart."

The hair on the back of her neck, tendrils that had slipped from her chignon, prickled. "Does he, now?"

The craftsman nodded. "I've known him a long time, and he's a good man."

If he was such an honorable man, then why was he flaunting another woman on his arm? "Do you know Laura Williams, the actress?"

"Of course. She's performed all over the Great Lakes. Even saw her in a hall in Cheboygan once, years ago." He rubbed his chin. "Captain Swaine brought her roses at the end."

"Oh."

He elbowed her gently. "Don't get so downcast. I think Miss Williams has been protected by him for years."

Like he tried to do for Sadie. "I see."

"I don't think you do." He smiled. "Let me tell you what Frenchie told me about her. You know I don't like to repeat gossip, but this just might be the truth."

"How would this Frenchie know?" It seemed disrespectful to refer to the elderly gentleman. Frenchie, who indeed was from France, had married Pearl and the two had helped raise her grandchildren until the Christys had adopted them. They still lived nearby the family.

"He said Miss Williams has a long-time secret beau, and it's not your captain."

"Not Robert?"

"Nope. When Frenchie was lumberjackin' near Cheboygan, he'd gone to the Opera House to see a show with Miss Williams. He loves all that kind of thing—theatrical stuff. He says the hotel staff, where she stayed, said Miss Williams and her supposed husband were stayin' there—together, but they were keepin' it all hush-like, of course."

Was she really married? And why keep it secret? Or was she one of those ladies from the stage who had a lover or was "kept" by someone?

Sadie's nerves began to jangle like the sounds on the tracks.

Adelaide unlocked the outer door to her office. Immediately inside was a rumpled envelope with *Miss Ada* scrawled across it in pencil.

She chuckled. Jack must have slid that under the door. On the one hand, it warmed her heart to find a note from him there but on the other hand, his father had told him to stay away from the Grand.

Adelaide bent and grabbed the envelope.

Peter—precious Peter—their love was blooming again with each visit. It was as if they'd never parted, in many ways. Had he sent a love note with Jack?

Adelaide placed her reticule inside her desk drawer and sat in her chair. She pulled out her brass letter opener engraved with AB and opened the envelope. The letter had hand-drawn flowers, birds, stars, and a sun with fluffy clouds in the background.

Dear Miss Ada,
I am glad my dad has you for a good frend. I miss my school frends. I feel sad a lot. Did you ges that? You look smart so I bet you no it.

He was right—she'd guessed, and known, that Jack felt sad. Especially after the incident at Arch Rock that had frightened them all. The boy had scrambled up atop the high arch in the rain. He could have slipped and fallen, but he didn't. Ben Steffan, not just a journalist but also a talented and sensitive pianist, intervened. Ben had discerned something that she and the boy's own father had missed.

Adelaide set the card down as tears welled in her eyes. She knew what it was like to experience loss. To lose her parents. She drew in a deep quick breath and then exhaled.

Thank you for offering to help me prepare for the Ohlimpiks. I would be very proud to represent the good ole U S of A when I am older. I don't mean no disrespekt, but are you sure you are able to pay for me to get trainors? When I run I forget my mom being gone. Same when I ride my bike. Mebbe more so when I ride other peeples bikes. The faster I go, the less I feel the bad stuff inside. It blows away.

Adelaide slowly breathed in and out for a moment, as her spirit warred within her. Jack was clearly more troubled than she'd ever realized. And he'd chosen to confide in her. Where was that boy today? What was he doing? Since the Arch Rock episode, the entire family and Adelaide had tried to keep an eye on Jack.

She needed to do more.

"I've never seen the like." Sadie stared in awe at the acres of red brick buildings, all new, some rising two stories with pillars in front.

The federalist-style buildings were like those she'd seen in books but having grown up in lumber camps and small villages, and then the island, she'd not actually seen such imposing structures. Her improved mood, at hearing that Miss Williams might not be a *miss* after all, caused almost everything to look better in the afternoon light.

"Pretty splendid, ain't it?" Richard Christy, a lumber camp boss, and at least a foot taller than herself, opened the wide, heavily embossed, engraved oak door to the Doctors' Offices building, a magnificent red brick structure, standing two stories high and what looked like a hundred feet long. The entryway was so tall, the giant of a man didn't have to duck.

"It's amazing." Sadie stepped in to inhale the scent of lye soap and ammonia water as Richard held the door. Two giggling young women in starched white uniforms stood just inside the entryway and quieted when they craned to look up at the lumberjack.

"Smells clean, don't it?" Richard snapped his suspenders against his broad chest.

Sadie bit her lip, unsure of how to respond. This man lived in a lumber camp, not among the most sanitary places in the world. "Um, yes, it does."

"Dr. Perry said to stop at the front desk."

Dark marble floors with a hint of pink threads gleamed as they crossed to a mahogany-finished desk. A dour-faced red-haired woman, her head bent over what looked like a list, jabbed her finger at each line.

The two waited a minute before Richard cleared his throat and the receptionist looked up, irritation etched on her sharp features. "We're here for Dr. Perry."

"Do you have an appointment?" The snap in her voice and the narrowed eyes suggested that she didn't think so.

"We sure do, ma'am. And may I say yours is the prettiest hair I've seen in these parts, save for my own sister's." The big man offered the woman what looked like a genuine smile.

"Thank you, young man."

Sadie glanced down the hall and spied a cherrywood door with a glass insert etched with STEPHEN PERRY, M.D. She directed her attention back to the receptionist, whose cheeks now bloomed a flattering pink tone, bringing some life to her face.

Sadie cleared her throat. "Should we go ahead to the office?"

"Let me announce you first, miss…?"

Mrs. Robert Swaine. The name flashed through her mind so quickly that for a moment Sadie felt dizzy. She wasn't Robert's wife. Might never be. But if what Garrett had told her was true, there was still hope. *You poor delusional girl—you're nothing but a project to him.* Her face heated at her terrible thoughts.

The secretary cleared her throat. "Your name?"

"Miss Duvall. Sadie Duvall."

With efficient movement, the woman strode from behind the desk and down the hall to the office. She rapped at the door and then entered. When she emerged, she waved them forward, beaming up at Richard as they passed.

Richard held the door open for Sadie and she stepped inside the office, which smelled faintly of fresh paint. Inside, two leather chairs flanked a wide walnut desk, behind which sat a young-looking physician. With flashing dark eyes and rosy cheeks, he looked more like a college boy than a superintendent of an asylum. But sunlight, filtering through his window, shone generous strands of silver streaks in the superintendent's dark wavy hair.

She recognized him now. This man had attended the psychiatrists' conference at the Grand Hotel.

The doctor stood and gestured to the chairs. "I believe you're here about our unknown patient?"

"Yes. We think he might be my father."

"Today, he's been asking for Opal and Garnet. We thought he meant jewels but—"

"My sisters." Two of them. Tears pricked her eyes. "May I see him?"

"Let me send someone to see if he's able to have visitors."

"Could I at least look to see if it is indeed my father?" Surely it had to be him to be asking for Opal and Garnet. *But not for Bea and her.*

The psychiatrist's dark eyebrows drew together. "I think we should first ascertain if he's up to a visit. But, yes, we could position him so you could see him in one of our group rooms and you could approach him from behind—see if it may be him. If it is, and he's up to a chat, then you can speak to him. If not, then…"

"I keep looking." She brushed away a single tear that trailed down her cheek.

He compressed his lips and then left the room.

Sadie closed her eyes. *Oh, dear Lord please let that be Pa.* She kept her eyes closed.

"Miss?" Someone shook Sadie's shoulder, waking her.

"Oh!" She looked up at Dr. Perry and Mr. Christy. "I'm so sorry. I dozed off."

"I reckon yer a might tired." Richard Christy peered down at her with a solemn expression.

"Sorry it took me so long to return. I ran into some difficulty on one of the units." The doctor's face flushed. "But, yes, our unknown patient is up to a visit."

How embarrassing. Sadie stood and brushed the wrinkles from her skirt. "Very good."

"I'll take you down to the atrium and have you approach him slowly from the side. Then you can decide if that's your father or not."

Sadie nodded.

"I'll come, too, if'n you don't mind."

"Certainly. You can both follow me."

They strode down long narrow corridors, with many doors which led to offices. Then they left the administration building.

"We'll head over to the Ferguson building. That's where he is." He gestured toward a large brick building with white pillars in the front.

It certainly didn't resemble what she thought an asylum residence would look like.

"He's in a glassy atrium with plenty of sunlight, so you should be able to view him clearly even from the entrance." Dr. Perry pulled a round brass ring as large as a woman's bracelet, from his pocket and quickly located a key. He unlocked the front door of the building.

Sadie's nerves thrummed. When something cracked behind her, she jumped. She turned to see a man, attired all in white work wear, pushing a wheelbarrow full of linens toward the sidewalk. He must have rolled over a twig, visible on the ground.

"Ain't nothin', Miss Sadie. Don't you worry, I'll take care of you if'n there's a problem in here."

"Thank you, Richard." Yes, Richard definitely suited him—not Moose.

They walked into the building, which smelled heavily of antiseptic which hadn't quite covered the scent of human waste. Sadie tried to breathe more shallowly. Richard visibly flinched.

"We do our best to keep the buildings clean, but. . ." Dr. Perry shrugged.

Dr. Perry pointed toward a row of several men, all seated in wheelchairs. "The one in the middle is our unknown patient."

Sadie focused on the center man. Painfully thin, his knees covered in a wool blanket, the man appeared to be significantly older than Pa. Unkempt silver hair peeked out from beneath a knit cap. Pa's hair had been graying, but not white. His profile, with slack features, wasn't that of Pa's.

She shook her head slowly, as her eyes filled with tears. Although she felt badly for the stranger, she certainly didn't recognize him.

The man in the middle, wheeled, chair turned to face them. His eyes widened and his head began to shake. As the man pushed to rise, an attendant rushed forward to help.

"We should go. He's becoming agitated." Dr. Perry gestured for them to leave.

Sadie froze in place, her breath catching. Then something propelled her forward and she stepped toward the men in the wheelchairs.

"Opal. . .Garnet. . .Bea. . ." The grizzled man's eyes focused on hers. "Sadie!"

Her heart seemed stuck in her throat as tears overflowed. "Pa?" The only thing she recognized were his eyes.

"Sadie!" Hands trembling, he reached for hers and clasped them hard.

She'd found him. At last.

Chapter Seventeen

"If Sadie goes away to nurses' school, who'll watch me?" Opal, dressed in her new nightgown and matching wrap, padded over the floor to where Robert drank his morning coffee.

Although Sadie had talked about wishing she could pursue such training, she'd not said she'd been offered a position.

Seated across the table, Garnet scrunched her face. "She'd take us, and we'd be in the Newberry School. It's a whole lot bigger than the island one."

He frowned as he stood. "Your sister has gone to see if the wounded man at the hospital might be your father." He pulled out the heavy chair for Opal and then pushed her closer to the table, which was set for breakfast.

"If it is, and he's recovered, then he'll probably want us to come there." Garnet cut her breakfast sausage into pieces.

Who knew what Frank would want, or what condition the man was in? Robert went to the sideboard and made the youngest Duvall a child-sized plate of food. He made sure he placed a few apple slices on the side—her favorite.

He set the china plate in front of the sweet child. "Milady."

"Thanks, my captain."

He chuckled. "You're welcome." Lately, after he'd started calling her milady, to tease her, the little girl had taken to calling him her captain. She'd also asked a lot of anxious questions about when he was going off to sail his ships again.

He'd told no one that he was accepting bids for sea-going vessels—except Laura, who understood that this had long been a dream of his to sail around the cape.

He sat down and scooted his chair forward. He tried to imagine Frank Duvall seated at the table with them—and failed.

"Would we live in a lumber camp again?" Opal grasped the vase of roses and Queen Anne's lace and pulled it closer to her and sniffed.

"Sadie said she'd let Pa take us to a lumber camp over her dead body, when he left before."

Robert took a bite of his toast, slathered in strawberry jam. "Let's cross this first bridge before we rush to the next."

Opal angled toward him. "What bridge? I wish we had a bridge to the island."

"Over the Straits of Mackinac?" Garnet scowled, looking very much like Bea at that instant. "What are you—crazy?"

Robert raised his eyebrows and sent the girl a warning glare. "None of that at the captain's table."

Opal set down her utensils and repeatedly slapped her hands on the tabletop, as Jack had taught her to do.

Robert dropped his chin to his chest. He might as well surrender.

"We're not pirates and Captain Swaine doesn't run buccaneer ships so you can stop that right now." Garnet's voice held the smug superiority of an older sister.

Opal stuck out her tongue.

These children had taken over his house and his life.

And that was not a bad thing.

"I wonder if Sadie did get to talk to those nursing lady teachers while she was there. She said she wanted to."

"They'll like her. Everyone likes Sadie." Opal chewed on a piece of apple.

"Who do you like more—Miss Williams or Sadie?" Garnet chewed her lower lip.

"Miss Williams is my friend." Robert reached for his coffee.

"So is Sadie." Opal frowned. "Yeah, but are you going to marry Miss Williams?"

"Shh! You aren't supposed to ask him that!"

Opal shrugged and speared a slice of fried potatoes.

"I am decidedly not going to marry Miss Williams." Since she was already married, but even if she was not.

"Then you better tell Sadie that." Opal held aloft a piece of potato and waved the silver fork like a scepter.

The nursing staff members had been very kind to her and told her they were impressed by her work with Mrs. Luce, but now that Sadie was back on the island, she wondered if they really meant their words. With Pa likely to be there for some time, if she got accepted to the training program, and brought her sisters to Newberry, they could all support one another. But as Sadie headed down the hallway toward the Lindseys' room, she couldn't help wondering if her sisters would be unhappy. And Robert had made a show last night, of professing that Laura was only his friend and nothing more. Garnet and Opal also told her that he'd said he could never marry Laura. She'd had a difficult time this morning, brushing back tears of confusion over what she should do next.

She needed to concentrate on the day ahead. Tonight would be another dance for the hotel patrons. Prominent community members sometimes attended as well. No doubt Robert would be there. She sighed. Sadie would never be part of this glittering gathering of the elite. She'd be assigned to the corner to watch or to clean up the mess afterward. Regardless, she would rise above her situation and be useful. She'd learn the nursing profession and become a valued member of a community somewhere far away from here.

She knocked on the Lindseys' door. It flew open and Miss Lindsey and her mother each took one of Sadie's arms and pulled her into their spacious room.

Sadie stiffened.

Dawn pulled the door closed and locked it. "What's happened, Miss Duvall?"

Sadie clasped her hands at her waist and kept her eyes focused on the pastel Aubusson rug on the floor.

"Something is clearly not right." Mrs. Lindsey touched her shoulder. "We saw you earlier looking very downcast. Didn't you find your father?"

"I did." Tears spilled over and Sadie wiped them away, her ammonia-scented fingers making them water even more. "But he's best left where he is."

Dawn handed her a linen handkerchief with embroidered edging. "I'm so sorry. Will he improve?"

Nodding, Sadie drew in a steadying breath. "It could take some time, but the doctors have hope."

Mrs. Lindsey smiled. "So not only have you found your father— we've discovered that Captain Swaine is besotted with you."

Sadie blinked back her tears and looked into the kind woman's soft blue eyes. "Perhaps he's only doing me a favor." But he *had* said he loved her. The only other time he'd said that publicly to a woman, he'd announced his engagement the next day—crushing Sadie's too-young heart.

The pretty matron shook her coiffed, bronze curls. "No. I recognize that look. It's the way Charles B. looks at Dawn."

She turned to face her daughter. "Show Miss Duvall what Charles gave you after she'd encouraged you to show him a little interest in return."

The pretty girl blushed but she extended her left hand, displaying a rose-gold ring set with a large oval diamond.

"It's beautiful!" Sadie wanted to embrace the younger woman, but she restrained herself. Dawn, however, opened her arms and gave Sadie a hug.

"Thank you for helping me see that Charles really was interested in me."

"And you, my dear, need to open your big blue eyes and notice that Captain Swaine needs you as much as you need him." Mrs. Lindsey sounded so much like Ma, that again, tears rose up.

Sadie sniffed. "Do you think so?"

Mother and daughter exchanged a long look and then bobbed their heads in agreement. "Mrs. Fox is going to help us get *you* ready for the ball tonight."

"What?" Sadie swiped at her maid's uniform. She must have misheard. She was only a maid and maids were definitely not invited to the Grand Hotel dances. "Get me ready?"

"Your captain doesn't know you'll be there." Dawn almost squealed in delight.

"We plan to surprise him."

Sadie shook her head. "Captain Swaine is only going because Maude and her fiancé will be there. He promised them."

"No, he'll be there to witness Miss Williams making her announcement."

"Really?" Was it true? Had Mr. Christy's friend been correct? Would *Miss* Williams share what he said was the truth of her so-called spinsterhood?

"We're now your official lady's maids."

"I…" She'd already worked several hours. Needed a bath, needed her hair washed, needed to make sense of things, too.

A knock on the door made her jump.

"Come in!" Mrs. Lindsey crossed the room as the door opened.

Mrs. Fox entered; her arms stacked high with boxes. "For our belle of the ball tonight."

"The dress already arrived earlier." Miss Lindsey stepped aside, revealing a blue silk moiré gown laid out on the bed.

Sadie sucked in a breath.

"Captain Swaine was admiring the Worth gown in the shop downstairs." Mrs. Fox set the boxes down on a nearby table. "He said it matched his sweetheart's eye color perfectly. And since Miss Williams's eyes are a renowned lavender-gray, we knew he meant you, Sadie."

"I couldn't possibly accept it. He's already done too much."

"Oh, *he* didn't buy it." Miss Lindsey exchanged a look with her mother.

"Robert wanted to order it." Mrs. Fox opened the top box, which contained a glittering necklace, bracelet, and matching earrings. "But I informed him that one does not purchase such things for anyone other than family members, such as a wife. It isn't done."

"But who has sent all this?"

"According to the gift shop clerk, the purchaser *refused* to be identified." Mrs. Fox's stern voice cut off any more of Sadie's queries. "But it was not Robert Swaine."

"I'm grateful to whoever my benefactresses were." She looked at the Lindseys, but they shrugged and gently shook their heads.

Ada Fox took Sadie's arm and led her to the full-length mirror and held the gown beneath her chin. "A perfect match with your eyes, indeed."

A gentle rap on the door preceded Laura Williams' entrance into the room, accompanied by the soft scent of gardenias. "Hello ladies! I'm here to help in any way I can. Heaven knows Robert has helped me and my husband, Tom, for years."

So, it was true. Sadie gaped. Laura was married.

"He's to arrive soon. And when he hears my good news"—she gently patted her middle, which had a small swelling beneath the ivory lace of her gown—"Thomas Kinney will be positively over the moon."

"He may even race his wheelchair down the hallway, if I know him." Mrs. Fox's comment was met by a shocked reaction from Mrs. Kinney.

"You know my husband, Mrs. Fox?"

"Yes, I attended him at a railroad investors' meeting in Detroit."

"He was without his private nurse?" Confusion danced over Laura's pretty features.

"Mrs. Fox!" Dawn Lindsey rushed to Mrs. Fox's side. "Is that a new ring I see?" She yanked the housekeeping director's hand upward.

Blushing furiously, Ada Fox nodded. "I'm marrying my first love."

Robert hadn't truly been Sadie's first love. She'd been so young and was merely his niece's best friend, who he'd treated with kindness. Her infatuation with him hadn't been reciprocated then, nor should it have been. Even now, though, when he seemed to hold her in high regard, and professed that he loved her, was it true? And to ask herself these questions, the problem pointed squarely back to herself.

Since Bernard's betrayal, Sadie hadn't believed in herself, hadn't esteemed herself. How could she trust that Robert did?

"Time to get Cinderella ready for the ball." Mrs. Lindsey feigned waving a wand.

"We can be the birds from the Grimm brothers' version who helped." Dawn fluttered her arms.

The only slipper Sadie really longed for, though, was a sturdy nurse's shoe. Once she had those, though, could she dance into her Captain Charming's arms?

Robert poured himself punch into a sterling silver cup etched with grapes, itching to be out of his new tuxedo. He already knew Laura's new secret. And while his long-time friend, Thomas Kinney, had secured a promise from him years ago, Robert's assistance ended tonight. Laura hadn't exactly manipulated him into perpetuating the notion that she was unwed, by being seen out with her. But by doing so, he'd nearly destroyed the chance he had in securing Sadie's affection.

Standing beside him, his niece Maude and her fiancé, Ben Steffan, whispered to one another.

"Do you really need me here?" Robert pulled his gold pocket watch from his vest. "This is a total waste of my time." He'd much rather be at home, reading stories to the girls. Sadie still hadn't returned home from work, and he was concerned, despite Mrs. Fox's assurances, upon his arrival, that she was fine.

Ben gestured to the grand ballroom, filled with guests. "*Nein*, something good comes of everything we allow God to enter into."

Good thing Laura was finally going to settle down with her invalid husband. She needed to stop kowtowing to her agent's demands for both secrecy and so much travel.

He slipped his watch back into his pocket. "I have too much on my mind to be here tonight."

Maude, dressed in a deep rose brocade satin gown, linked her arm through Robert's and patted his arm like he'd done to her so many times when she was a child. "When Ben and I marry, maybe there will be a double wedding."

"Your father and Mrs. Fox?" He narrowed his gaze at his niece. "They may have known each other a long time, but many years have passed since they've kept close company." The same could be said of he and Sadie. If he had his way, they'd keep *closer yet* company for the rest of their lives.

Maude exchanged a meaningful glance with Ben as a waiter passed by carrying a tray of canapés. Robert swiped several off the tray and Ben extended a china plate embossed with the hotel's gold lettering for him to set them upon.

"I didn't mean Father. I believe he and Ada might marry before we do." Maude stared beyond Robert toward the ballroom's entrance.

A collective gasp sounded behind him.

Ben grinned his toothy smile.

Robert wasn't about to turn and gape at some young debutante, attired in her finest, to snare a husband. Beauty went far beyond good looks. Beyond clothing. Beyond wealth. In fact, when he next saw Sadie, he was tempted to drop down on one knee, in front of all these patrons and propose to her even if she was still dressed in her maid's uniform.

"I'm leaving." He spoke to Ben, but he was still distracted by Mrs. Fox's earlier assertion that Sadie *had* to stay late at the Grand that night. Was the manager overworking her?

Sighing, Robert swiveled around to speak with his niece. But his breath stuck in his throat as he realized why the crowd had quieted. Dressed in the gown that he'd said would match his beloved's eyes, Sadie stepped carefully over the highly glossed wooden ballroom floor and toward them. Mrs. Laura Williams Kinney flanked her on the left and Mrs. Fox on the right. Miss Lindsey and her mother followed them until Charles Bobay stepped out from the crowd to direct the Lindseys to a table. Charles might be just as much in love with Miss Lindsey as Robert was with Sadie.

Crystals glittered atop Sadie's hair, which had been coiled into swirls. The sapphire jewelry from the shop, hung from her creamy neck and the matching earrings dangled from her earlobes. The electric lights overhead, made the jewels glitter. He swallowed hard. Had Sadie been born into wealth, she'd have been married years ago—off to the highest bidder. Her gaze met his and didn't falter. She looked as nervous as he suddenly felt.

Laura signaled the band leader to begin playing a waltz, as she escorted Sadie forward and placed her gloved hand in Robert's. "I believe this first dance is for you."

When he was unable to move, looking down at Sadie, so beautiful, her hand fitting perfectly in his, Laura nudged him. "I'm afraid I've monopolized you far too long, Captain. And I *do* have another dance partner."

Pushed by a porter, Thomas Kinney, veteran of the Indian wars, lacking the use of one hand and only partial use of his legs, was wheeled into the room. As the crowd gaped, Laura began to "dance" with her husband.

Robert directed Sadie onto the floor.

"Do you know the power you have over me at this very moment?" He took her into his arms and swept her into the dance that he, Maude, Sadie and Greyson had all practiced years earlier. So much had changed since then. This was a grown woman in his arms.

"I don't want to have command over you, Captain Swaine."

He looked down at her pensive face. "Would you consider sailing your ship alongside me in my fleet, until we figure a way for us to both share the helm?"

Sadie drew in a deep breath and slowly dipped her chin as the dance commenced.

His heart thudded in his chest, pounding out her name as they moved through the steps. One-two-three turn his beautiful Sadie, one-two-three show this roomful of people that she was his, one-two-three accept that she was her own person—and on it went.

When the waltz ended, he escorted her to the side and leaned in. "Could we sail aboard the same ship?"

"I believe I may understand your suggestion." Her breathy voice stirred a longing in him so strong that he almost shook. "But I have some things to work out before I could give you the answer that I think you want. I have my own course to sail just yet."

This wasn't working out the way he'd planned, but still he had hope. "I'm a patient man."

"Things I need to do for me—and for us—if I'm to feel. . ."

"Ready?"

Sadie nodded.

"Can we at least agree to sail our vessels in a parallel direction?" He winked at her. "That's what I was suggesting."

Her beautiful smile was all the answer he needed. But, oh how tempted he was to lean in and kiss her just as he had during the fire.

From the gleam in her blue eyes, Sadie may be thinking the same thing.

Chapter Eighteen

Your engagement party is a real lally-cooler, Miss Ada." Jack tipped his head back and swallowed his fruit punch.

Poor Alice. Found dead on the rocky slope by the Moores' cottage. And Lily Swaine accused of murdering her. The last few days had been dreadful with all manner of police crawling all over the Grand. At least Adelaide now knew for certain who the Pinkerton at the hotel had been.

Bea leaned in toward Adelaide and Jack. "If you consider the ladies here are simply gossiping about Miss Lily, saying she killed her maid." She rolled her eyes. "If that's how you define a success, Jack Welling, I'm sorry for you."

Jack made a face of disgust. "We all know Lily was at the Canary. She was with us."

"Your father's and my party has twisted into a murder mystery guessing game here at the Winds of Mackinac." She raised her eyebrows in frustration. This event proceeded as she imagined book clubs that read murder mysteries did—because every guest conjectured about what exactly had happened to the young maid who'd died on the West Bluff.

Adelaide's premonitions had finally come to fruition—something dreadful had happened on her watch. But why had someone killed poor Alice? Lily, although accused, had been with the family during the murder up at the Cadotte Cottage, where Lily was now being moved to after her interrogation by the police. The murder had occurred at the Moore's home. Adelaide shuddered at the thought. That poor girl, Alice. And she was sure Mrs. Stillman had something to do with the entire thing. Her Pinkerton had told her all about the nasty woman's function as a madam at a brothel downstate. Adelaide knew first hand how vicious such a woman could be—she had the scars to prove it.

Bea, who wasn't supposed to be working at the party, carried a tray of bonbons to the main food table.

Jack jerked a finger at Adelaide and she bent over, but only slightly. The boy was sprouting up. "Miss Ada, I am pretty sure Izzy did it."

"Izzy? The doctor's dog?"

"Yeah."

"Did what?"

"Killed Alice."

She straightened, gaping at the boy, aghast that he could jest about such things. But Jack just laughed and ran off.

The pastor's wife, Jillian McWithey, joined her. "Boys." She arched an eyebrow.

"Indeed."

Jillian squeezed Adelaide's hand. "We're so looking forward to your wedding." She leaned closer. "But did you know that a florist from the mainland has informed us that they'll be bringing in hot house flowers—hundreds of them?"

"Well, one of us wished to be frugal while one," She hoped to imply that it was Peter not she who, "desires the church to be fragrant with the hopes we have for our future."

"Oh." Jillian offered her a sweet smile. "That is so very romantic."

"Isn't it?" Adelaide flexed her left hand, upon which would soon sport a wedding band that had far more significance than the others had. She'd loved her husbands—but they were never Peter Wellington. Her heart was full to overflowing to know that soon she'd be his bride.

Jillian joined Maude, Sadie, Garnet, Opal, and Rebecca Christy who encircled the large oval cherrywood table in the receiving room. The ladies would have light refreshments inside, and the men would join them in a bit, for the party.

Her assistant, Florence Huntington, arrived attired in an unexpectedly frothy afternoon gown, with massive ivory satin balloon sleeves. Flo must be softening her attire now that she was engaged to Anthony. Perhaps Adelaide's generous raise helped, too.

Florence embraced her. "Mrs. Bishop, I'm so happy for you." When she pulled back, her cheeks were red. "Sorry, I meant Mrs. Fox."

Adelaide exhaled and waved her hand dismissively. "Fortunately for me, Adelaide Bishop's fortune and businesses will increasingly be managed by an intelligent—and lovely—young woman and her future husband."

"I appreciate your confidence in me, in us." Florence's eyebrows drew together. "And I pray we'll continue to have much success."

"You two have handled my businesses beautifully. So many improvements. And you've only been with me for a year. You both deserved your promotions and raises and I've approved the hiring of two new staff members." If anyone could keep a secret, it was Zeb—his wife, Dessa, too. "Teach them the ropes and you can also have them do as I used to do for my meetings—go work as servants to glean information."

"We spoke with them both yesterday, at the Grand Hotel, after—" Florence placed her satin-gloved hand on her throat, "after that poor girl had been found." Flo and her fiancé had only just gotten ensconced in their rooms at the Grand when they'd learned of the tragedy.

"Dessa took it very hard."

"Yes, but now let's turn our attention to celebrating." Flo pointed to the hallway, where several more guests, friends of Peter's from town, had entered. "We can't bring that poor girl back, but she's said to be a Christian girl. She's dancing in heaven now, on streets of gold. We must remember that."

"Yes, indeed." Adelaide spied Sonja Penwell. "Florence, I want you to meet a dear friend of mine, Sonja."

The Penwells had arrived from Shepherd but were staying here at the inn.

"She's the other bridesmaid, right?" Florence's eyes sparkled.

"Yes, you and she will need fittings tomorrow afternoon, here at the inn."

Adelaide led Florence over to Sonja and made introductions. The trio then went to the tea table and selected their choices.

The room was filled with the scents of roses, geraniums, and violets as well as the ladies' perfumes. Their tea gowns ranged from a more subdued mossy color worn by Mrs. Christy to a lemon-yellow linen skirt and blouse that set off Bea's red hair to perfection. Adelaide had selected that ensemble herself for the girl.

Adelaide sipped her Ceylon tea slowly, the china cup light in her hand. Tiny rosebuds and violets intertwined around the rim of the cup. Adelaide had ordered the china as an early wedding gift for Maude and Ben. Maude had graciously allowed Adelaide and her father to use the new teacups, saucers, and sandwich plates for the party. Perhaps Maude had sensed Adelaide's reluctance to use that which her mother had selected for the inn. It had not seemed right to celebrate using china that had belonged to Peter's deceased wife.

Nearby, Maude whispered, "Poor Alice."

"Poor *Lily*." Sadie, attired in a peachy ensemble that set off her complexion moved alongside Maude. "I'm outraged that the police hauled Lily off like they did. Lily—the poor dear—looked absolutely mortified."

"What about Dr. DuBlanc?" Maude's pretty face contorted into an expression of horror. "Can you imagine having your fiancé accused of murder?"

"I know Garrett Christy tried to comfort them both." Sadie shook her head. "I saw Mr. Christy with Dr. Cadotte at the ferry. They certainly seemed very chummy. I didn't realize they were friends. Did you?"

The island was a small place; everyone knew everyone. Still, Adelaide had never seen the hotel's craftsman engaged in conversation with the island doctor.

"Cousin Françoise?" Maude drew her chin in and gave her head a tight shake. "No."

"They were thick as thieves." Sadie raised her brows in an expression that Adelaide knew well.

If the topic weren't so serious, Adelaide would have laughed. That young woman's emotions were so easily read. She'd just implied, with that gesture, that Garrett and Françoise had, indeed, been up to something. But what?

Bea carried a tray of Mrs. Christy's fabulous lemon scones around to Adelaide. She bent over and whispered, "Was this what you had in mind for your tea party? All these nosy folks gossiping about that murder?" Her tone, typical of Bea, was infused with sarcasm.

Adelaide held back a snort but couldn't help the tiny bit of chuckle that escaped. "Not quite."

Bea straightened. "You all look so pretty in your tea gowns."

"You look beautiful, my dear." Adelaide took the tray from the girl and set it on the table. "Stunning."

Sadie joined them. "Our fairy godmother sent exactly the right color and style for each of us."

To Adelaide's surprise, Bea's eyes glistened. "I've never had anything so pretty. Never."

Her own eyes welled up and Adelaide swallowed hard. "When I was about your age, I went from living as the daughter of a prosperous sea captain in a grand Massachusetts home to a Poor House in lower Michigan."

Flo moved closer, holding a cup of coffee. "It's true." She gave Bea an appraising glance. "Are you a modern young woman? Interested in business?"

Bea blinked hard. "I'm interested in anything to better myself."

A slow smile of satisfaction blossomed on Florence's face. "Do well on your classes this next year and you could come down and attend business school—maybe hire on with my company."

Adelaide and Flo had agreed that she'd refer to the business as Florence's—particularly since she'd now assume primary operation for oversight. She smiled. "I imagine you could find her a nice scholarship and room and board, too? Am I right, Miss Huntington."

"Of course."

Adelaide pressed her eyes closed for a moment. She'd vowed to not interfere with other people's life's and yet here she was doing it again. When she opened her eyes, Bea's face glowed. "I'll do my best. I'll work hard this year, so you'll choose me."

Someone pulled the lace on Adelaide's sleeves. "I'm hungry, Mrs. Fox."

"Come on, Opal, let's get you some food." Sadie took her sister's hand.

Adelaide and Florence followed them. They both selected cucumber sandwiches and pecan tarts. It warmed Adelaide's heart to have her protégé here with her. Flo had quickly gotten to know Adelaide and had grasped business skills in a dizzying fashion. As the daughter of a wealthy industrialist who'd lost his fortune, Florence had acquired accounting skills and possessed a keen awareness of changes in business. In only one year, she'd mastered what had taken Adelaide years to set up.

"Mrs. Christy has outdone herself, hasn't she?" Mrs. McWithey placed a tiny blueberry muffin on her plate and a lemon tart.

"She's catering the wedding, too." Adelaide couldn't help her grin. "With your husband officiating, and the Christy Tea Shoppe catering, I don't think we can go too wrong."

Mrs. McWithey smiled warmly at Adelaide. "And with two truly lovely people getting married and forming a new family with Jack—I know heaven will be smiling down on you."

Little Opal Duvall waved from the other side of the table. "I don't know how heaven could smile. How would it do that?"

Garnet elbowed in between Sadie and Opal and rolled her eyes. "It is an expression. It just means, well, I guess the angels and God would be doing a little jig about it up there."

"Oh." Opal dipped the silverplate spoon into the candy bowl. But when she dropped the candies on the floor, she set the spoon down. Sadie was engaged in conversation with Maude as Opal grabbed a handful of candies from the top and stuffed them in her mouth.

Garnet, bless her heart, gaped at her younger sister. She cast Adelaide a mortified look. Adelaide mouthed, "It's all right," and Garnet pulled Opal away from the table. Somehow the little girl had managed to place a small piece of almost every item on the groaning table onto her plate.

"I don't need a crystal ball to predict that someone is going to have a tummy ache later." Mrs. McWithey clucked her tongue. "I understand Jack likes to invite his pals over to the inn. If you think the Duvall girls are a handful, wait until school starts back and Jack and his buddies are playing here."

Adelaide sighed. "Peter and I are discussing moving to his farm, downstate."

"You want Jack to be closer to training opportunities and races?" Bea slid in beside them, a small plate with miniature ham and cheese biscuits and strawberries on her plate.

"That's our plan."

"But we'll sure miss all of you."

Adelaide knew that Bea was particularly fond of Peter but hoped that now that Frank Duvall had been located, that Bea would accept their move. "We'll be back to visit." For now, she'd omit that she owned a hotel in Mackinaw City where they'd stay. She didn't want to have to explain about that to their guests.

Sadie rejoined them. "I'm going to miss everyone while I am at nursing school, too."

"But you'll come back to the island afterward, won't you?" Mrs. McWithey cocked her head. "Since Robert and the girls are here?"

Oh my, from the look on Sadie's face, Mrs. McWithey had just opened a can of worms.

Adelaide took Sadie by the elbow and pointed her toward the side door that led outdoors onto the lawn. "Why don't you go and ask the menfolk if they're ready to join us?"

"Certainly."

As Sadie departed, Jack sped into the room, skillfully dodging the ladies. When he reached Adelaide's side, he panted.

Adelaide arched an eyebrow at him.

He grinned at her. "The men have been talking about Mr. Parker and Mr. Butler—I saw those two up at the hotel. They did look like criminals. And that Mrs. Stillman did something bad to do with a brothel—but no one will tell me what that is."

The boy was getting old enough to hear what was what. "I'll tell you after the party."

His eyebrows shot up. "Really?" He gave her a quick, sweaty hug that left dampness marks on her blouse.

"Yes. My goodness," she looked into his eyes, "you've gotten almost as tall as me this summer."

He grinned but then the smile faded. "Oh, and another thing the men are betting on is that one of those old bad guys killed Cousin Françoise's dog. We think they shot Izzy, too, after they shot Alice."

Maude's face crinkled in disgust, making her look closer to her brother's age than almost a decade older. She poked Jack's chest. "That dog was ancient. And no one said Izzy had been shot."

"Maybe they just didn't find the bullet. Maybe it went through. Did you think about that, huh, Sis?"

Maude huffed a sigh. "Françoise would have said."

"Maybe it's a secret. Maybe those state cops and Pinkertons told him to keep it quiet." Jack crisscrossed his hands at his mid-section.

"Good Lord, give my new stepmother-to-be extra patience." Maude lowered her head reverently.

Jillian laughed. "She'll need it."

Jack ran over to Garnet and Opal, both seated at the divan. Whipped cream dotted Opal's pert nose. "Hey, did you girls hear that Izzy got shot? I think it was one of those thugs that killed Alice who did it."

Opal's jaw dropped open. She looked about to burst into tears.

"Excuse me." Adelaide went to the children. "Now Jack, that dog was very old. Someone said almost fourteen. That's very old for a dog."

Jack crossed his arms. "I want a dog."

Someone cleared their throat. Peter slid his arm around her shoulders. "Every farm must have a dog and a cat. I believe it's state law."

Robert slipped around them and lifted Opal easily from the couch. "Do you want a cat or a dog, little miss?"

The girl stuck her index finger in her mouth.

"We want a dog for us and a cat to sit on Pa's lap when he comes home." Garnet nodded solemnly.

"I'll have Reverend McWithey say a blessing over them, for a good long life just like Izzy had." Jillian clasped her hands at her waist, a look of longsuffering on her face. Adelaide could only imagine what things, what secrets, the pastor and his wife had listened to over the years.

Time to let more of Adelaide's skeletons in her closet out, too—to Peter.

If he wished to cancel the wedding, so be it.

Chapter Nineteen

S adie Girl, have you seen what those new folks up by the fort are building?" Mr. O'Reilly doffed his hat as he halted the two large Percherons who pulled his dray.

The Canary stood only a hundred feet ahead and a warm bath awaited there once she got out of her uniform. 'I couldn't care less,' was what she'd love to tell him, but that would be rude. Still, the older man had known her long enough that he'd have laughed at her retort. She crossed her arms over her chest and tapped her toe. "I'm sure you'll tell me."

"Ah, so you haven't seen it then." He laughed. The horse on the right stamped its right front foot.

"Some of us are a little busy working inside all day long." Sadie pointed to her maid's uniform. It had been a long hard day. What a different day from her day off—when she'd attended Mrs. Fox and Mr. Welling's engagement party. That had been lovely. And she'd been so happy that Mr. Welling had invited Robert. They seemed to be putting their differences behind them. She and her sisters had also been invited and they'd all had a jolly time except that Opal kept her up that night with her stomachache. At least it gave Sadie a chance to practice her nursing skills.

She still hadn't heard from the Newberry State Asylum as to whether they would hire her as a nurse in training. But Pa was reportedly improving since she'd visited. They'd inquired as to when she could return for a visit. *Not until I have that student position.*

O'Reilly tapped his forehead. "I'm thinkin' ya might want to go take a gander."

"Right now?" Her voice came out more irritated than she meant.

"For sure and for certain. Or are ya diggin' in your heels like a stubborn Duvall would?"

She scowled at him. How was she going to be a sensible and proper wife to Robert Swaine? He deserved better. How had she ever thought, in years past with Bernard, that she'd have even been a good officer's wife? She wasn't accustomed to all these manners and things expected of her. Mr. Hastings, Robert's butler, had spent an hour training her on which silver utensil was for what food dish. Her younger sisters understood far better than she had.

The islander winked at her. "Everyone knows you could live the life of Reiley, if you'd marry Captain Swaine."

She'd once thought that ditty about Reiley was funny, but now it annoyed her. She put her hands on her hips. "I imagine Mrs. O'Reilly would say that life with you would be preferable to that of Mr. Reiley in the song."

He scrunched up his face. "Now that you mention it, I'm sure you're right. That fella wasn't appreciatin' what he already had." He began to hum the *Is that Mr. Reilly* melody.

Was she, also, not valuing what she had? Could she not be content with being a wife and mother? The wife of a successful captain and businessman? She shook off the thought. "I'm sure you didn't stop me to give me romantic advice, did you?"

"No!" He slapped his free hand on his knee. "Listen, lass, about what's being built. They're calling this wee building they've built a 'playhouse' but it's an almost exact replica of your folks' cabin."

Sadie stiffened. Were these new people mocking her and the Duvall family? She huffed a breath. "You're jesting."

"No. They've started building their huge cottage on the cliff and on the back grounds they've completed the playhouse for the children."

As if living in a two-room log cabin in a formidable climate was child's play.

"Who built it?"

"One of Patrick's boys."

Patrick Byrnes was one of the island builders who had a reputation for excellent craftsmanship. As far as she knew, he harbored no ill will toward her nor had Byrnes' son, who'd attended the island school with her. "Why did they copy our family's cabin?"

O'Reilly's horses both twitched, and one stamped its foot again. "I don't know, but I best get on my route now. Go see for yourself."

"I think I will." She'd go now. She'd borrow one of Robert's many bicycles and set out. The sun wouldn't set for several hours.

She should change out of her uniform, but she'd no doubt perspire on the ride, too. She'd ride the back streets so fewer people might see her and then go up to the construction site. She strode to the front lawn and grabbed the Arnold, Schwinn & Company bike that someone had carelessly laid on the grass. *Jack, no doubt.* Sadie pinned her skirts up and out of the way so that she could freely pedal the bike. Once she got her next paycheck, she'd purchase a pair of riding bloomers like Maude had. Forget that thought—once she got her next check she'd have to pay toward her father's care at the hospital. She swallowed hard as she mounted the bike and set off. She could be back in under twenty minutes if she kept a good pace.

As Sadie neared the back of the fort, she spied Jack on his own bike. Hopefully it was his own bike and not one he'd "borrowed" from some unsuspecting tourist.

Sun pierced the overhead tree canopy as she neared the site, illuminating a log cabin structure—a replica of her family's own home in town. She slowed, and then coasted up the dirt path that led to the building. How dare they? What audacity that they'd copy her family's cabin and then treat it as if it was simply a children's play space. There was even a chimney on the building and real glass windows. Sadie's hands shook in anger.

"Can you believe their nerve?" Jack sped in beside her, his bike kicking up dirt as he halted.

She scowled at him.

Jack nodded. "Yeah, I can see you're real mad like I am. I haven't told Bea yet. I think she'd have a conniption."

"You're right, she would." With good reason. The people building here were supposed to be business associates of Robert's. Were they trying to rub his nose in about her or were they relaying a message of what they thought of Sadie? Was that it?

"But I think old Patrick just wanted to play kind of a joke on those new folks." Jack dismounted and laid his bike on the grass.

"What do you mean?"

"Come here and I'll show you." Jack ran off toward the log cabin.

Sadie exhaled a long breath, unpinned her skirts, and followed him.

Jack touched the logs. "This here is real cedar wood hauled over from Cedarville. Same as was probably brung here for your folks' cabin back in the ancient days."

Maude would have corrected her brother's grammar, but Sadie wasn't about to do so. "The seventeen hundreds were not exactly the ancient days."

"Yeah, they were."

She rolled her eyes. "Yes, this looks the same."

"Well don't ya see?" Jack removed his cap and slapped it against his thigh. "That stuff lasts forever. Cedar doesn't rot."

"That doesn't matter though, when all those ancient log cabins on this island have been destroyed by people building elaborate summer homes?"

"Yeah, but see—Patrick showed them. He built *another one* right here! And fooled them into having one on their property. Only they're calling it a playhouse." He cackled.

There was something to be said for Jack's logic. "From what I know about Mr. Byrnes, I wouldn't be surprised if you are right."

"Sure and for certain I am. I overheard his son talking about it down at Horn's."

"Jack Welling! What were you doing there?"

"I get a lot of my information there. My dad says it's the one place I stay quiet."

Sadie stared at the child. "I can't believe he takes you there."

"Him and Miss Ada do. They hold hands while they are there." He made a face of disgust.

She laughed. The boy had lightened her mood and defused her anger. He'd be her nephew if she married Robert. Her nephew and her best friend her niece—now that would be something. She had to admit she loved this boy like family and of course Maude, too. "Want to look inside?"

"Sure. Oh and look!" He pointed. "Did you see he even put a pump outside here and a little outhouse?"

She saw them. "Oh, my goodness."

"Not that those city folks' kids will use them."

"They might." If they got desperate.

"Yeah, and call it play." He chortled and bent over, his hand on his stomach.

Sadie shook her head slowly. Life at the Canary was nothing like living in the tiny cabin her family had shared.

"Come on Sadie, let's look."

Inside stood a large fireplace, with stone masonry almost exactly like at the home they'd lost. She touched the wood mantel. "This looks like it could be actually used."

"They must have money to throw away because they sure as shootin' won't be here in the winter."

"No wood stacked by the side, like we always had." That seemed odd.

"They built in the seating."

"That can also be used for sleeping." Sadie pointed to where a long bench stood. "You pull those together and put the mattresses on top so you can sleep." Jack had never visited the cabin. Nor had anyone else in town stopped by much. That had changed when the Christy family had arrived.

Jack's eyes widened. "You mean you and Bea slept like that?"

"Uh huh. And Opal and Garnet, too. We'd pull the two long benches up by the built-in ones and cover them with our mattresses." If one could call the miserable, thin, cushion a mattress. "And we'd have our wool blankets and quilts." Moth-eaten blankets but lovely quilts that the church ladies had given Ma over the years.

"Wow. No wonder Bea almost cried when we showed her the attic room."

"A bedroom to herself and no one there to kick her in the head, either." Sadie laughed. But inside, right now, her emotions skittered like mice were scrambling through her clothes as they'd sometimes done in the cabin at night.

She and Robert were from completely different backgrounds.

Maybe this cabin was a reminder to her that she shouldn't try to get above her station.

Robert knew he shouldn't have steamed open Sadie's letter. It was wrong. So wrong. But curiosity had gotten the better of him. Now he sat at his desk, staring at the words he'd feared.

Congratulations Miss Duvall. You are offered a position in our new class of nursing candidates. Our program completes in a one-year curriculum. You'll be offered room, board, instruction, and will be paid a stipend during your nursing practicum.

The amount, while modest, was double Sadie's pay at the Grand.

Not only would she have training, but Sadie would also be near her father. Robert closed his eyes. *Lord, I thought you were bringing me back here to be a husband to Sadie. Help me understand.*

In his heart, he knew she'd have to accept this offer. Her pride was not going to allow her to marry him and let him make her life easier.

Support her. That still quiet voice had a message that was different than the help which Robert wanted to give.

Meet her needs. Again, that nudging in his spirit was at odds with his motivation because he thought he *was* trying to meet her needs.

Clarity struck him. She wanted this training. Sadie longed to be self-sufficient. Sadie needed to be near her father and to show her siblings that a woman could make her own way.

He quickly slipped the letter back into its envelope and then pasted it shut again.

Could he really set his own wishes aside? He loved her.

"I've been accepted into the nursing program!" Sadie grasped the letter hard and waved the paper aloft. Opal and Garnet stepped in and wrapped their arms around her.

Robert walked into the parlor; his hands shoved in his pockets, "What's all the commotion?"

"Sadie's gonna be a real nurse!" Opal ran to Robert and threw herself into his arms.

He lifted her youngest sister up into his arms. "Well, isn't that something? Congratulations, Miss Duvall."

Miss Duvall? She caught his gaze. Robert appeared very calm and composed. Businesslike even. Was he glad that he would be relieved of responsibility of her? He'd tried to tell her other ways she could be useful to society, as his wife—as a community leader, in the church, as caregiver to her sisters and so on. But he apparently didn't realize that anyone who knew her as Frank Duvall's daughter, especially on this island, would never accept her as such. She was an outcast regardless of being his sweetheart and his niece's best friend.

"Thank you. I'm so excited."

"Is there lodging for us, Sadie?" Garnet reached for the letter and scanned it.

"I. . . don't know."

"I want to stay here." Opal stuck her index finger in her mouth—a habit she'd quit.

Robert set Opal down.

"I thought you'd stay with me. There's a boarding house that may have room for children."

"The girls can stay here if there's no housing for them in Newberry." Robert's tone was kind, but distant. "The program is only for a year, after all."

She stiffened. How had he known which curriculum she was in and that she was in the one-year track? She'd not told him. Had he opened her mail? Was that why the envelope seal seemed over-glued? She blinked up at him. His eyes wandered to the envelope and then back to her face. He blushed.

He knew that *she* knew. Were they so connected that even now he understood her thoughts? Robert had known her for much of her life. He understood her better than any other man did.

"I'd be happy to support you in any way that I can, in your efforts to. . ."

To better herself? Wasn't that what this was all about? Was she risking losing him? Yes, she loved him, but she didn't feel worthy of his love in return. "Thank you, Robert. I'll send an inquiry about the rooming house."

"I want to see the school over there. Can we make a trip to see?" Garnet bounced on tiptoe, like a much younger child.

"I'm sorry, Garnet. I can't do that. There's not time nor money."

Her sister hung her head.

Robert stepped forward and lifted the girl's chin. "If you start school there and despise it, I could come and get you."

"If we stay here, when would we see you?" Opal tugged at Sadie's sleeve. "Would you ever have time to come back?"

"I hope I'll have time and be welcome to come. . ." she almost called this place *home*. But it wasn't her home.

Not yet.

Chapter Twenty

At the last moment, instead of bringing in hothouse flowers to decorate the church, Adelaide had late summer roses, ferns, and late-blooming wildflowers used to make arrangements for the church. Of course, she'd still paid the bill for the previous order and had those donated to a large hospital near the florist.

"Are you nervous?" Maude looked beautiful in her tailored puff-sleeved jacketed gown with a gently pleated skirt.

Adelaide patted her hair, which had never looked better. "A little anxious, but mostly I feel. . ." How did she tell Peter's daughter that this felt right—that this was how it was supposed to be—and not offend her mother's memory? "I feel God's hand in this."

Her soon-to-be stepdaughter smiled.

Florence Huntington appeared almost ethereal in her color periwinkle, silk, satin brocade gown with a gauzy shawl on her shoulders.

Sonja held Florence's and Adelaide's bouquets as Maude helped the two make final adjustments. "I don't think I've seen a lovelier bride."

Adelaide laughed. "Ask your husband what he thinks. I believe Louis will name another lady."

Sonja blushed and grasped her mid-section. "Oh! I think I felt something." Her eyes glistened as sun streamed through the nearby window. "It's baby's first movement."

"It's probably gas." Jack crawled out from beneath the tablecloth covered table nearby.

Maude strode straight to her brother and grabbed his ear. "You are the worst boy in the universe."

"Doubtful," Florence commented dryly. "The odds are far against that possibility."

"You're supposed to be in helping Father."

Jack shrugged and broke free. He was definitely taller than he'd been when summer began. And stronger it seemed.

Maude adjusted her gown and looked about to swat Jack's behind as he departed, but Sonja stepped in and touched her arm.

"Jack," Adelaide called out, "straighten your suitcoat before your father sees you."

He turned and saluted. Only his knees looked worse for the wear. He pressed a hand over his heart. "Ladies, you all look splendid." Was that a fake British accent he used? "Simply splendid." It was.

"Get out," Maude's teeth looked clenched as she pointed to the door.

As the boy departed, Sonja gasped. "Yes. It's movement. Like a flutter. A butterfly. Or. . ." Her eyes widened. "Angels' wings."

The sun's rays grew stronger. Sonja and Louis had waited years for this baby. When Adelaide reached forty, some years earlier, she'd accepted that she'd never have a child. And now, she'd have two— Jack and Maude. "That's so exciting. I pray God blesses your baby and those to come."

As Adelaide stepped in to hug Sonja, Florence held her back. "Don't you dare wrinkle that dress."

They all laughed.

"Or crush the flowers." Sonja handed them their bouquets.

Adelaide drew in the heady scent of the roses and fingered the frothy ferns. This was really happening.

Someone knocked.

"*Alle Damen bereiten sich vor.*" Ben Steffan's deep voice carried through the door.

Adelaide tried to translate the German. Something about all the ladies.

"*Fraulein Huntington, Frau Fox, Frau Penwell? Gleich beginnt der Organist. Maude, bitte komm raus.*"

Maude lifted her skirts. "He must be on edge to forget to use his English."

Florence cleared her throat. "He wants us to all prepare because the organist is about to start what I presume are the wedding marches."

Flo continued to surprise Adelaide with her skills, even now.

"And he wants me to come." Maude beamed.

Yes, that was it. Her German was getting rusty. Adelaide took a last look in the cheval mirror. She wore a trim ivory linen skirt with a matching bodice and a veil adorned in Irish lace. That was a nod to her adoptive parents. She could imagine the young woman she'd once been, instead of the woman in her forties, reflected back.

Her adopted parents had died young. Her father had only been near her age when his ship had gone down off of Charleston, in a hurricane. And her adoptive mother only a few years later, after a brief illness. But her birth mother, if her father told the truth, had been killed after the brothel owner had learned that Adelaide had been spirited away.

This is not the time to be thinking of this. But this was who she was. She was the child of a runaway slave who'd married a poor Virginia farmer and whose horrible owners found her and sold her off into a life of prostitution in New Orleans—taking Adelaide with her. She pressed her fingertips against the locket that held a bit of her mother's hair. Mother had pinned it on her dress the day Adelaide had been spirited away. She became the child of a captain whose unsavory habits had brought him to the brothel. His compassion for the child, or perhaps desiring to give his wife a child, had led him to bring Adelaide back to Massachusetts. To an adoptive mother who didn't truly want her and who likely understood exactly what Adelaide was.

You're a child of God.

Adelaide blinked back tears. She'd spoken those same words to sweet Sadie the day before, when the young woman said that as Frank Duvall's daughter, she had a hard time keeping her chin up on Mackinac Island. Sadie was a child of God—and so was Adelaide.

Thank you, God, for making my dream come true.

When Maude exited, Ben motioned for the bridesmaids to come out. "*Die Trauzeugen*, I mean the groomsmen, are waiting."

Louis Penwell and Anthony Zandi, attired in dark cutaway jackets and matching waistcoats and pants waited in the hallway.

Her heart swelled with pride. Louis had completed college because of the help she and Peter's father had given him. Florence, who'd only joined her one year earlier had become one of her closest and most trusted confidantes. And the young woman had proved herself indispensable in her management skills.

The organist sounded three long chords, the signal for Adelaide and her ladies to come down the aisle. They were doing things a bit differently because neither she nor Peter were young, nor did she need to be given away by her father—a man who had bought her freedom.

Father may have had his faults, but if it hadn't been for him, she'd not be here now.

They entered the foyer, and then doors were opened. Inside, their friends and family stood. But she had no family. No father to walk her down the aisle.

She and Peter had agreed that she would walk on her own.

As Florence and Anthony moved forward, the door behind Adelaide creaked open. She turned to see the sexton speaking with an older gentleman, attired in a workingman's suit, clutching something in his hand. Perhaps one of Peter's friends, whom she'd never met.

The sexton hurried toward her; his face flushed. "This man wishes to speak with you."

The stranger stared hard at her and swiped at his eyes.

Adelaide took a deep breath and turned. She followed the sexton several steps back to the man. He held a black leather-encased item, which he extended to her. When he rotated his hand, he revealed the ambrotype image of her young mother and a young curly-haired girl clutching what was surely Adelaide's tiny quilt.

She gasped.

"That's my wife, Satilde, and our daughter." The man's gravelly voice held a strong Virginia accent.

Adelaide tried to breathe as she stared into Pa's moss green eyes.

He pointed to her locket. "I gave my wife that broach."

Then she hurled herself into his arms and wept. Solomon Lightfoot was here. Her Pinkertons had found no trace of him in Virginia.

"My baby girl." Pa sniffed. "I can't believe I finally found you."

"If that ain't something?" Jack elbowed Sadie and she nearly dropped her cake, plate and all, onto the church hall floor.

Maude leaned in; fork raised. "Isn't that, or wasn't that, something?"

"What?" Jack scowled. "Is there something else besides Miss Ada's dad showing up?"

Maude huffed a sigh.

"Mr. Lightfoot lives in Mackinaw City. I've seen him there." Ben shoved a large forkful of the white wedding cake into his mouth.

"Mackinaw City?" Sadie raised her eyebrows. "I thought he was from Massachusetts."

"That guy is dead." Jack closed one eye and lowered his chin. "Her adopted dad, Captain Fox, died."

"Solomon Lightfoot is not her adoptive father," Ben shook his head. "I can see our Mrs. Fox, or rather Mrs. Welling, has more secrets."

"Yeah, she's got a lot." Jack made a motion of raising a key to lock his lips.

Maude laughed. "If anyone knows her secrets, that would be my sneaky brother."

"I'll never tell." Jack ran off to where Sadie's sisters were circled around a small ice sculpture of a dove.

"A memorable wedding." Robert raised a cup of punch to his lips. He seemed distracted, his focus jumping around the room.

Sadie was packed and ready to go. Was Robert ready to let her leave?

The longest week in Robert's life had finally passed. He sat at the table with Opal. They awaited breakfast, and Garnet's arrival, while he sipped his coffee wishing Sadie was still there. Ada and Peter had left for a honeymoon spent at his farm. Not very romantic in Robert's opinion, but perfectly so in theirs. To each their own. They'd given Ada's father a promise that they would stay at her hotel in Mackinaw City once they returned, so that she could visit more with him. What a nice surprise and relief that Ada owned that hotel nearby. It lessened Robert's guilt considerably about Peter not inheriting anything because of Mother's codicil.

He lifted his newspaper, and the front-page headline caught his attention. If anything could tempt Robert to pursue his dream of sailing a ship internationally, the opening of the Kaiser Wilhelm canal was it. The feature story in the *Wall Street Journal* lauded the finish of the eight long years of construction. The waterway connected the North Sea to the Baltic Sea, through the Jutland peninsula. Over sixty miles long, this channel spared ships a good two hundred fifty or so nautical miles. Not only that, but mariners could avoid the Danish straits, which were storm prone. He glanced out the window and could view the Straits of Mackinac in a state of turbulence today, much like he felt internally.

If once Sadie completed her training and she took a nursing position away from Mackinac, then what was preventing him from returning to the water?

Getting his mother's codicil to her will removed, that was one thing that kept Robert here—for now. As it stood, the heirs had to remain on the island to keep their inheritance. Not only that, but only descendants could keep property. Anyone who married into the family, like Peter, were frozen out—like the Straits in the winter. That didn't sit right with Robert.

One day I will get that corrected, if I have to consult every lawyer in Michigan.

"I miss Sadie already." Opal jumped from her chair, pushed his newspaper aside and climbed onto Robert's lap.

He tweaked her tiny nose. "You know she'd be at work if she was here."

"I know." She sighed and snuggled her head against his shoulder.

Robert could easily provide for her, but Sadie—who seemed ready enough to run off with the lieutenant the previous year—now believed she must provide for herself. So much, so very much, had happened since 1894. It seemed like many years earlier. Both he and Sadie had changed. They'd matured in different ways, but both had been touched by grief after the local epidemic claimed their loved ones.

"It's not the same without Sadie." Opal patted her pintucked shirt, near her heart. "Knowing she's off the island makes me feel lonely. Our fambly is split up."

He knew she meant family, but he didn't correct her. He took a deep breath. Robert felt the very same way. Not an hour went by that he didn't think of his Sadie. Their Sadie. "She's our rock, isn't she?"

Opal leaned back. "She's not a rock. She's a girl."

He laughed. "You know what I mean."

"Nope." She laid her head back on his shoulder. Would he and Sadie have children of their own one day?

The scent of hot chocolate and something yeasty wafted toward them as Matilda carried a silver tray loaded with goods into the room. "Cocoa or juice today, Miss Opal?'

The child leapt from his lap. "I want coffee with cocoa and milk in it like Sadie makes for me."

Frowning, Matilda cast Robert a quizzical glance. "Coffee?"

Robert raised his eyebrows and stood. "I'll take care of that. I happen to know exactly how Sadie makes this special drink."

Opal clapped her hands. "Yes. Thank you."

Robert went to the sideboard. He would have to place his body squarely between the child and the tray, so she'd not see him. Only a splash of coffee was placed in her mug, then a generous dose of cream, and the remainder hot cocoa.

Matilda, a smile tugging at her lips, winked. "Well, now I know how to do it right and proper, Captain Swaine."

He winked back. "Thanks, Matilda. I'll take it from here."

"Yes, sir."

Matilda had been stalwart during their efforts to procure more staff for the house. "Thank you again for your assistance with bringing in our new cook and his kitchen helper. And for showing our new maids the ropes."

She dipped a curtsey. "They're all working out well."

"If you chose my boat crews, I'm sure everything would be shipshape upon my return." He grinned.

She wagged a finger at him. "Don't be leaving us just yet, Captain Swaine."

He nodded. "Now, Opal, you go back to your chair and await my creation." He dolloped a large portion of whipped cream on top of the drink.

She laughed but complied. "I bet it's not as good as my sister makes it."

Was anything as good as what Sadie made it? Life was certainly better with her in it. Meals more enjoyable. Nighttime strolls and outings with her were the best. "I did what I could, but no guarantees."

"Aw, it's all right. You're a boy."

Jack ran into the room. "Hey, what's wrong with bein' a boy?"

"Nothing," Robert said as Opal chimed in, "Everything!"

Jack swiped a cinnamon roll from the tray.

"Hey that was mine!" Opal declared.

"Not now it isn't." Jack shoved half of it in his mouth.

"That's not fair." Opal came alongside Robert, arms crossed.

"Your name wasn't written on it." Jack gave Opal a saucy grin as he took another gooey bite.

"He's so mean." She burrowed against Robert's arm.

"Oh, no. I think he meant to save you the biggest bun, didn't you Jack?" Robert pointed to another cinnamon roll.

"Huh?" His nephew leaned in; eyes wide.

"That's just the one for dear Opal." Robert lifted the plate away before Jack could reach for it. "And I'll give her some more of my frosting, too."

"Hey!" Jack scowled.

"I'm sure that's what a *gentleman* would do for a young lady. Or should do, my dear nephew." Robert pointed to the nearby chair at the table. "Now go and pull the chair out so Opal can sit down."

Eyes rolled heavenward, the boy stalked around to their side of the table and pulled the chair back.

"What are you doing here, Jackie boy?" Opal asked in a sing-song voice.

Robert cleared his throat. "Thank Jack for helping with your chair."

"I don't have to. Boys are supposed to do that for girls."

There were long days ahead of them. Hopefully Garnet wasn't in as much of a snit as her sister was, over Sadie being gone.

Jack reached past him and grabbed a napkin, surprising Robert. The boy snapped it open and laid it across Opal's lap. "Little mademoiselle, may I bring you one of our fine drinks?" He pretended to twist at a nonexistent moustache.

Robert shook his head but passed the cocoa mug to his nephew. "This is what she special ordered."

"Ah, very good, very good, the best we have in this fine establishment, mademoiselle Opal."

Someone clapped.

Robert turned to see Garnet, attired in an old-fashioned dark patterned dress. Was that one of Mother's? Three costume jewelry broaches pinned tight a bright scarf that covered her hair. "I see you got here just in time for our practice for our play, Monsieur Jack."

"Yup." Jack set Garnet's drink down, then scampered around to examine Garnet. "Gee, this looks just like an old crone's outfit."

Old crone? That looked like many of the matrons in this community had worn a generation earlier. In fact, some of them still did—especially that bunch who used to attend those seances that had finally ceased.

"We found the clothing in a trunk in the attic."

So, the dress was one of Mother's. "I thought that looked familiar."

"Mr. Hastings thought you wouldn't mind. He said the stuff was supposed to have gone to the charity box, but Maude said no one would use any of it."

Jack snorted. "She's got the right of that. Who'd wear something from a hundred years ago?"

More like a generation. Robert sighed. "Garnet, you can have that third roll there. I'll just take my coffee. But could you please share a little of that frosting with your sister? I'd already promised extra to her."

"Sure." The girl could be so easygoing—unless you tried to make her stop reading a book. Maybe being the middle child had its advantages. But Opal was more like Robert—the baby of the family. The two of them often wore their emotions on their sleeves.

He kissed the top of Opal's head. "I'll be in my office if any of you need me." He grabbed his newspaper and was about to head off when it occurred to him that he shouldn't appear to be favoring the youngest Duvall sister. Wasn't that some of the source of friction between himself and his older sister? He moved to Garnet and patted her shoulder. "You, too. If you need anything, please seek me out."

"Can we be bridesmaids?" Garnet looked up with wide eyes.

This should be an interesting play they were putting on. "I don't know why not." He shrugged.

"Sadie didn't say we could," Opal protested.

"I don't know why she'd care if you're play-acting being in a wedding. And she's not here."

"No. We mean your wedding, silly." Opal ran and linked her arm through her sister's. "We want to be *Sadie's* bridesmaids."

His tongue suddenly caught like it had when Uncle Al foisted his failed attempts at a caramel-taffy sauce on Robert as a child. That particular combination never did make it onto any ice cream at his shop or someone who have broken a tooth.

Jack grabbed a serving spoon and waved it. "Enough of that wedding stuff. We've got a killing to plan!" His nephew cackled like a hyena. "There's murder afoot!"

God help the woman who ended up married to his nephew. But she'd never be bored.

Opal poked Jack. "I'm not killing anyone."

"Yes, we are. We have to get rid of that bad guy at the end." Garnet's countenance grew serious. "Remember? He killed the dog."

"Oh, yeah," Opal whispered. "Like poor Izzy."

He wanted to tell them, yet again, that no one had killed his cousin's beloved pet. But it was useless. They'd decided the rumor was true that Mr. Parker, on Butler's orders, had killed Alice and Izzy. They'd even created an elaborate explanation that grew longer each time he asked. So, he didn't anymore.

They would certainly be the death of him, yet. Sadie couldn't get back soon enough.

But that really wasn't because of the children.

He needed her beside him. They weren't even married but he felt he'd lost half of himself when she left.

Would he be sailing around the cape in a year? Alone?

Chapter Twenty-One

Newberry, Michigan
October, 1895

What fantasy had she been spinning? Sadie had invented her own storybook idea—like something borrowed from Garnet and Sadie—where everything would go perfectly in her nursing training, and she'd return triumphant and independent.

Not independent.

Not really.

Because in her mind she'd always wanted Robert there, too. More than ever, she felt her emotional dependence upon him—and his absence.

"Miss Duvall. Penny for your thoughts." One of the young psychiatrists offered her the smile that would cause most of the nursing candidates to almost swoon.

"I assure you my thoughts are far more valuable than a penny." She offered him a tight smile and clutched her books to her chest and continued to walk on.

When he grasped her elbow, she pulled away and turned to give him a stern look.

Two other nursing students giggled as they passed by on the walkway.

The doctor's handsome face reddened. "I beg your pardon."

"Sadie?!" Robert's voice boomed from not far behind them.

She swiveled to spy Robert and Opal hurrying toward her. Tears filled her eyes. It took everything within her to not run and launch herself into his arms. She gasped in air and forced herself to breathe normally.

Although she'd expected the psychiatrist to hurry on, instead he remained frozen next to her. "Who is that man?"

She almost said, "my husband," but that wasn't true. It could have been true. If only she'd not pushed him away and doggedly pursued this plan of hers.

Robert looked like a steam engine chugging down the tracks straight toward the doctor. "Is there a problem with this man? I saw him grab you."

The psychiatrist straightened. "I didn't grab her. I merely took Miss Duvall's elbow. I had something to tell her."

"Well, I'm her fiancé, Robert Swaine, and anything you have to say to her you can tell me as well." Robert bent and kissed Sadie's cheek.

Her fiancé? He'd never actually asked her. "Robert," was all she could manage to say.

Opal threw her small body against Sadie. She wrapped her arm around her sister and gave her a squeeze. "You've grown an inch."

"Yup. But Garnet hasn't. She's at the add-men-stray-shun building." Opal pointed at the physician. "Who's he?"

"I'm a colleague of Miss Duvall's and what I have to share with her is confidential." His thick eyebrows bunched together.

Robert scowled. He looked ready to put his purely ornamental, brass-headed cane to use. "We have an appointment at Superintendent Perry's office, so tell her quickly." He sounded very much the captain that he was.

"About Mr. Duvall?" The doctor's full lips quirked beneath his moustache.

"Yes," Robert bit out. "What are you doing out in the yard, Sadie? We came looking for you. Garnet stayed behind in case you arrived there a different route."

"That's what I was about to tell you, Miss Duvall. I apologize for touching your elbow, but you're wanted at Dr. Perry's office."

"Then you could have said so and been about your business." Robert slipped his arm through Sadie's, warmth surging through her. He looked so handsome. So smart looking in his tailored gray and navy suit. "Is that how things are run around here? I'll take up this gaff with Dr. Perry."

She'd never seen Robert so in command. He was, though, a ship's captain as well as owner of a fleet of ships and an investor in railroads and commerce.

Cheeks aflame, the psychiatrist tipped his hat. "Good day to all of you."

Another cluster of nursing students passed by, two of them staring with open admiration at Robert. He did cut a striking figure. She'd never hear the end of it tonight, in the dormitory.

Opal pulled away. "Is it true about Pa? Is he doing better?"

Exhaling a sigh of relief, Sadie nodded. "Yes, he's much improved. I see him every day after my studies, and he's gotten most of his memory and his skills back."

Robert frowned. "Did they tell you they plan to release him?"

She stiffened. "No."

Opal jumped up and down. "He's coming home."

"But, but. . ." Sadie wasn't through with her course of study. And who would take care of him? Where would he go? "He believes we all still live in our old cottage. He doesn't understand that it's gone—sold off." The little cabin had been in their family for generations.

"He'll like the Canary much better." Opal bobbed her head.

"I don't know about that. He's been telling me all these old family stories—things I'd never heard before—that he remembers." Light snowflakes drifted down, and she shivered.

"Come on. Let's get over to the administration building and have that conversation with Dr. Perry." Robert kissed her cheek. "It will be all right."

He took her hand in his and Opal grasped the other. Together they followed the walkway over to the big brick building. Every few steps, Sadie snuck a look up at Robert's face. So handsome. He was so kind. And he'd be her husband. She imagined herself walking alongside him as he pushed a pram holding a little dark-haired boy with hazel eyes like his father. Tears filled her eyes. "I've missed you so much."

He grinned down at her and Opal pressed her head against Sadie's shoulder. "We're looking forward to your return at Christmas, for the holidays."

If she went back to the island for the holidays she'd likely never return. She chewed her lower lip. "I've learned a lot while I've been here." About herself, too.

"We heard you were doing extra studies." Opal leaned away and pulled Sadie's hand. "And that you are the top student in your class."

Pleasure stirred within her, but her cheeks heated with modesty. "I wouldn't say that."

"You don't have to—your instructor told us on the way to get you." Robert's face glowed with pride. "She said you could practically sleep through the second half of your studies, and you'd still be a wonderful nurse."

"I wouldn't sleep. I've worked hard." Some of the young women there seemed more intent on finding a husband than on learning to be a good nurse.

"Jack Welling used to fall asleep, and Mr. Huntington didn't like it."

"I imagine not." Sadie made a face of mock horror and her sister laughed.

"Mr. Huntington is gone now, though. To Pickford." Opal crinkled her nose. "He married a girl who dressed like a boy."

Ah. Maggie Hadley, the dray-driver. That poor girl had done what she needed to do, though, to help her family—just like Sadie had done.

"Did he, now?" Robert chuckled. "I missed out on that. I'm guessing islanders were scandalized."

"Nah."

"You're starting to sound like Jack." Sadie cast Opal a sideways glance.

"Nahhh." Opal stuck her tongue out at Sadie and ran off ahead of them.

When they reached the administration building, Garnet held the door open for them. Once inside, the two sisters hugged. "You smell good, Garnet—like lavender and carnations."

"I won a miniature bottle of cologne for reading the most books so far this year."

"Very good." No surprise, either.

The secretary rose from her desk. "Follow me, please." Her hard-soled shoes echoed with each footstep down the hallway.

She stopped at the superintendent's door and knocked.

"Enter!" came a muffled voice from within.

They all stepped inside. The place smelled of pipe smoke and the faint odor of ink and paper. Perry gestured for them to take a seat.

Sadie's hands shook as she lowered herself into the wooden chair.

"I'm sure that Miss Duvall had informed you of Mr. Duvall's progress." He looked expectantly at each of them.

Opal shook her head and clutched her toy bunny.

Garnet sniffed. "She said he's all mixed up."

"Well, yes he has some confusion."

A lot of confusion, but Sadie bit her tongue.

Robert leaned in. "Is Frank able to care for his own needs?"

"Oh yes, he's managing his self-care beautifully, according to my staff. And I've observed him in the gardens. He could possibly take on work as a gardener as long as he was given very specific tasks."

Sadie chewed her lower lip. Pa needed much direction.

"There's actually not much more we can do for him." Dr. Perry steepled his fingers together. "So, as you see, Mr. Duvall is almost ready to be released."

"But I'm still in my studies." As soon as the words slipped from her mouth, Sadie realized how silly that sounded. Her father's progress had nothing to do with her training. But it had everything to do with her comfort level in having him out without nursing care.

"We cannot keep him here much longer. Certainly not until your graduation, Miss Duvall. Surely you understand this is a psychiatric facility and not a care home."

Sadie clenched her teeth.

Robert leaned in. "So, he knows who he is and can care for his needs?"

"But he believes, he's convinced, that he'll be living in our family home. And it's been sold." As much as she didn't wish for Dr. Perry to hear her personal business, this fact was important.

Dr. Perry shrugged. "We can make that a focus of treatment for the transition team."

Robert squeezed her hand. "I'll look into what we can do, on the island. It will depend on whether the new state parks commission on the island has purchased the land and cabin for specific usage."

Perry smiled. "Isn't it amazing what they are doing? Moving from one of our first federal parks to the state taking it over. We had a wonderful conference on the island last year, at the Grand Hotel."

Sadie bit her lip. She'd been about to say that she'd cleaned the psychiatrists' rooms and had seen what messes those men had made. She'd also discovered that many enjoyed too much drink and gambled on anything that moved. Robert's niece, Lily, was about to marry a wonderful psychiatrist though, Dr. DuBlanc. Dr. Perry and his colleague, Dr. Bottenfield, were also among the few doctors who kept their rooms tidy.

"Do you have a target date for Frank to be released?"

"The end of next month."

Sadie swallowed hard as Garnet and Opal clapped.

"We wanta see him." Opal stood.

She hoped and prayed her sisters would not be dismayed once they'd had their visit.

God had answered so many prayers already. Surely, he had room for one more request.

How strange for Adelaide to be back in Shepherd, but to have Peter with her—her husband. She went to the door to call him for lunch. She'd fried sausage with squash, tomatoes, and peppers and had stirred in some jarred pickled corn that their neighbors had sent over. She opened the heavy oak door with inset glass windows covered by red-and-white checkered curtains.

Peter, covered in dirt, stood at the bottom of the steps into the farmhouse. "How do you feel about being a farmer's wife?" He'd been out in the fields and in the barn for most of the morning.

"My dear husband, you do realize there was a reason you never became a farmer."

He huffed a sigh. "I know."

"But this place makes a perfect hideaway for us." Especially now that Peter understood exactly who he had married.

Peter sat on the steps and removed his boots. "And it's a short train ride to your office."

"And close to Jack's trainers." She waved to the boy, who was running toward them from the back acreage.

"And we'd rob the Wenham family of their additional income from this land if I tried to farm it." He waggled his eyebrows.

She laughed. "Exactly. You mustn't even try because you'd affect their livelihood."

The farmers had used the land to extend their own farm, for the past few years, with a lease from Peter's father.

He scratched his chin. "Wouldn't want that, now, would we?"

"No." She definitely would not. Adelaide had no idea that Peter had never absorbed his father's knowledge, in all the years he'd worked the farm. Well, perhaps a little.

"I was surprised a bit at how Jack wanted to stay on the island for at least part of the year."

"He was all right with staying at our hotel in Mackinaw City, though, too." Adelaide raised her eyebrows. "As long as he got to see his friends and family on the island regularly."

"The Winds of Mackinac is Maude and Ben's home now, not ours."

"Jack will always have a room there, though. And before we know it, he'll be all grown up—like his sister is."

"Oh, don't wish that! I want to enjoy the last of his childhood."

"And I don't want this honeymoon to end. It's been over ten weeks of bliss so far." As he leaned in to kiss her, Adelaide was struck by the amount of time. A very strange sensation captured her.

Was it possible? As Peter drew away, his arms still around her, his eyes locked on hers. "What is it?"

"Do you remember when you told me that you didn't care that I was the daughter of a runaway slave?"

"Yes. And it absolutely doesn't matter."

"What if your child was the grandchild of a slave?"

"What do you mean?" He cocked his head to the side. "Neither Jack nor Maude is. They are descendants of the Ojibway. Some of them may have been enslaved at some point, but I've never heard."

The fatigue, the morning nausea, the changes in her body—could it be?

Chapter Twenty-Two

Mackinac Island
November, 1895

So, the Duvall cabin is definitely to be made part of the new state parks exhibit?" Robert scratched at his winter beard.

"That's correct." Ben Steffan pointed to his notepad. "They've acquired even more land than the feds had, including the Duvall cabin."

A red rubber ball flashed past Ben's head and Jack flew into the room. "Sorry!"

The scamp picked up his ball. His nephew had come to the island to visit with family and friends. He joined them at the desk and wrinkled his nose as he patted an image of the Duvall cottage. "Wow, that playhouse they built up by the old fort really does look like a repeat of this one."

"A replica," Robert corrected.

"Yeah, that, too."

Ben grinned. "It is indeed *die Nachbildung*. No matter how you say it, those people evidently modeled their play building after the Duvall's historic cabin." He pressed his hand to his chest as if affronted.

"Sadie was real mad when she saw it last summer. But then we talked to Old Patrick later."

Robert raised his hand. "How many times have your sister and I asked you to not call Mr. Byrnes that?" The man was only in his fifties.

His nephew threw his arms up in the air. "That's what he calls himself! Go down to Horns' sometime and see."

Ben's eyes widened. "*Die bierhalle?*"

"Yes, the beer hall, but Dad lets me go with him."

"*Nein.* Not good."

Robert closed his eyes. His mother would be rolling in her grave if she knew her grandson had been hanging out with the local men, after work hours, and Jack so young.

"My new grandpa takes me to the tavern to watch the singing, but he never orders beer. Grandpa Lightfoot is real nice. So are my new uncle and cousins."

Ada's half-brother owned a business on the mainland. He had a wife and five children.

Jack jabbed his finger at the photo of the Duvall cottage. "Why don't ya ask them newcomers if they'd sell ya their playhouse that looks like this? And promise 'em you'll have old Patrick make 'em a new one."

"Jack, you are my brilliant nephew." Robert clapped Jack on his back. "That makes sense."

Maude entered the room, still wearing her heavy wool cape. "What makes sense?"

"We can't buy the Duvall land." Robert crossed his arms over his chest. "Nor the cabin."

"What a shame."

Ben moved closer. "But perhaps we can purchase the new *blockhaus*, the play cabin, and have it moved."

"Oh, I like that idea." Maude removed the pins from her hat and set them in Mother's pin bowl atop the side table then set the hat alongside them. "But where would we put it?"

"Lilac Cottage is for sale." Robert gestured to his right.

Maude frowned. "But they just built that place."

"Financial problems." And too much gambling this past summer on horse races.

"But how would that help you if Frank needs to live in the cabin?" Maude removed her knit scarf.

"There is room at the back of the property for it."

"And Lilac Cottage would be a wedding gift for Sadie?" Maude's tone was teasing and held a question. The *when* question.

He raised one eyebrow. From Sadie's letters, she clearly was considering returning, and staying, with her father. "It's winterized."

"It *is* right next door."

"Can't beat that." Ben helped Maude out of her overcoat.

"And if they won't sell to me then I could clear the Canary's backyard for the cabin." Robert splayed his hands.

"But we're having the reception for Lily's wedding in the back." His niece's eyebrows arched high.

Jack shrugged. "If it doesn't snow."

"*Hoffentlich nicht*. Let's hope not." Ben mussed Jack's hair and the boy ran off.

"We've had many a snow before Thanksgiving." Robert knew all too well how snow could disrupt plans.

Maude cast him a stern look reminiscent of her mother's warning glances. "Robert, you know we haven't worked out all the details but surely Lily is entitled to some of the property that Uncle Terrance would have received."

He had grown up in this house. Robert had imagined living here with Sadie. But it was true that Lily likely had a right to this place too, even though she'd not asserted that right. And their attorney, Mr. Hollingshead, still hadn't offered them a solution to the codicil that their mother had placed in the will.

"Lilac Cottage is brand new." Maude sat down at the table. "You wouldn't have to do anything to the place if you moved in there."

"And who would live here?" His voice came out much testier than he'd intended.

Ben straightened his gray cravat. "In case you had not noticed, you will have three young sisters-in-law who could stay here."

"With supervision." Maude tapped her fingertips on the tabletop.

"While I and my bride have solitude in the house and my father-in-law living right out back?" Robert snorted.

"Maybe the playhouse owners will let you have use of the little cabin this winter and you could move Frank when the family returns next summer."

"That has merits to be sure. But I don't know that Frank could live so far from us, unsupervised." By next summer, Robert would need to be back in port some of the time, managing his ships. At least Sadie would have her family there nearby. But she wanted to complete her nursing studies. And what would she want after that?"

"I have something I wanted to share with you." Maude's features tugged in an expression of secret glee mixed with contrition.

"What?" Robert shoved his hand back through his hair.

"François's nurse may be quitting." She clasped her hands at her waist.

"*Was ist das*?" Ben touched her cheek. "How do you know this?

"Quilting bee." She wriggled her shoulders. "And Rebecca Christy confirmed it."

"So, is *tratsch*? Gossip?"

"You have a lot to learn, Ben, if you don't understand that the ladies have their own reliable sources." Robert chuckled. "I've got a lot to look into."

"Ja. If you are to get a wife soon and your future father-in-law settled, you'd best make haste."

"Fine then. I'll see you all later." He headed out to get his coat, hat, and gloves.

Hastings assisted him. "Shall I send for the driver?"

"No. But send word to the stableboy to ready the carriage and horses."

"Yes, sir."

He'd talked with the elderly man about whether he wished to retire to the mainland, but Hastings refused, even when Robert explained that he'd still receive payment. Hastings had said the house was full of life again, and he enjoyed being part of it. That had touched Robert's heart.

Ben and Maude joined him. "I didn't mean to run you off, Uncle Robert."

"What's that expression?"

"Strike while the iron is hot. Or would you like the German version?"

"No, that's fine. Wonderful article you did in the paper recently about the increase in motor cars and the problems some have. Thinking about buying one myself."

"Where would you keep it?" Maude wasn't fond of motorized vehicles.

"St. Ignace. I know of a few others who've stored theirs in a garage on the edge of town."

"Electricity coming to all the cities, horseless carriages, and women studying at colleges—the world is really changing." Ben loved most things that were new. He was after all, a newspaperman.

"It's exciting." Maude linked her arm through Ben's. "I feel like we're on the cusp of a wonderful new era."

"I wonder what the new century will bring." Would he and Sadie be married, living in this house, would they be surrounded by children?

"Will this place be full of more family?" Maude must have been reading his mind. She released Ben's arm and turned around slowly, examining the large room.

"Well, I'm off to pressure Françoise," he winked, "that is, persuade our cousin that he could have the top student at the nurses' program as his new nurse."

"Wouldn't Sadie have to agree?" Ben made a dour face and Maude slapped playfully at his shoulder.

"Of course." Robert left the house and strode to the carriage house, behind.

Snow threatened overhead in bunchy thick clouds as Robert drove his carriage himself, east toward his cousin François's medical building. With the summer residents and tourists gone, the place was almost empty.

From the other side of the street, Jerry Meeker waved at him. The young man drove a dray covered with hay past—some no doubt to be delivered to the cottage. Robert nodded at the young man.

Wind swelled the Lake Huron waves in a slow but steady dance. Out on the water, if Robert had stood on one of his ships, he'd have still walked sure-footed. He missed the call of the Great Lakes. He yet heard the call of the Atlantic, too.

Robert stepped inside the neat and clean, but empty, waiting room. The receptionist smiled at him. "Good to see you, Captain Swaine. Doc Cadotte will be out in a moment. We had a bike wreck this afternoon."

"Anyone I might know?" Robert tensed. This was one of the very reasons that he could agree with his niece about cars. How many more bicycle accidents, or even fatalities, would result as use of motorized vehicles increased?

"One of the Christy girls tried to race her sister out to Arch Rock. Said if women could be in contests across the world, then she could start racing on our little old Mackinac Island."

"Makes sense."

"Yes, but not if you have done nothing, and I do mean absolutely nothing, to keep your skirts out of the way of the chains and spokes." She arched a thin brow.

"Ah. Right." He scratched his beard. "I imagine the Christys weren't too happy."

"Heavens, no." She shook her head. "And since our nurse quit, well, Doc has got his hands full."

"She quit?"

"The midwife is helping us out some. . ." She lifted her palms. "But we must have more nurses in here, come summertime."

Or possibly even earlier. "Did he mention to you that we'd asked him about help with Mr. Duvall?"

Her face began to mottle red. "Why do you think our nurse quit? She heard she might be assigned Frank Duvall as a patient."

"Oh." Oh no. This conversation might not go well at all. François was already in a fix and because of Sadie's father and their request for him.

Sadie sat atop her narrow bed in the dormitory. She raised the wick on her oil lamp's chimney and re-read Robert's terse letter. His scrawled handwriting suggested he'd been in a hurry. Or possibly agitated. It was like there was something he wasn't telling her.

Investigating housing options. Your Duvall heritage home is now property of state of Michigan, and they will not release it. Frustrated. But there are other options. Do you remember the place Jack showed you last summer? I'm working with the owners on some possibilities

As far as a trained nurse to sit with your father, there is no one at present. However, Dr. Cadotte is interviewing new nurses for his office. He will also interview for someone to help with your father as will we, privately. If you know of anyone at the school who might be interested, please advise him, and of course me, promptly.

Did she know anyone? Yes, she did.

Chapter Twenty-Three

I am dying. Robert struggled for breath.

Standing in the corner, Cousin François shook his head. "You'd better send for the rest of the family." He'd used his most sorrowful doctor's voice.

"What about my sister?" Bea's voice sounded like an accusation. *Sadie.* The name went up like a prayer.

Cadotte straightened. "Best send for her, too."

Robert's head needed to be pulled free from the vise it was trapped in. If he had to live like this, he'd rather go home to the Lord.

"Sit up, sir." Matilda placed a hand behind his head. "The doctor wants you to drink this real slow."

Pungent liquid passed over his lips and Robert resisted the urge to spit it out.

"Swallow it." That was Garnet's voice.

The bitter elixir coursed down his throat. *Oh God, help me. Restore me.*

Sadie. He needed her.

Robert began to shiver violently, and the girl pulled the covers up around his neck.

"If that fever doesn't break soon. . ." Cadotte's voice was low and full of dread.

He knew that feeling. He'd dreaded losing his ships and yet he had. *Gone.*

Robert began to cough and Cadotte reached behind him and sat him up in the bed. The spell wracked Robert's entire body. Everything hurt. So weak. So tired. So ready. . .

Sadie. Please bring her, Lord.

Mother and Father stood at the end of his bed. They were much younger. And smiling. A young man appeared at father's side. It must be his brother. Another stood next to Mother. The brother who'd died for the Union. They stood there, expectantly. He sensed their love.

"Are you here for me?" He asked them, but they remained silent.

A warm hand patted Robert's forehead. "Robert, Uncle, it's Lily."

He ran his tongue over his lips. "He's here."

"Who?"

She must not see them. "Your father."

Somebody murmured something.

He removed his arm from the cover and reached out. "Terrance?" he croaked.

Someone began to sob.

Take care of Sadie and the girls. Robert wanted so badly to say the words aloud, but he couldn't manage them all.

"What's happening?" His niece, Maude, stood beside Lily.

"I don't know."

His sister Eugenia, Maude's mother, joined the rest of his family standing at the end of his bed. She looked so beautiful—a glow surrounded her. "She's here," he whispered.

"Who?" Maude's flushed face was very distressed.

Robert had been upset, too, to see them all after so many years. But now he was so very fatigued. The roar in his head turned to a dark buzz. "Eugenia."

"No! Don't go! Do you hear me?" His niece shook his shoulders. It hurt. He coughed.

"Maude, stop." Dr. Cadotte came to Robert's rescue.

These people needed to leave. They needed to give him peace. It was all he wanted. Eugenia nodded in agreement, for he understood that she could hear his thoughts as could Mother, who gazed at him with love and extended her glowing arm toward him.

"Robert? Robert?" Sadie's voice called out to him, but she wasn't there. Something thin, like a mist, but strong, coiled around him, tying him there. Her unspoken voice, her thoughts of him, shot through time, through space, unhindered and to him.

Sadie's love anchored him to that bed and wouldn't release him.

I need to go.

Newberry Insane Asylum

"And if the patient struggles too much, here are some other techniques to try." The instructor droned on.

"Sadie." Sadie heard Robert calling her name as clearly as if he'd been sitting right beside her on the uncomfortable wooden chairs in the lecture room.

She shook off the feeling. She rubbed her arms as chills coursed down them.

"Sadie, I need you."

She turned and looked around the room but there were no men there, only her fellow female nursing students.

"And here's the best method for getting a recalcitrant patient to swallow his medicine."

She'd only felt this tug in her being once before—when Ma had died. She closed her eyes and bowed her head. *Lord, I don't know what is going on, but if Robert is in dire trouble, I need you to help.*

She dabbed at her eyes. She had to get home. Home. That's where Robert was. Where she should be. "Excuse me." She slid past the two students seated adjacent to her. *Oh Robert, please be all right.*

"Miss Duvall?"

"I have to go."

She gave her a curt nod.

Once outside the brick building, Sadie hurried across the walkway toward the dormitory. When was the next train?

Richard Christy loped across the frozen lawn toward her, holding a telegram, a sad but determined look on his face.

She covered her mouth. *Lord don't take Robert from me.*

Sadie owed the Christys all a great debt. Richard had gotten her to St. Ignace. Josephine accompanied her to the island. Clem's wife Marie had sent Ojibway herbal medicine. And Garrett brought her up to the cottage.

Carriages were parked all along the roadway. A chill wind, carrying tiny snowflakes whirled around them, penetrating her cloak. She inclined her head toward the many conveyances. "That cannot be good."

"Keep hope. Keep faith. We're all praying for Robert." A muscle twitched in Garrett's cheek.

"Thank you, Mr. Christy."

He stopped and she got down, then turned and grabbed her bag. She hurried up the walkway to the house, dreading what she might find.

Ben Steffan ambled toward her. "He's hanging on."

She could almost hear his unspoken words, 'for now.'

The door opened and Maude hurried out. She waved at Sadie. "I don't know what happened but he's beginning to improve a bit."

"Everyone's praying." Ben compressed his lips. "We're going home."

Maude joined them, her breath making puffs of mist in the cold air. "We were up all night."

"Thank you, Ben and Maude." Sadie shivered. Whether from the cold or what lay ahead, she wasn't sure. "Keep those prayers coming."

Maude chewed her lower lip. "Sadie, with his asthma, this pneumonia has severely affected his breathing." Her eyes filled with tears and a half-sob escaped her.

In that moment, her training and her faith kicked her emotions aside. "Now listen here. We'll not borrow trouble."

Both Ben and Maude nodded.

"You go rest and I'll take care of Robert. I'll need relief tonight," particularly after the bone-rattling journey she'd had, "but for now please get some sleep and leave this to me." *And the Lord.*

"But François says there's nothing more—"

Sadie raised her free hand. "I've seen what can be done with people who were given up on." Like Pa.

"Ja. You're right." He patted Maude's hand. "Come on, we go now."

Sadie hurried off toward the house. Hastings held the door for her. Once inside, she set her bag down and the butler assisted her from her winter overcoat.

"He's been asking for you, Miss." His face looked even more careworn than usual, with a grayish cast around his deep-set eyes.

She nodded. "I'm here now." She removed her gloves, hat, and scarf.

Matilda descended the stairs, a stricken look on her face. "He's sleeping comfortably, Miss Duvall."

Jack ran down the stairs, rushing past the servant, who cast him a scowl. "He's stopped babbling about our dead old family members being here, so at least we have that."

Sadie raised her eyebrows. "He saw the departed?" That wasn't good. She'd heard many stories of this at school—of people near death reporting that their loved ones had come to accompany them to heaven.

Jack shook his head. "He got kinda crazy for a while. Claimed my mother was at the end of the bed lookin' at him." He made a horrified face.

She touched Matilda's arm as she passed on the stairway. "Is there clean water and soap in the room?"

"There is but let me fetch you some that's fresh."

"Thank you." Sadie lifted her skirt and hurried upstairs.

She hesitated on the landing. She'd never entered Robert's room before. The notion of doing so seemed strange and improper. But she was here now to make sure he lived so that that one day he could carry her into that bedchamber as his bride.

She continued upstairs, the normal scent of flowers and beeswax absent and the faint odor of sickness lingering in the air.

Opal emerged from Robert's room, her face pale and tear-stained. She ran to Sadie and threw her arms around her.

"There, there." Sadie patted her sister's silky head. "It's going to be all right."

Her little sister sniffed and drew back. "But Ma died."

"Yes. But we're not going to let Robert die." Sadie shook her finger. "And you're going to help me."

Opal stared. "How?"

Sadie pulled the packets that Marie had given her out from her bag. "Take these to the kitchen and have Cook add each of them to a cup of boiled water. Then let them cool."

"What will I do while they cool?"

"Jo Jeffries, Mr. Christy's sister, sent some special treats from her bakery in St. Ignace. You can have one or two while you wait." Sadie handed a small tin of cookies to Opal.

The child headed off down the stairs.

Sadie stepped inside Robert's room; the air overly hot. After that cold journey, she felt like she'd stepped into an oven. *That will be remedied.*

Lily, standing by the foot of the bed, gave her a weak smile. "I'm so glad you're here."

She set her bag down on a small cherrywood table. Bea and Garnet shot her worried looks, tears in their eyes as Sadie stepped around the bed and bent over the man she loved.

"Robert?" Sadie's voice came out a whisper. She stared, open mouthed, at the gaunt man in the four-poster bed. *I cannot lose you.*

"It's all right." Garnet leaned in. "You don't have to whisper. He's not been responding to our voices today."

"Not for a couple of days." Bea shook her head. "I think you've got here just in time."

"No. I'll not have it." Sadie ran her hand across Robert's brow. He was perspiring but that could well be from the overheated room. "I don't believe I feel a fever."

"His fever's broken but he hasn't woken." Garnet set her book aside and stood.

Bea exhaled a sigh. "Might not wake up, according to Dr. Cadotte."

"He'll wake up." Sadie glared at her sister. She hoped the steel in her voice would stop Bea's negative comments.

"I pray you're right." Garnet bit her lower lip. "Dr. DuBlanc said that part of healing can be mental or emotional. He said we needed you here."

"He was right." Sadie's hands trembled as she reached to feel her beloved's pulse. "I'm glad you all sent for me."

Garnet pointed to a corner divan, with a knitted burgundy and tan afghan and a tasseled pillow. "Maude and Ben stayed in here last night. They took turns resting."

"I sent them home to get a good sleep." Trying to sleep in a sickroom wasn't the same for a caregiver. "I'm here now. I'll take over." And she would.

Matilda entered the room with a shiny, white, enamel wash basin, glass carafe of water, soap, and a clean towel.

"Thank you." Sadie pushed her sleeves up. "I'm going to wash his face."

"Very good, Miss Duvall." Matilda cast a long glance at Robert. She carried off the items that she'd replaced.

"Do you think that's a good idea?" Bea frowned as Sadie lathered the soap onto the washcloth, with the warm water.

"Yes, and once he's feeling a bit stronger, we'll even wash him up a little more and change his sleep shirt." Hygiene and cleanliness might not be focused on by Dr. Cadotte, but in her nurse's training they were vital. "And we'll want new bed clothes."

Garnet and Bea frowned.

"Let's open those windows and let's give him some fresh air. All this miasma of hot air is not good for him." She felt stifling herself, as she pulled off her wool vest.

Robert didn't stir even as the girls made noise to wake the dead as they pushed up the sashes on the windows, groaning with their efforts.

She patted Robert's cheek. "Now, sir, we've had enough of this. You open those beautiful hazel eyes of yours and welcome me home."

There was absolutely no reaction. His breathing didn't change. No twitch. No change. She took a deep breath and caught her sister giving her a sorrowful glance.

"Sadie?" Lily called from the doorway. "I'm so sorry for not offering earlier. Can we bring you up some tea?"

She exhaled slowly. "Yes. Thank you. Tea and a sandwich would be lovely." Josephine had tried to get her to eat, at her bakery in St. Ignace, but Sadie couldn't.

"I'll bring a tray."

"Oh, and Lily, I want a camphor-soaked plaster for Robert's chest. And one for his back." Sadie searched the room and located a cork-topped, glass bottle of camphorated oil.

"I'll have some flannels brought up."

"Thank you." The door closed behind Lily.

"Bea, I want you to help me sit Robert up when we put the plasters on him. And I'm going to pound his back to see if we can loosen his cough."

"All right. But Doc Cadotte had us stop the ointments. Said it didn't seem to be working."

"It will work." Sadie wasn't about to put up with any nonsense. "And if you can't speak of his recovering then send someone else up to help me."

Bea scowled. "I suppose you want Opal."

"In fact, she's downstairs right now waiting on some Ojibway medicines that Marie, Clem Christy's wife, sent over for him."

Cool, or rather, cold air began to billow through the curtains.

"I want Cook to put on, and keep on, a kettle of boiling water. Go down and tell her, Bea."

Then she looked at her sister, really took in her appearance. "Bea Duvall, when is the last time you've bathed and changed your clothing?"

Bea burst into tears.

"She's not slept in days." Garnet held up three fingers. "And she barely eats."

Sadie opened her arms, went to her sister, and held her close as Bea sobbed into her shoulder. She patted her back.

"It's. . . too. . . much. Too. . . many." Bea sniffed.

She knew exactly what her sister meant. Too many losses.

"Listen. Pa's coming home next week. I'm coming back." She pulled back. "And Robert Swaine is not going to die if I can help it. So, you go eat, sleep, take a bath, and come back tomorrow when I'll need help getting him up and walking."

Bea's green eyes looked doubtful, but then she smiled. "Yes, Nurse Sadie."

Who was this woman in charge of his care? Robert heard someone barking out commands all afternoon. She reminded him of his ship's steward. Maybe they'd finally finished building his replacement ships. The lady would say something, then all manners of hands were on him, turning him, rubbing ointments on him. They'd even sat him up and pounded on his back until he'd coughed, and coughed, and coughed.

Now the strident voice turned gentle. "Please, you need to drink this medicine." This sounded like. . .

"Sadie?" He ran his tongue over his dry lips.

"Robert!"

He opened his eyes. Sadie stood over him, her eyes wide.

"Water," he croaked.

She wagged a finger at him. "You'll drink this medicine first."

"Let's sit him up, again." Stephen DuBlanc stood and gestured Jerry Meeker and Peter Welling forward.

"I told you we'd need men here to get him up." Sadie beamed and kissed his forehead. "I want to get fresh clothes on him and new bedsheets.

The men pulled him up to sitting and placed what seemed like a half dozen pillows behind his back.

Sadie carried a cup to him that smelled like it had rotten cabbage in it. He pulled back. Hadn't someone been dribbling this tincture into his mouth earlier? The taste was putrid. He shook his head.

"See here now, Captain Swaine. I'm in charge now. We're going to get this down you and you'll be happy for it."

"I doubt it."

"You'll have bone broth next, if you'll cooperate."

The men began to pull the bedding off.

Jack ran around and stared at Robert. "You better do what she's says. You're finally getting better after a whole week."

"A week?" He'd just opened his mouth and Sadie shoved a tablespoon of the wretched liquid into it.

"Swallow." She held his lips shut. How did she know he'd wanted to spit the bitter solution out?

He forced it down. He was awake. He'd not gone on to Glory. He took a couple of deep breaths. The rattling had ceased in his chest.

"That's much better. Jack, go ask Matilda to bring that bone broth up."

His nephew saluted, then swiveled around on his heels—like a proper cadet.

"Nurse Sadie?" Robert grabbed her free hand.

"Yes?"

"Will you marry me?"

The men stopped yanking the bedclothes off and applauded.

Jack stopped at the door and turned around. "Bea and Garnet said you never asked."

Opal wriggled in underneath Sadie's arms. "Did you 'fishally ask her?"

Sadie, whose face reflected both bemusement and a little irritation, swiveled around to face her helpers. "I'm not going to agree to marry someone whose body and bedsheets need a good washing."

The men laughed.

Peter waved Sadie away. "You're not married yet, so you go on now while we handle this."

"We'll come and get you when we've got him all set." Stephen looked like he could use a change of clothes himself, out of that rumpled shirt, vest, and pants.

Sadie faced Robert, again. "You'll feel a lot better once you're clean, in new pajamas, and new bedclothing on."

And even better when she answered his proposal.

Chapter Twenty-Four

Adelaide's father kept her hand clasped in his for a long moment before they were seated at their booth inside the Mackinaw City Tavern. "I can't believe after all that looking and searching, that I finally found you."

"Like Jesus's parable about the shepherd with the one little sheep he kept searching for." Peter patted her shoulder.

She caught the waitress's eye and made a circle. "Coffee all around, please. To start us off."

"Yes, ma'am."

"It's a mite chilly outside today, isn't it?" Pa took his place. "But that coffee will warm us up."

"I am glad that you left Virginia and moved north." Adelaide slid into the wooden booth and arranged her skirts around her.

"I had to leave that place." Her father swept a hand back through his thinning hair. "I couldn't bear living on my farm anymore and always remembering what had happened to my wife and baby girl."

"So, you sold the Lightfoot farm in Ladysmith." Adelaide had heard part of the story when they'd gathered with her half-brother and his family, the month before.

"Yes, to my neighbors, the Swaines."

"The Swaines?" Adelaide exchanged a long glance with Peter.

"They were the ones who encouraged me to try to purchase farmland in Northern Michigan. Swaine's son had married a woman from Mackinac Island."

"Jacqueline?"

"Yes. That was her name."

"That was my mother-in-law."

Her father gaped at Peter. "You don't say."

"Yes. She was Peter's first wife's mother. My stepchildren's grandmother."

Her father shook his head. "If that don't beat all."

"Not only that, but the Swaines, in Virginia, were the Grand Hotel's singer, Lily's, grandparents." Adelaide passed the brief menu sheet to her father. "She was born there after you had left."

"I heard that gal sing here in town, once, last summer. She had a beautiful voice."

"Yes, she does," Peter agreed.

Their waitress set steaming mugs of hot coffee in front of them. "I'd recommend pasties with gravy on a day like this. Or our stew."

"Pasties all around?" Adelaide glanced at her father and then Peter. Both men nodded.

The waitress took their menu and headed off toward the kitchen.

Adelaide added cream and sugar to her coffee and stirred it. "So, you took Mr. Swaine's advice about relocating to Michigan?"

"It was mostly those Northern Swaine boys who encouraged me. Seems they'd heard the stories of what had happened to Satilde and you, Adelaide. The one young buck, Terrance, seemed like he'd fit right in, though, on the Swaine's plantation." Pa cupped both hands around his mug, like she remembered him doing when she was a child, and he lifted the steaming coffee to his lips.

"He died for the Confederacy," Peter grunted out.

"I doubt that. I'm thinkin' he died for his Grandpappy Swaine." Her father set his mug down. "Old Mr. Swaine always hated that his son had run off North. But those folks sendin' the boys back South for visits—for the one, that Terrance, he was mighty close with his grandpap."

"The other son served the Union." Peter added cream to his coffee until it began to turn almost white. Peter took a drink of his creamy beverage and smiled. He might as well simply add a dollop of coffee to a mug of cream. He grinned that devilish boyish smile he used to give her when he'd done something naughty.

"He was a good boy. Does he live on the island? I'd like to see him sometime."

"No. I'm afraid he perished in battle."

"Ah, so that's why I've never come across him up here." Pa tapped the side of his mug with his long fingers. "I'm sorry. We Lightfoots were some of the earliest settlers in the Commonwealth, but it shamed me what my fellow Virginians did."

Peter tapped his fingers on the tabletop. "Understandably so."

"The younger Swaine boy convinced me that this place was as near to paradise as I would find. His grandpap bought me out and I left."

"Speaking of grandfathers," Peter leaned forward. "I believe you're about to become one, again."

"Adelaide?" Her father's eyes widened. The joy she remembered flickering on his face when she'd done something special shone again, now. "I reckon I couldn't be happier."

"If it's a boy, we'd like to name him after you."

"Well there, you've gone and proved me wrong. I'm even more joyful that you'd consider such a thing." Her father blinked back tears. "And if a baby girl?"

"Satilde. For a brave woman who ran to freedom, lost it, and then sacrificed herself for me."

Robert pointed to a spot on his Weber terrestrial globe. Bea had polished the oak stand to a gleam and now she leaned in with Sadie, Opal, Jack, and Garnet to watch as he pointed out an ocean voyage that he hoped to make one day. Only a week earlier, he'd been making a different passage. Sweat broke out on his brow as he remembered Mother and Eugenia standing at the foot of his bed, waiting for him—not them, but perhaps a spiritual representation of them to give him comfort on his journey to heaven.

"Isn't that really dangerous?" Jack scratched his cheek. "Ya just got better. Why not take the easy street?"

Bea elbowed his nephew.

"Ow!"

"Don't you have any sense in your head? Mr. Byrnes almost got run over by a runaway horse yesterday in the street. Right after they moved that cabin replica into the backyard."

"Yeah, bad stuff can happen anywhere." Garnet nodded solemnly. "In one of my stories, a girl fell out of a low branch of an apple tree and broke her neck."

"Or brained herself, ya mean." Jack crossed his arms, looking smug. "Like they thought I'd do up at Arch Rock last summer. But I'm as nimble as a gazelle."

"How would you know? Have you ever seen one?" Bea sneered at Jack.

"No, but my mother has."

Everyone stared at Robert's nephew, including himself. Jack had already taken to calling Ada his *mother*? To Robert's relief, no one corrected the boy. In fact, this was a good sign. Jack needed all the love and connections he could make and having a new mother was already bringing healing. He could see it in the boy's demeanor and general happiness.

"My new mother went on safari trips in Africa. She's gonna take me and Dad." Jack compressed his lips.

"How'd she do that?" Bea's green eyes flashed. "Stop making stuff up, Jack."

"I'm not. She's been on lots of trips—just ask her."

"Speaking of trips, I'm grateful the Christys are bringing Pa back with them next week." She waved her hands overhead, the scents of antiseptic and rosewater mingling. "I'm so relieved because now I can make sure Robert doesn't overtax himself."

She was still babying him, although Robert was almost well enough to walk all the way into Hubbard's Annex, to his friends' homes. "And I'm sure I'll soon feel well enough to help the Duvalls prepare for their father's return."

"Pa has changed so much." Sadie shrugged. "It's like we're getting a different father."

Garnet shifted her weight from foot to foot. "The psychiatrist's letter said Pa doesn't show any inclination to drink alcohol—that's a big change."

"They say he's like a child." Opal twisted a knot in the front of her dress. "I don't know if I want a Pa who seems like he's never grown up."

Sadie brushed her little sister's hair from her forehead. "He's going to need some care, but he can also take care of some things on his own. But from what I saw at the hospital, he's quieter, he's polite, and Pa does make effort to regain skills. I'm proud of the progress he's made."

"Maybe when he gets back here, he'll do even better." A muscle in Bea's cheek twitched. She'd expressed her concerns about Frank's return.

Robert would see if he could do something to allay their concerns. "We're waiting to hear about a nurse from the mainland coming to join us this winter, to help. That will give Sadie, and all of you girls, a break if your father's needs become too taxing."

"I really think he'll be fine—especially now that he'll be settling in that little cabin. It will feel like home." Sadie gave Opal a quick hug and then moved closer to Robert.

"Now, let's focus on what Robert wanted to tell us about some possible exciting plans in the future."

"Thank you." He cleared his throat and pointed to a path from Boston down around the cape in South America. "I'd come up into Mexico and visit there for a while." He had an idea for an investment in a new shipbuilding company there.

"He'll have a nurse on board, too." Sadie took his hand. "At least an almost-nurse if I don't get to complete my studies."

"Cousin François thinks he has a plan for that." The doctor said he may be able to train Sadie at his practice. Robert squeezed Sadie's fingers, feeling Mother's sapphire ring that he'd retrieved from Greyson Luce and placed there. "Maybe by that time, we'll even have some little Swaines on board."

Sadie blushed so violently, she reminded him of Mother's pink summer peonies in the back garden. "Robert Swaine!"

The youngsters all giggled.

Robert took Sadie's hand and squeezed it. "No matter where we go, our hearts will always be anchored at Mackinac."

"And we'll always return." That was a promise that Sadie would keep.

THE END

Author's Notes

This book has sections that were originally published in novella form in "His Anchor" in Barbour's *First Love Forever* collection. Sadie's story was originally intended to be a full-length novel, book two in my Brides of Mackinac series. When the rights were reverted to me, I knew I wanted to expand Sadie's story but in the meantime, I have moved more toward writing Contemporary Women's Christian Fiction. Ada Fox AKA Adelaide Bishop and a few other faux names, the second heroine in this novel, also finally gets her own storyline after all these years. Sadie's character development also changed dramatically. *Anchored at Mackinac* now has both Historical Christian Romance and with a Women's Christian Fiction "feel" to it. I hope you'll enjoy it! Did you know there isn't actually a Historical Women's Christian Fiction subgenre per se?

Adelaide/Ada made a cameo mysterious appearance in *The Substitute Bride* and is also in *My Heart Belongs on Mackinac Island* and *Behind Love's Wall*. I was inspired to create Adelaide Bishop's story when I read, a while back, about one of the wealthiest women in the world having been found dead in her sparse tenement. She'd lived like a miser, and no one had a clue about her. I thought, what a waste of the blessings she could have given so many people and what a miserable way to live. I wanted to create a character who has reasons why she hides from people but who *overcomes* the desire to hide from others and to hoard her wealth. She's a dear character to me, as I've written Ada/Adelaide into stories beginning almost a decade ago. If you want to know more about Adelaide's mother, read *Love's Escape*, a James River Romances novella in which Satilde is a minor character.

If you've read *My Heart Belongs on Mackinac Island: Maude's Mooring*, you'll recognize many characters in this novel. I recommend reading that novel first, however this book can also be read on its own. Sadie Duvall, one of my heroines in this novel, is Maude Welling's best friend. The prologue in this novel is one year prior to Maude's story, beginning in 1894, but then the story parallels Maude's tale in the beginning chapters before moving into the months beyond August 1895. Also, if you've read *Behind Love's Wall*, (Barbour, 2021), Lily Swaine's story also is part of this series that isn't quite a series! The rights to *My Heart Belongs on Mackinac Island* revert back to me in 2022 and eventually all three of these novels will be part of the same series.

There really was a famous Madame Patti, an opera singer, who performed in Paris in the late 1800s. She was known to have used henna in her hair as Adelaide has done at one point. The singer would have been about a decade older than Adelaide would have been, as Madame Patti was born in 1843. Of course, Adelaide is fictional so she couldn't have known Madame Patti. The army did introduce a new "forage" cap in 1895. I "fudged" a bit and allowed Sadie's lieutenant to have one in 1894.

The Kaiser Wilhelm Canal was indeed a marvel and completed during the time of this novel. You can well imagine why its name was changed to the Kiel Canal! If you want to see the inspiration for the Duvall's log cabin, then visit the French cabin, called the McGulpin cabin, part of Mackinac State Parks' exhibits, downtown Mackinac Island. And visit all of the parks' many wonderful sites!

Mackinac Island is nestled in the Straits of Mackinac, where Lake Huron and Lake Michigan intersect. Some hydrologists consider it one lake: Lake Michigan–Huron or Lake Huron–Michigan. Limestone, beneath the water, contributes to the gorgeous turquoise- and sapphire–blue hues viewed there. It's a beautiful place between Michigan's Upper and Lower Peninsulas and is also populated by other islands. Even today, Mackinac Island allows no motor vehicles, save for emergency use except in the winters when residents use snowmobiles. A new issue in recent years has been the increase in electric or e-bikes, and although there are regulations on the island for them, it's a thorny current issue.

When the Grand Hotel was being constructed, workers had to pull the lumber over the icy Straits. I had the privilege of hearing the hotel's historian, Bob Tagatz, repeat a story he'd heard from one of the men's daughters. She'd recollected how distressed her father had been upon return from each haul. The men had to remain dead silent on the transport from the mainland to the island to listen in case they heard the ice begin to crack. And then they had to go back and get more! I could picture Sadie's father, Frank Duvall, becoming unhinged from this activity and turning to drink.

What later became Newberry State Hospital was a brand-new asylum, built in the 1890s. The institution also housed a nursing school. Centered in the middle of the Upper Peninsula's booming lumber and mining industry, the town also became a center for treating psychiatric conditions. I grew up in Newberry, and my father, uncle, and other family members worked at the hospital. I lived only a few blocks away. I used to be on those grounds almost daily. The location is now a prison site.

Fairy Arch was indeed a real place on Mackinac Island. I had maps from the 1890s that referred to the Fairy Arch, Fairy Lane and so on that I'd found at various times but in modern times I had never ever heard where Fairy Arch was hiding on the island. There was a reason for that—it was destroyed. I was very sad to read that. It sounded like the perfect romantic and fun place for Victorian times.

Beeman gum was produced at the turn of the century. I grew up loving Beeman gum—my Great Uncle Fred, who served in WWI as a medic, used to give me some, but it's hard to find today. Schlitz beer has been around since the late 1860s, and Stroh's Bohemian beer was the Blue Ribbon Winner at the Columbian Exposition in Chicago.

I reference one of my favorite books, *Little Women*, by Louisa May Alcott, in this novel. Although I found information that the book, as we know it today, was published in two tomes, I wasn't able to determine the exact time frame when the merger into one novel happened. But, likely in 1895, my heroine's sister, Garnet, would have been reading one of the two Alcott volumes. And a real other book, *Cinderella,* did have three different versions. I reference the book by Charles Perrault, with the fairy godmother, and the story by the Brothers Grimm, with the helpful trio of birds.

Daylilies, as Adelaide and Peter discussed upon their reunion, were not cultivated widely until the early 20th century. And, yes, like Peter said—they are so hardy and they've been in America for so long, that it's not uncommon to find them in ditches near an abandoned home site. When we lived in New York state, in West Falls, I was astonished to go on my walks and find hundreds, perhaps even a thousand, beautiful day lilies blooming in a roadside ditch alongside an empty lot. The area had first been inhabited by European settlers in the early 1800s. One home on our short street had been built in 1815 (our rental was "newer" having been built in 1850!)

Fires happened on Mackinac Island, and across the country, due to the heavy use of wood for building, plus various other fire hazards. When my family and I were taking the ferry home from the island, after a book signing in the summer of 2017, we observed a fire on the island. The danger of any such fire is of it jumping to other wooden structures as well. It was truly frightening. Firefighters from the island, and ferried in from Mackinaw City and from St. Ignace, battled the flames—and won. God bless them all!

I "borrowed" a lot of names. Thank you to Cousin Laura Williams Kinney, and her husband, Tom Kinney, for permission to "borrow" their names. Thank you to my friend, Dawn Lindsey Bobay, for the use of her name. High school classmates' names were used for the family's attorney, Steve Hollingshead, and for the psychiatrist, Stephen Perry. Psychiatrist Bottenfield is the brother of my wonderful Beta reader Anne Rightler. I didn't get Mr. Foster's agreement—he was a naughty little dog, one of many we have adopted over the years.

Acknowledgements

Father God, You know I couldn't do anything without You. Thank you to Jeff and Clark Pagels, who have been rooting for Sadie for some time and have accompanied me on my travels to the Straits of Mackinac. Thank you to my critique partner, award-winning author Kathleen L. Maher, who went above and beyond in her assistance. Thank you also to author Kim D. Taylor for critiquing the early chapters. Much appreciation to my fabulous Beta readers: Tina St. Clair Rice and Anne Rightler. Thank you also to my wonderful advance readers Sherry Moe, Susan Johnson, Betti Mace, my *Anchored at Mackinac* Promo team and my Pagels' Pals members.

Thank you to the administrators of the Addicted to Mackinac Island Facebook, especially Linda Borton Sorensen and John Hubel, and to the members. It's a wonderful group and I've received a lot of support there both for my writing ministry and my love of all things Mackinac!

I can't even say how much I fully appreciate the owner of the Island Bookstore, Mary Jane Barnwell, and the manager, Tamara Tomac. And to the readers who visit their fabulous store. Most of my Mackinac set books can be purchased there (often autographed) or ordered from their online store. If you get to the island, be sure to stop by the bookstore—you'll be glad you did!

With appreciation to Mackinac Island Public Library's Anne St. Onge for access to the historical resources room, and to Bob Tagatz, Grand Hotel historian, for his wonderful lectures at the Grand Hotel. I love all the great history on Mackinac Island and the surrounding area!

Thank you to my readers! Without you I wouldn't have my writing ministry! Be blessed!

Bio:

Carrie Fancett Pagels, Ph.D., is the award-winning and bestselling author of over twenty Christian fiction books. Twenty-five years as a psychologist didn't "cure" her overactive imagination! A self-professed "history geek," she resides with her family in the Historic Triangle of Virginia but grew up as a "Yooper" in Michigan's beautiful Upper Peninsula. She loves to spend time in the summer at the Straits of Mackinac—where this novel is set!

Connect with me at: www.carriefancettpagels.com While you're browsing my website, be sure to sign up for my newsletter via the Contact page. You can also send me messages via the Contact page form. You can see some of my other books on my website Books page.

You can also find me on Facebook, Instagram, Pinterest, Twitter, and YouTube (where I share some videos of me reading sections of some of my stories!

If you enjoyed this novel,

a review is always appreciated!

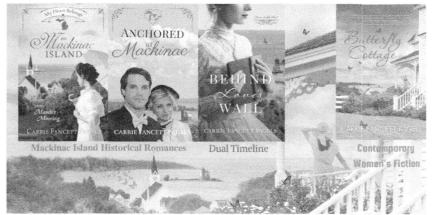

Mackinac Island Romances & Women's Fiction

Christian Historical Romance:

My Heart Belongs on Mackinac Island (Barbour, 2017) - A Romantic Times Top Pick, Maggie Award Winner.

    1895 – Maude's story

Anchored at Mackinac (2022)

    1895 – Sadie's & Ada's stories

Dual-Timeline:

Behind Love's Wall (Barbour, 2021)

    1895 – Lily's story

    2020 – Willa's story

Contemporary Women's Fiction:

Butterfly Cottage (2021) – Selah Award Finalist 2022

    2018 – Three generations: Jaycie, Tamara, & Dawn